# THE WAY OF THE
# SHADOW WOLVES

## The Deep State
## and the
## Hijacking of America

By Steven Seagal & Tom Morrissey

FOREWORD BY SHERIFF JOE ARPAIO

5th Palace Publishing

www.tommorrisseybooks.com
5th Palace Publishing

*We dedicate this book to the Native Americans who were victims of genocide by the early invaders from Europe;*

*To the tribal police, who combine the old ways and the new to defend our border with intelligence and integrity;*

*To the US Marshals, most of whom represent the ideal of the Texas Rangers, the goodness of the Nation in one man, one badge, riding alone;*

*And finally, to the average American citizen, awakened and finally, perhaps, ready to confront the Deep State and restore our Constitution.*

*This is a work of fiction and any resemblance to anyone living or dead is purely coincidental.*

*But always remember that the truth comes in many forms.*

# TABLE OF CONTENTS

# FOREWORD

I strongly identify with this book because in many ways I lived what is portrayed on its pages. During my over twenty-six year career in DEA I worked as a young agent in the mountains of Turkey, often on my own, chasing illegal drug merchants as part of the war on drugs. Many times, although unknown to me, I had to work side by side with individuals who were actually sabotaging my efforts and even putting my life in danger. This was because they were on the payroll of the illicit drug underground.

I was promoted to Regional Director of the DEA Office in Mexico and Latin America. What I experienced during that time brought me an understanding of the mindset and customs of the drug cartels, which drive those organizations to this very day.

As the longest serving elected sheriff in Maricopa County, Arizona history, I brought my experience to that organization. Arizona, today, is and has been, Ground Zero, concerning illegal immigration and drug running. The deserts of this great state contain the hidden highways used by drug cartels as they pour across our unsecured borders. That flow has slowed under President Donald Trump, however, there are powers known today as the Deep State, working against his efforts.

The activities of the "Deep State" operatives are a grave danger to our country because they are working against the effort to secure our borders. It is my belief that books, such as this, bring a better understanding through fiction. This will help to bring an awakening which has been smothered by the entrenched leftist mindset that dominates the creative media in this country today.

I know and have worked with Steven Seagal, who is a law enforcement officer, along with being an international movie star. He has an unusual understanding of the world in which this story takes place. During his time with my office he proved his skills as a fugitive hunter when he arrested one of our top fugitives within forty-eight hours after beginning the search for him. He brought us a new and extremely effective way of getting the job done. I first met Tom Morrissey when he was a Chief Deputy US marshal for the federal district of Arizona. We came to be close allies and united our agencies as we fought the good fight against the evolving threat of illegal drugs that were moving through Arizona. Both of these men bring their experiences to life on the pages of this book.

It is my hope that you have not only enjoyed the story line of *The Way of the Shadow Wolves* but you will also think about the message portrayed here. It is less than a hair's breadth from the frightening truth of what is actually happening today in America.

Sheriff Joe Arpaio

# PREFACE

What if the Deep State is not, as some strive to suggest, unelected government officials, generally in the secret intelligence community and the military, who run amok outside the rule of law? What if abusive elements of the federal government are very much a part of the Deep State, but they should be seen as the best of the servant class—not the masters?

What if the Deep State begins with one of the world's largest churches and one of the world's most powerful families who control London and Wall Street as well as the central banks—all privately owned—in every country of the world? What if governments failed to nationalize the central banks, leaving the Deep State to be controlled by one of the world's largest churches and one of its most powerful families with their personally appointed agents throughout the world of finance?

What if the greatest crimes against humanity occur at the banking level, where bankers are able to manipulate interest rates and foreign exchange rates, create billions in digital cash without backing, manufacture "derivatives" that they sell to unwitting investors, and start wars to impact the price of oil and other commodities?

What if beneath the bankers are the political parties, generally two parties per country that conspire to exclude all other political parties and Independents from power? What if, in the United States, one party controls 17 percent of the eligible voters and the other major party controls 13 percent of the eligible voters? What if another 20 percent belong to small parties, while fully 50 percent are Independent, No Party Preference, or Not Interested? What if many active politicians could be assumed to be compromised? What if they are being bribed or blackmailed by multiple parties, including the secret intelligence services of their own and other countries?

What if co-equal to the political parties are the secret intelligence services? What if in addition to spying on and blackmailing politicians and judges, the secret intelligence services engage in drug running, illicit arms trading, money laundering, and child exploitation (pedophilia) as a means of manipulating specific individuals?

What if the "mainstream media" is a complicit partner with the banking, political, and intelligence communities? What if it communicates to the public a broad range of false information and mixes a broad range of mindless entertainment with outright "fake news," while failing to do serious investigative reporting or provide any foundation for citizens desiring to be informed about current events, the true costs of policies, and more?

What if the universities are also complicit in the Deep State narrative? What if most history taught is a lie? What if few realize that the Pulitzer Prize was created to honor the man who invented "yellow journalism," the original "fake news," in which massive lies were told in order to justify wars? What if universities have refused for decades to actually study and publicize the true cost of specific policies, products, and behaviors because they have been incentivized by commercial interests to overlook the fact that most of what the West produces is both wasteful and harmful to human health and the environment?

What if some religions are also complicit in the Deep State? What if they are used to comfort and distract the masses, offering a promise of an afterlife intended to reduce demands for economic and social justice in this life?

What if, put most simply, the Deep State is the totality of the institutions of governance that are used to concentrate wealth and power among the 1 percent, while excluding the 99 percent from having effective voice and vote?

What if the Deep State is our common enemy? What if we the people have the power to say no to the Deep State? What if we the people have the power to demand election reform? What if we the people have the power to demand that integrity be restored to our government, our economy, and our society?

What if this book is dedicated to the Constitution and to the Republic? Would the answers to the preceding be in some ways answered?

# THE WAY OF THE SHADOW WOLVES

## The Deep State
and the
Hijacking of America

# 01: Tribal Police—America's Front Line in the Desert

*IN A DARKENED Arizona movie theater, a somber male voice provides commentary over the Native American chanting and drumming that plays in the background of a documentary film.*

"Perhaps the greatest morality play in American history is what occurred in the struggle between the Indian tribes and those in the US government who were hell bent on 'civilizing' them.

"Throughout history, the conquering of the land that once belonged to the Native American tribes, which were actually nations in their own right, by those who migrated here from other parts of the world was a legacy of cruelty and bloodshed.

"The history begins with the brutal relocation of many of the two hundred fifty different tribes throughout this country, manifesting in such tragedies as the infamous Trail of Tears. On to the creation of the Bureau of Indian Affairs. Moving to the great contributions of the over twenty-five thousand Native Americans who served with exceptional ability in World War II.

"The government encouraged the creation of tribal constitutions, out of which came the tribal police departments. Within these departments was the genesis of the great trackers, many of whom were Shadow Wolves."

*The closing moments of the film arrive, and the credits start to roll as the narrator continues.*

1

"Native Americans have an innate and powerful spiritual connection with the earth and its creatures. An understanding of the 'true nature' of all that is on this planet and how it works in the perfect balance of cause and effect. An elite group within the Native American communities, known as Shadow Wolves, are part of this perfect balance and are the 'best of the best,' with the ability to see what can't be seen with the eyes. They know without having to be taught. They blend easily with the night. True right from wrong is ingrained in their souls, which makes them able to stand against evil, no matter the cost. To see footprints on rocks."

———————

A man sits alone, quietly watching the film in the back of the darkened theater. He stirs in his seat and comments to himself, "It's about time." John Gode rises slowly from his seat and continues viewing as he backs up, slowly making his way out of the theater into the lobby.

## 02: Deep State Sign in the Desert

THE ARIZONA DESERT sky was full of color as the sun set, and the spirit of the night began to stir. The clouds, a brilliant orange, were hanging on the horizon with sunrays lighting them from the bottom up as the daylight crept behind the mountains, off in the distance but not too far from where a man named John Gode was standing. A dust devil was dancing across a place between him and the setting sun. This tall, lean man, who in the approaching darkness could have easily been confused with a saguaro cactus, was breathing in the beautiful scene before him. He was fully aware of a man standing behind him about eighty feet away in the desert foliage. At first, that man seemed to be taking photos of the evening desert that lay some thirty miles south of Phoenix and less than ten seconds from Washington, DC.

The Native American, John Nan Tan Gode, had classic chiseled features and was born and raised on the reservation, leaving it at age eighteen after graduating high school to join the United States Marines. It was clear even in boot camp that he had something unique going that had its genesis in the words of his grandfather who had taught him the "old ways," starting when he was thirteen years old.

His spirit was totally connected to this land. He knew that when he walked this desert, he was stepping where the many brave, bold, and sometimes naïve men who preceded him once walked. He could feel their energy and sense their spirit with the way things were playing out in their culture. How they had been led down a path of total dependence by an elite group of politicians who were concerned only with absolute power. Nothing more. Nothing less.

He could hear what sounded like clicking behind him as the sound rode the desert air to his animal-like ears. There were others who had joined the man, but there was no conversation accompanying their arrival. The one with the camera device used hand signals to communicate with them.

About twenty feet from where John was standing was a rise in the land. He proceeded with what he was doing despite the action behind him, moving slowly toward it while shaking his fist in the air. This was his grandfather's "old ways" method of bidding the sun a good-night and asking it to return in the morning. As he was ceremonially dancing and chanting toward the rise, he suddenly dropped to his knees. There he began his shaman-natured ritual celebrating the spirit of the wolf, the dominant creature of the night. As he chanted, a shadowy wolf slowly approached him out of the encroaching darkness, kissed his forehead, and stood there for a moment, watching him. After a moment, the animal turned and looked at the men who had stopped dead in their tracks as they approached from behind. The mysterious wolf's fierce eyes glared at them as they froze in place. He then slowly turned his glance back to the kneeling Native American, kissing his forehead again before disappearing back into the shadows. At that point, John heard movement coming from what sounded like three men. He got back to his feet and continued dancing his way into the darkness. He went behind the rise from where he was able to observe them, but they could not see him. He was a Ghost Warrior known as a "Shadow Wolf." One who could easily blend with the night. Disappear into the darkness at will.

They spread out, moving swiftly without making a sound, closing in from different directions on the place where they last saw him. All three had been startled by the appearance of the wolf and prepared themselves should it attack them.

John's first thoughts were that they were sent by one of the drug cartels to take him out because of his success with intercepting their supply lines into Arizona. He remained part of the darkness, blended with the desert landscape, observing them, totally hidden from their eyes, his Sig Sauer in his hand, poised at the ready.

As suddenly as they appeared, they were gone. Motionless, John held his position for another ten minutes to make certain they weren't doing the same and waiting for him to move. After a short time, the night sounds of the desert and his spirit wolf helped him to know they were gone.

"I thought that we had gotten them all, but maybe I was wrong. Never underestimate the Deep State," was John's lingering thought.

———————

A few days earlier, things had started to get strange when he began hearing from a confidential informant that there were black SUVs doing a lot of driving in the night "out where nobody was." He mentioned a young tribal member who might be of some help to him . . . for a price.

John made it his business to find that person so he could get an idea of what he knew about the goings-on so far out in the nighttime desert. The big lawman tracked him down at the casino where he worked part-time as a "gofer" errand boy. He quickly engaged the errand boy in conversation after showing his badge and telling him he had some questions about the SUVs he had seen out in the remote desert.

"How come you were out there?" John asked the young man whose nickname was "Sweet Tooth."

"I was camping."

"Out there? Why?" John asked.

"Wanted to be alone. Trying to find myself."

"I'd call that being as alone as you can get without being on the moon," John said sarcastically.

"I like being alone. That's all."

"How many nights did you see the SUVs, Tooth?"

"Oh, I don't know . . . Couple a' times . . . maybe."

"How long ago was this?" John asked pointedly.

"Maybe a month or so back."

"And you're telling me that you like camping out there enough to spend a couple of nights? Stop shitting me." John faked annoyance.

"Come on, man! Before you go acting like you don't believe me, you want me to show you where it is, and you'll see what I'm talking about?" The rangy young Indian was gangly and of average height,

5

dark-complexioned, with long, black hair and a constant, slightly hopeful smile. He wore a black "Billy Jack" style flat top cowboy hat. In his early twenties, he didn't light up the sky with his brilliance.

John didn't have to think much before taking him up on his offer, but he took notice of how quickly the offer was made to show the area where he had seen the SUVs. The tall lawman drove with him to the campsite. It was a long ride in John's dust-coated, black SUV. The dirt trail wound around saguaro cactus fields, which seemed endless, and low brush for about twenty miles. It ran up and down the rough landscape of the Arizona desert.

It was early afternoon when they got to the "campsite." John found an assortment of tire tracks indicating there was more than a little traffic running through there. This was a remote area, loaded with snakes and scorpions, and despite Sweet Tooth's claim of "wanting to be alone," it made no sense for him to be out there, in the middle of any night, alone. But it made a lot of sense for the vehicles to be there. It was simple—maybe the cartel had a new corridor through which to transport their drugs and people.

"Tell me, exactly how many camp-outs you been on, Tooth?" John asked with a serious tone to his whisper-quiet voice.

"A few. Like maybe three or something around that," he responded quickly. "Why?"

"You finding yourself yet?" John asked, not looking his way as he studied the tracks and the direction they were moving in while he spoke. This was a common occurrence in the Arizona desert between the Mexican border and Phoenix. Something, he thought, extremely dangerous and, if left unchecked, could cause the eventual destruction of the United States. The Deep State within the mainstream media kept the eyes of the country on the flood of illegals that were coming across the border. They painted them as simple people in need of a better life. It was a cunning distraction to take the eyes off the drugs that billionaire drug lords were pumping into the US. John knew why it was working and saw it as collusion between the paid-off media and the drug lords. His sense was that the then presidential administration in Washington was using the media as their potent tool for forwarding their open-borders agenda. He felt that they were poisoning the minds of the many who drank up what they were spewing like thirsty nomads in a desert oasis.

What troubled John even more was that the country was asleep when it came to the "OTMs" or "Other Than Mexicans" coming across a virtually open southern border into the country and possibly assembling for what America had never known before—a jihadi caliphate. His fear was that they were already spread throughout the country without anyone understanding how big a threat it was, especially in the American cities they could be targeting.

"What's your name, man?" Sweet Tooth asked in a friendly tone.

The tribal police officer turned toward him, looking him up and down without saying a word. He wondered about the world this kid lived in. Did he have a strong male role model in his life? Did he have anyone in his family who gave a damn about him? He felt a sudden surge of sadness fill his heart as he recalled his own upbringing by a mother who struggled to make his life good and a paternal grandfather who taught him the "ancient ways" from the time he could understand until he went off to the Marines. He thought about the way he was guided and kept on the "path" by two people who cared about him and the way his life should be. Did Sweet Tooth have anything like that in his life?

"My name is John Gode . . . John Nan Tan Gode," he answered with a trace of sensitivity.

"Cool . . . I like that. You are this quiet guy who moves around like no one I have ever seen. You are a 'rez' man, and yet . . . you ain't." He had a curious expression on his face. But he seemed sincere in a crude way. "How does a dude get himself into a job like you got?"

"A 'dude' gets himself a high school diploma, for starters. You got one of those?"

"Yeah . . . I graduated high school a few years ago. What do I have to do to get started? How do I become a cop?"

"You ever been in trouble?" John asked him, anticipating his answer.

"Sure . . . You know anybody who hasn't been in trouble?" he responded quickly, looking at his boots before looking back up, smiling.

"What kind of trouble, wiseass?"

"Oh, I don't know . . . I got drunk and raised some hell at a bar in Phoenix."

"What else?" John continued, looking at the tire tracks and a few footprints he had found while he was talking. He knew right away that they didn't belong to Sweet Tooth because they were from running shoes and were a few sizes larger than his.

"I got into a fight or two."

"And got your ass kicked, didn't you?"

"Wouldn't exactly say that. Got in a couple shots to the face before I took off running and left the asshole in the dust." He laughed. "I can move when I have to."

"Did the people in the vehicles see you out here?"

"No one sees me if I don't want them to see me," the youngster said smugly.

"What's your secret, Tooth?"

"I'm magic . . . pure magic . . . Officer," he said, smiling, his arms opened wide.

"So . . . what did you see the people in these vehicles do?"

"One night, they moved some scared-sounding folks from two vans into a box truck." He thought for a moment before saying, "Then on another night, two small trucks met up with a dark SUV, and three or four guys moved a bunch of small boxes from the truck beds into the back of the SUV. Then the two guys in the SUV counted whatever they put in their car and when they got done, handed them a small bag. At least, I think it was a bag."

"Any other time you saw them?" John was getting really interested now, and Sweet Tooth sensed his growing interest.

"Yeah, it looked like they dragged someone or something out of the truck bed and went off into the darkness. They were gone for about an hour and came back empty-handed." He was disturbed, telling that story. The memory of it caused him to realize that he was extremely fortunate to not have been discovered by those men while he was "camping out."

John didn't buy all of his story, but the part that he did buy caused him to fully understand that what was taking place out there under the cover of darkness was not something to be celebrated by good people.

There was a feeling about this place that disturbed John, but he couldn't put his finger on what that feeling was. It stirred something in his memory that made him feel uneasy, though he couldn't quite get where it all came together. It seemed to take him back to things his grandfather had warned him about when he was spending time learning from the old man. He remembered being told that he had the spirit of the snake in his bloodline and that "gave him power over some people and many snakes." It wasn't until he became a full-grown man that he totally understood what that meant. But what he had going on in that place, at that time, was unsettling at best.

As they began the ride back to the reservation, Sweet Tooth made some small talk while John said nothing until he asked, "What's your name, son?"

"You know that already. You been calling me by it since we've been talking. What'chu mean?"

"I'm gonna ask you again . . . What's your name?" He wanted the young man to understand that he wasn't in the mood for games. He looked at him with intensity.

After a futile shrug, he answered. "Henry."

"Henry what?" John signaled his impatience.

"Begaye . . . Henry Begaye." He thought for a moment before asking, "Why do you want to know?"

"I'm curious. And I need it for my report."

"Report! What report? Why are you doing a report? I thought this was just between you and me . . . I'm just trying to help you. I don't want to be in no report, man." He was upset.

"Look . . . ain't nobody gonna see any of this . . . provided—" He stopped dead in the middle of the small dirt road and in the middle of his sentence when he noticed several coyotes pawing the ground just off to the side of where they were driving. John got out quickly. He then paused for a few seconds before beginning to walk cautiously toward the animals. The younger man stayed in his seat, not wanting to move until he knew what was going on. He froze when he saw John draw his weapon slowly. The big man was hoping he wouldn't have to use it on the dogs as he moved to within fifteen feet of the small pack. They took off when he made some strange sounds and spoke words in a language the young Native American had never heard before. He shook his head,

9

saying to himself, "I believe those animals understood every word this guy said. This is some crazy shit, man."

He sat absolutely still, watching closely as the big man holstered his weapon and knelt down, picking up something small. He examined it slowly. The young Native American didn't know it, but John had discovered a tooth lying on a flat rock. There was a slight blood trail leading away from where he found it. A strange energy came over John as he folded it into a page he tore from a small notebook he kept in his hip pocket. Dropping it into his shirt pocket, he had the sense that it was something more than just a piece of a tooth. Something that sent a strange chill through his body. He stood up again and walked over to the place where the coyotes had been digging. Kneeling on one knee again, he began pushing the dirt around in front of him.

The younger man knew something bad was there when John threw his head back in disgust and looked away for a moment from whatever he had uncovered. Sweet Tooth got out of the vehicle and started making his way toward John.

"Stay back . . . don't come over here," the tall lawman commanded. Tooth froze at the ominous tone of his voice. He didn't want to piss him off, but at the same time, a familiar grim feeling started coursing through him. A feeling of dread of what John might have found.

"What'chu got there, horse?" Tooth asked, hoping against hope that it wasn't a body. "You find a body or something?"

John didn't respond. He held his hand up in a "stop" signal as Sweet Tooth resumed walking toward him. "Stay there!" John commanded as he looked at the handless and footless body of a Caucasian woman lying in the fresh shallow grave he had just discovered. Her face was totally covered with caked, bloody dirt and her teeth were all missing. He realized that he most likely had one of them in his pocket. The need to keep this to himself until after he had run a DNA and dental records ID check was firmly entrenched in his gut.

Henry was nauseous with fear that it might be the body of his brother, Jimmy, who was the reason why he was camping out in the "no-man's land" where his brother used to hide when he got into trouble. He was hoping to find him or learn something about where he could be by hanging around out there. Jimmy was four years older and quite a bit more adventurous. He was bolder and extremely prone to take chances that often made his younger brother afraid for him.

John dialed on his phone to report what he had found and to request a crime scene investigation team, then walked over to the younger Native American. He guided him back to the vehicle.

"What's there?" Henry asked with a shaky voice.

"A body."

"Shit." He suddenly broke away from John and ran back to the body. Looking at it closely, he wretched, almost vomiting, fearing what he might see. Then a breath of relief came slowly out of his mouth as he realized that it wasn't his brother lying there.

John walked back to him slowly and asked, "Who were you expecting that to be?"

"My brother Jimmy," he confessed flatly.

"Your brother? Why did you think that?"

"Because he's been running with some bad people. Really bad people, man." He tried to put the brakes on what he was saying, but it was too late.

John started putting it together as soon as the words left the young man's mouth. "You know, kid, I'm glad it's not your brother, but I'm wondering why you didn't mention this right out of the gate?" John hardened his tone.

"I don't know why. I just can't talk about it with anyone. You wouldn't understand any of this shit, man. It's like, family stuff."

"What kind of family stuff?" John watched his reaction to the question closely.

"Stuff like, I thought he might have gotten himself into some bad karma and it caught up with him."

"You want to tell me the story? The whole story. Then maybe I can help you."

Sweet Tooth looked down as he spoke. He shook his head, expressing his self-pity. "Not too many people into helping me these days."

"Well, maybe you just met one." John was stoic, but his sincerity came through when he wanted it to. "My feeling is that you got something on your shoulders that maybe needs to be lifted off. Talk to me."

The younger Native American wanted to trust John, and he actually had to fight back the tendency to do so. He had been burned by a lot of people he had trusted before and had adjusted his thought processes to stay away from anyone but family when it came to an issue like this. Maybe it was because the longer his brother was involved with whomever he was involved with in Mexico, the more desperate he was becoming, and the possibility of someone jumping in who could help was causing him to lower his guard. "I got a question for you, Gode."

"What?"

"Do you know anything about the Mexican military running practice shit on this side of the border?"

"Practice shit? What kind of practice shit you talking about? Maneuvers?"

"Yeah, like that. Is it something they can do?" He was skirting the issue somewhat, trying to find a way to ask the question without blurting out everything he knew about it.

"Not unless the big dogs in DC know about it." John was getting more and more interested in this conversation.

"Have you never heard about this stuff? You're a cop . . . you would know . . . right?"

"A cop is not a soldier. We don't get let in on what happens with the military on a lot of things they do."

"Yeah, but something like this . . . wouldn't you guys get involved? Like you work with the Border Patrol, don't you?"

"Sure we do, but they're law enforcement. Not military . . . " John was trying to get him to a point where he could say what was truly on his mind.

"They sure looked like they was military guys . . . " Sweet Tooth blurted out and seemed to regret that he had done so.

"Who are the 'they' you're talking about?" John jumped on the statement.

"Uh . . . the guys in the SUVs and the trucks."

"You saw all this, and no one saw you? That's hard to believe." John stared at him with a quiet intensity before he continued. "How did you get all the way out to that spot where they were doing business?"

"Business?"

John persisted. "How did you get there, and if you're going to tell me that you drove, where did you hide your car?"

"So like, I got a dirt bike, and it gets me around where I need to go . . . when I need to go," he said proudly. "When those guys showed up, it was always dark, and I just kept it lying on the ground, in the brush." He watched John for a reaction.

"There's more to this than you're telling me, Henry." John's eyes were like molten steel when he didn't hear what he wanted or if he felt he was being played—and at that moment, he felt like he was being played. He bent toward Sweet Tooth's face, since he was a good six inches taller, and said, "Stop bullshitting me with half-stories, man. You're not telling me anywhere near what you know, and it's making me not want to help you, Henry."

"Don't call me Henry . . . It's Sweet Tooth or just Tooth. Okay?" He was taken off guard by John's changing demeanor, and he didn't like it.

"Again . . . tell me what's really going on, or I might forget that I am trying to help you. Understand me?" John intimidated the young Native American, and he knew it.

Tooth stared at him, deciding if it was okay to unload what he knew. He decided to do it. "Okay . . . Okay, here it is." He took a breath and hesitated until John nudged him again.

"About a month ago, my brother shows me this wad of bills he's carrying around in his pocket. More money than I ever seen in one place ever before. He says, 'Keep this in a safe spot for me. Go ahead and buy our mom something nice, and buy yourself some ice cream. The rest goes in a place that only you know about, and it stays there until I get done with the job I'm doing.' "

Tooth adjusted his black, flat-brimmed Billy Jack cowboy hat, thought for a moment, then got right back into his story. "I asked him where he got all that money. I was afraid that he had done something stupid."

"Something stupid? Like what sort of something stupid?" John tried to get him to move along with the story before they would be interrupted by the crime scene investigators headed their way.

"Something stupid like robbing somebody or selling drugs to the wrong people. You know what I mean?"

John just nodded in response.

"Then he tells me that he's hooked up with some Mexican guys who run nighttime 'exercises,' he called them. Right out where we just were."

"Exercises? What kind of exercises?"

"Damned if I know. But whatever it is, he told me they do them a lot. He said that they were some heavy-duty hombres."

"Mexicans. No Americans? Just Mexicans?" John pushed him, trying to get a fix on whether or not they might be Deep State operatives.

"No, they weren't American. But he said that there were these heavy-breathing Arab guys coming out with them."

"Heavy-breathing. What was making them breathe heavy?"

"No, it doesn't have nothin' to do with breathing. It's like, the way they talk, man. He said they sound like they're gargling when they speak. They got some bad accents." Tooth tried to explain it as best he could.

"Did he tell you anything else about these guys?"

"Yeah, he said that they had him get them some women and hashish for when they're done with whatever they were doing out here in the dark."

"That was his job? You're telling me that your brother's a pimp and a drug dealer?"

"Yeah . . . and that's what worries me. He said he was going back down to Mexico with the rich guys and was going to stay there for a while because they were hiring him to help them with some 'projects.' "

"Projects? Did he say what kind of projects?"

"No. That's all he said and then he took off. He's got him a nice ride now. It's an Audi with Sonoran license plates. He's been strutting around, all proud, like he finally made something of himself."

John ran Tooth's story through his head, thinking that this was shaping up to be something that couldn't be classified as a happy ending for young Henry Begaye. The way people go missing in Mexico was becoming more and more expected in some circles of society these days, and Jimmy Begaye seemed to be traveling in those circles.

"That's the whole story?" John pressed him.

"No, there's a little more. Jimmy finally shows back up a few days ago and looks really worried, like he did something stupid. I ask him

14

what's up with everything, and he says 'get in the car, I want to show you something.' Then he takes me to the casino hotel and wants me to see some chick he has lined up. We get there, and she's not in her room, like she said she would be—and he freaks. I mean like he did something dumb with this chick. Like he regretted being there, and I think he was worried about being caught. I thought that maybe she was married, and her old man picked up on her screwing around with Jimmy or somethin'. Ya know?"

The Crime Scene Investigations Unit showed up and interrupted the conversation. John walked them over to the shallow grave while briefing them on how he came to find it. "I'll do a report and have it ready by tomorrow for you."

He motioned Sweet Tooth back into his vehicle and they began driving back.

"What's this going to do to my schedule?" Sweet Tooth asked as they rode the dusty desert trail.

"What schedule is that?" John looked over at him in the bouncing vehicle.

"Well, like, I'm gonna, like, be your assistant on this. Right?"

"My assistant?" John looked at him with a slight smile. There was something going on with this kid that John found worthy. "Now, let me think this through. You're going to be my assistant . . . My assistant what?"

"Your assistant, uh, cop . . . I guess."

"You guess?" John was beginning to enjoy his newfound friend's naivety. But that coupled with his sense that somehow, some way, Jimmy Begaye might be messing with some dangerous people. He couldn't shake the notion that this could have something to do with the international Deep State. The hidden actors who played hard with the truth and understood the real game and its dark rules.

## 03: Hot Girl, Bad Boys

THAT DAY, AFTER he dropped Sweet Tooth at the casino, John drove to his task force headquarters.

"Where you been, Moose?" Bellamy, one of task force members, asked when John walked through the door into the squad room.

John didn't respond because his attention was taken by what was lying on his desk. It was a picture of a beautiful young woman posing in a seductive red dress. Her hair was copper, flaring around her tan face. Her eyes captivated him immediately. "Who's this?" He nodded at the photo.

"Some gal who says she needs to talk with you, and right away."

"What's with the picture?" John asked curiously.

"I guess it's a motivator to get you to get in touch 'right away.' That would work for me." Bellamy had a smile on his face.

"She say what this was about?" John took off his black jacket, which had a patch on the left sleeve with an insignia of a wolf encapsulated in an arrowhead, and draped it across the back of his chair.

"She said it was about something you might be interested in knowing. Claimed she's an investigative reporter following a story you might wanna hear."

"Why didn't she talk to you about it?" John asked.

"I guess because I ain't you. Believe me, I offered to listen . . . intently . . . but all she wanted was you . . . you stud, you." He smirked as he spoke in mock admiration.

"This her number?"

"Yeah, and I'd get right on it, man. You don't want something that looks like that going elsewhere for help."

"Her name is Maria?" John looked closely at the piece of paper. "No last name?"

"That's all she gave up."

"When was it she stopped by?"

"About two days ago." Bellamy smiled. "Hope she's still around . . . so maybe I can be of some help to her, just in case. Uh, she said that she wanted to meet you for coffee because she knows what a coffee freak you are."

"Now, how could she possibly know that, Bellamy? You giving up my secrets?"

"She said to tell you, and I quote, 'that more things are revealed over coffee than on a golf course.' "

John jerked his head back in mock reaction as he half laughed, "What?"

"Yeah, I know. I almost said the same thing to her. But the word's out, Johnny Boy—you are a coffee freak, and apparently the world knows it."

John's curiosity was raised as he dialed her number, but it went immediately to voicemail, a message saying that she would return the call as soon as possible.

"What's she got, Big John? Is she into cops, ya think? Does she want to thank you for your service, before the fact?"

"Bellamy, Bellamy, Bellamy . . . why is it that you think all that women want is a cop to love?"

Bellamy turned around in his chair and threw his feet up on his desk before saying, "Now, that makes no sense. If that was all women wanted, how could she have resisted this beautiful specimen?" With mock pride, he pointed both his thumbs at his chest.

Although John liked Bellamy, he thought him a bit nosey. And he was, at times, somewhat annoyed by his seemingly constant barrage of questions.

Bellamy was a man in his early thirties and a former mixed martial artist who believed that the only way to win a fight was to believe he could. He was part of the fugitive task force operating on the reservations and all the cities around Arizona. Bellamy was on special assignment from the Maricopa County Sheriff's Office, and his specialty was Intelligence. His blond hair was cut in the military style he had kept after his tour with the US Army in Afghanistan.

"So . . . John Nan Tan Gode, what have you been up to?" Bellamy pressed him for an answer, sensing something bothering the big lawman.

John shook his head as he looked down at his desk. "There's this kid who has something going on that makes me wonder what is actually going on. He tells me that he has an older brother who may be in with some bad hombres. The brother supposedly gave the kid a wad of money for safekeeping." John relaxed into his chair as he continued. "This kid was hanging out in the desert, checking on his brother to see if he showed back up, just in case he might need his help with what he was doing. The brother had told him that he had some dark-of-night business that sometimes brought him to the open spaces south of Phoenix. Supposedly on the Tohono Odom Reservation. So he winds up spying on what he claims is a lot of middle-of-the-night traffic moving north and south under the cover of darkness. He somehow seems to have gone unnoticed by the traffic, which is amazing if he's observing who I think he is."

"Yeah . . . sounds a bit strange. But you know how dark it is out there when the sun sets. You know better than anyone, John."

"Not dark enough for those folks. No, I think my little buddy is not telling the whole story yet. But it's worth taking a look at one of these nights, real soon. But there's more. Today I take a ride with this kid to the place in the desert where he claims to have seen all this traffic. When we get there, sure enough, there's all kinds of tire tracks that seem to indicate that he may be telling the truth. Possible it could be another route for the Mexican cartels that we should be giving a look-see."

Bellamy jumped in. "Let's put something together. Tonight? I like this story, and we both know how quickly things can change. So let's check this out. Might be something good."

"Wait. I'm not done. We start riding back and maybe a tenth of a mile or so up the trail there is a small pack of coyotes furiously digging at something right off the trail, in the brush. So I stop to take a look at what's got their attention, and what do I find but a woman's body in a really shallow grave? Only covered by an inch or two of dirt." John paused.

"No shit?"

"Yeah, no shit, Bellamy. Her hands, feet, and teeth were gone, and her face was caked in blood so bad, it was hard to see her features."

Bellamy said eagerly, "I think that we should put a team together and get out there tonight to take a gander at what's going on."

"You got nothing else to do tonight, Bellamy?" John chided.

"Sure, I always have something going. That's the way it is in 'Good-Looking Bachelor Land.' I can always do that, John. But this may be tied to some of that 'Fast and Furious' shit, and you know how I am about the business of our fine, upstanding federal government."

As John was running Sweet Tooth's story through his mind again, he decided to call the forensics lab to arrange a DNA analysis on the tooth he found. He was keeping it to himself, so he went to a technician he had worked with many times before, asking her to keep this under the radar. The tech, Jill Ramone, agreed to do so without question and suggested he run it over to the lab while she was still on duty. He did so and returned to task force headquarters within an hour. He had the lingering sense that there could be something much bigger than a simple murder case here. Why would the handless and footless body of a Caucasian woman be lying in a shallow grave in the middle of nowhere in the desert? It didn't make sense at that moment. Maybe someone was trying to send a message. And what that message was, exactly, remained to be seen.

As John returned to the task force headquarters, he saw Bellamy talking with two other officers. "What's this guy's name who showed you the tracks in the desert?" Bellamy asked.

" 'Sweet Tooth.' I guess it's because he has a sugar addiction he got that nickname." John was keeping Sweet Tooth's real name to himself.

"Yeah, that's it, 'Sweet Tooth.' Sugar addiction—don't we all suffer from that? How many donuts have passed through that door?" Bellamy laughed as he pointed to the entryway.

John headed right to the office of the task force commander, Armando Grant. He belonged to the Phoenix police department and had worked undercover narcotics for over eight years. Grant was prone to work with his officers' hunches, and John was always operating on his. He totally trusted his gut. And his gut was leaning toward looking into the area where Sweet Tooth had camped.

---

Armando was comfortable with the idea of letting John lead the group on a scouting expedition to determine if what he heard from his new informant was right. Within two hours, the whole squad was assembled in the big meeting room next to the task force commander's office. John briefed them on the information he had. Bellamy followed up with some sketchy intelligence about possible border incursions. They were mostly based on reports received by the US Border Patrol, and two of them had been confirmed as actually having occurred by the Mexican military or people dressed like Mexican military over the past six months. There were also coincidental reports of finding dead bodies in the desert where the incursions happened. Bullet-riddled bodies of men, mostly in their early twenties. There were also other bodies that had been beheaded.

Task Force Commander Grant cautioned the group about what they could find out there and reminded them that if it was the Mexican military that the informant was seeing, it would be highly sensitive State Department stuff that could bring federal heat down on them. "So don't be a bunch of cowboys, any of you. I don't want my ass hauled before a congressional committee because we started a war with Mexico." That was greeted with laughter and some "Oh yeahs!" from the group of law enforcement officers.

"I'm putting John here in charge." The five-foot-eight-inch fireplug of a man nodded toward the big man. "It's his baby, and I believe you all know that he has an accurate gut. And his gut is telling him this is something to run with. But . . . if you get into the weeds on this, make sure you find me immediately. I'm gonna assume you all understand that . . . and should, if for some reason it becomes necessary, you keep the media in the dark. Until we know anything about the shit that's going on . . . for real, we have nothing to say to anybody outside this room. So be careful, and that means no cowboy shit." He looked around the room, squinting with intensity as he continued, "Okay, Gode, it's yours." Then Armando Grant sat down slowly in a chair in front of the group.

John moved back to the front of the room and looked everyone over before saying, "I think he said it all. Anyone got any questions?"

Noche, a forty-year-old Hispanic/Native American who was one of John's "trusted few," asked quietly, "Big John, how come you are moving on this without looking into the facts a little further? Not your usual MO, my man."

He was right. John was not one to rush into things. Especially something like this. Noche liked to needle John and knew he could because of their brotherhood background as "Shadow Wolves," those who were trained in the old ways because they had the natural instincts of a wolf and could do things like track people and animals based on factors that others couldn't see or smell. "Ghosts" or "Shadow Wolves" were legends in the Native American culture, no matter what the tribe or nation. No matter where in the country, it was understood that these folks had "spirit power."

John put his hand up and turned it from front to back, then closed it from pinky to thumb in a circular grasp known in martial arts as the "talon fist." It was the way a hawk grasps its prey and a method of gaining everyone's attention. "Listen. I see this as a 'look-see.' First, we take a 'look.' Then if we 'see,' we hang back and follow what we see. If those who we see get wind that we see them, then we need to have enough firepower to deal with it. We have to find out what all's going on here . . . first. Okay?" He looked at everyone for agreement and got it. They all respected his instincts after having worked with him for over a year on the task force. They had all learned not to disagree with him when he said, "I feel it in my gut."

They loaded their SUVs with ammo for their Sig Sauer hand weapons, their shotguns, and their AR-15s. "Hey, John, what about taking a mortar or two?" Noche kidded his friend as he loaded his vehicle.

"Asshole," John uttered quietly in response.

They rode in black, four-wheel-drive SUVs. John had Murphy, a young Phoenix PD SWAT member on temporary assignment with his task force, riding with him.

The three assigned to Noche were: Deanne Higgins, a woman agent with the DEA who could hold her own as a member of this or any other task force; Anthony Quadrino, a leather-skinned veteran cop wise beyond his years who was built like a linebacker with a round face and stood about five-foot-ten; and Maurice "Scotty" Random, a black man pushing thirty who had the body of a man who looked like he lived in the gym. The latter two were both tough Tempe, Arizona, cops.

John named Bellamy as the leader of his team, which included the other woman on that task force team, Bonnie Simms, who was on loan from the ATF. She was trained in the Chinese martial art of Bagua, one of the deadliest of the Chinese internal martial arts. The other two officers assigned were Tyrone Homer, a Chandler cop, whose specialty was finding fugitives, and his partner Pete Satorio, who excelled at whipping ass and quick thinking and belonged to the Pinal County Sheriff's Office.

As the sun was setting, they rolled out of South Phoenix in convoy toward the desert to the south of the city, fully aware of what might lie ahead of them. Bellamy did a com check with the team and recalibrated the GPS to ensure accurate coordinates so their whereabouts would be exact in case they needed backup.

John led them along the dirt path he rode earlier with Sweet Tooth, checking the fading landmarks as they went. It was just about dark when they arrived where most of the traffic had been. They dispersed into the brush, turned on their surveillance equipment, and waited as darkness completely overtook the desert. John was in the second vehicle placed in the middle of where the other three were sitting. The night grew more intense with each passing minute and they depended on that to keep their profiles hidden. A pack of four-legged coyotes ran past John's vehicle without stopping to investigate.

Bellamy called John on his mobile to ask him, "You watching the coyotes?"

"Yeah, I am. Why do you ask, Bell?"

"Just wondering if you know the difference between coyotes and dogs."

"Ah . . . so here comes the first pearl of wisdom for the night . . . go ahead, why don't you tell me?"

"Well, a dog would have come straight to the car and pissed on it. Coyotes don't do that."

John rose up in his seat with mocked excitement and responded to Bellamy, "Let me write that down. Holy shit, Bellamy, this could change everything we know about dogs and coyotes."

"Calm down, asshole." He smirked. "Small observations like that can lead to great vision. All creatures are subject to pack mentality, and pack mentality shows natural patterns. And since we are all animals and subject to the same laws of nature, it could be a useful tool one day, compadre."

"I already know that. Maybe I'm rubbing off on you." John laughed quietly. He thought that maybe his statement might have more truth to it than jest, but his knowledge of these types of things was deeply engrained after learning the old ways from his shaman grandfather.

"King two to king one," a static-filled message came through the radio.

"King one," John keyed his response.

"Something's moving our way. At eleven o'clock from where you are. It looks like a truck running dark and slow. It should be coming into your view in a few seconds."

"Stand by, two and three." John caught sight of the vehicle, about two hundred feet from where he was sitting, as it moved north on the dirt road. It was rolling at about fifteen miles per hour and seemed to be on a steady course. John watched it with his night vision binoculars.

"That's Border Patrol. Hold!" A Border Patrol light truck was something that should not have been surprising to the task force, but when the expectation is to see bad guys and instead you see good guys, it can throw off the "pattern" somewhat.

They held their positions and watched the truck move by. Five minutes later, another vehicle appeared on the same track following behind the Border Patrol vehicle.

"Here comes another one," Bellamy transmitted, watching it move slowly.

John observed it through the night glasses. "This one is not Border Patrol. Just a van. King three, follow that one. Stay far enough behind so they don't get spooked." He pulled out his phone and called Armando Grant. "Chief, we got something that needs some looking into."

"Go ahead, John." Armando sounded like he had been awakened by the call.

John said, "I need someone to follow a Border Patrol vehicle and a van that is following it. They're driving north, and I'll bet they'll be coming out on Riggs Road."

"Why do you want to put a tail on a Border Patrol vehicle?" Grant was puzzled.

"Gut," John answered matter-of-factly.

"That's it? Gut?"

"Yeah." John was solid on that one.

"Okay . . . how much time do you estimate before they get to Riggs Road?"

"Probably forty minutes from now. Maybe a few minutes more. They were moving real slow, running dark when they went by our checkpoint."

"Let me see what I can scramble. Hope I get someone there in time." He didn't sound fully awake.

"Hey, Chief, I have a feeling that something's not right here. Please tell the 'tail' to stay low."

"I'll try to get a few cars on this. Be careful, John. Bye."

"Look." Bellamy pointed to a third vehicle lumbering along the road, following the same path.

John dialed Noche, who was in the vehicle following the van.

"Hey, John," Noche answered quickly.

"Noche, there's another van coming up behind you. Just get off the road and wait for it to pass you by, then get behind that one. I think they're probably all heading for Riggs Road."

"Okay. Why do you think that's where they're headed? I noticed at least three other cut-offs between where we just were and the one at Riggs."

"Gut," was John's stoic answer.

"Yeah, man. Shoulda known. Bombs away." Noche totally understood John's gift and connection to the spirit and did not question his friend and tribal brother. He drove into the brush and parked about fifty feet from the road, waiting for the next van.

About three minutes later, Noche's team caught sight of the following van as it rolled slowly along the dirt road. Letting it pass, he waited about a minute before rolling back out onto the dirt road and resumed trailing what could be prey. The heavy darkness made Noche feel invisible and confident that those he was following had no idea they were being followed, at least until they hit the pavement on Riggs Road, just south of Phoenix. The van they were trailing suddenly peeled out and sped toward the highway. There was no sign of the Border Patrol truck or the van that was following it.

Bonnie said, "They made us, Noche."

He voice-dialed John and relayed what was happening. John told him to pursue and make a felony stop when they could. "Remember what you could be dealing with, Noche. These people make the Jamaican Posse look like boy scouts. I'm rolling your way, so keep me posted on where you're heading."

Noche took off with emergency lights flashing and siren wailing. The mood in the SUV became extremely serious and focused as they readied themselves for the worst. Two police units that had arrived just minutes earlier and were sitting in wait for the van joined in the pursuit on Interstate 10 when a Phoenix PD helicopter suddenly appeared overhead. They weren't on the highway long, exiting about eight miles north onto Ray Road. Blowing through another light, they headed west into the foothills of Ahwatukee. More units joined in the chase, and the sky was now lit up with red and blue flashing lights as they rolled into the bedroom community just southeast of Phoenix.

John was moving up the dirt trail, with Bellamy's team following, pushing toward the Riggs Road exit. They hit it in just about twenty minutes from when they started. Noche gave him the area they were speeding through. Luckily it was late enough at night that there wasn't much traffic on the roads and few people on the streets.

The van blew a tire as it quickly turned onto a side street. Everyone in it bailed out, running in the same direction. Noche directed the squad as they jumped out of their vehicle and pursued on foot. The suspects jumped a block fence by a big house four hundred feet ahead of them. All four of the squad moved stealthily behind them, bending low to make a smaller target if they were shot at.

John raced up the highway with Bellamy close behind. As they peeled off onto the Ray Road exit, they were waved through the light by a marked PD unit.

John called Noche for a status and location report. He got what he needed from his Shadow Wolf brother and sped to their location. There was a "knowing" that the Shadow Wolves shared that came from their spiritual connection, and it came in real handy when they were tracking or heading into danger.

When Noche's squad approached the fence they had observed the suspects going over, he put up his hand, stopping them. He pointed at himself and then pointed two fingers at his eyes, indicating he would "take a look." There was streetlight behind them that would have made anyone going over that wall a nice target, so he went around the fence to the other side of the house into a cluster of small, ornate trees that would make him less visible. He pulled himself up, surveying a large backyard and swimming pool.

He heard a heavily accented voice say, "*Culero* . . . Hey, look what I brung you, man."

*Bam, bam!* Two shots rang out. One hit the cinder block right below his chin and the other rang by his right ear.

"Son of a bitch," was all Noche could get out as he dropped to the ground and moved back behind the small trees, hoping he was invisible. He heard a door open and people trying to rush out. A woman screamed, followed by the sound of a door slamming shut.

Noche shook his head and called John. "We got us a hostage situation," was his greeting.

John flew toward them. Pulling up to the patrol unit, he left his vehicle like a tiger coming out of a cave, moving low and rapidly toward Noche. Bellamy was right behind with his team, and Murphy followed, feeling in his pockets for his phone.

"What happened?" he asked, sensing his Shadow Wolf brother's angst.

"What happened is this . . . we hauled ass trying to stop the van these guys were running in, and when they blew a tire, they bailed, ran to this fence, and jumped over. We followed and when I popped my head up, they took a couple of shots at me."

"You okay?" John checked his face and voice for the answer. Seeing he was all right, he asked, "How many we got over the fence?"

"I saw five, at least. Did you hear me on the phone about hostages?"

Murphy crawled up beside John and Noche. "I got a view into what looks like the den, and they are holding two people—a man and a woman. They have them kneeling on the floor with guns to their heads, and the woman is freaking out."

"How many, Murphy?"

"I don't know. I could only see one of them for just a second. Now they've drawn the drapes."

John's eyes were narrow and looked like the eyes of a cobra. His chiseled facial features showed no emotion.

A loud, wailing woman's scream came from the house. They knew something bad was happening or about to happen because of the nervous intruders who might hurt the couple.

John said to Bellamy, "You and me are going in the front door high and low, cutting the pie. Noche, you, Bonnie, and the rest of your team cover the back. We'll try to push them toward you into the yard. Try to take them alive, but if they don't want to cooperate, then take them out." He said stoically, "This has got to be lightning-quick. Can't allow them time to kill the hostages. If we do, they will."

Noche's team took their positions along the back side of the fence where he had been when the shots rang out. Murphy and Deanne Higgins followed John and Bellamy toward the front of the house.

"SWAT's on the way," a police officer told John as he made ready to hit the door. He took a flash bang from his field jacket pocket and said, "We don't have time to wait." He nodded to Bellamy as he crouch-walked up to the front door and put his foot to the handle, knocking it wide open as he threw the device into the house. There was a quick explosion as it went off.

They went in, each covering the other's half. Three shots rang out from the den, hitting the walls in the hallway ahead of them. John saw where they came from, and as one of the perpetrators started to drop behind a couch, the big man put one in his head. The home invader fell backward.

Standing in the middle of the room was a heavyset, intense-looking man with a black bandana tied around his head. His huge mustache moved when he yelled, "*Payaso* . . . I'm gonna kill this bitch if you don't—"

It was all he was able to get out as Bellamy put a hole through his forehead. The middle-aged woman was frantic and collapsed on the floor screaming, "My husband, my husband, they took him in there." She pointed toward a side bedroom.

"Come out, assholes. You don't have a chance. Don't make us have to kill you," John shouted as he and Bellamy prepared for whatever was coming next. There was mumbling near the door. "Okay, okay, we're done . . . we're coming out . . . don't shoot." Three young, Hispanic-looking men came out of the bedroom single file with their hands in the air, walking slowly.

"Get on the ground," Bellamy ordered as Murphy and Deanne came through the door and patted the three down after cuffing them. John found the husband unconscious on the bedroom floor, but he was still breathing. It looked like he had been hit with a pistol butt, from the gash on the side of his head. "Get the EMTs in here quick," John shouted as the police moved in and started searching the rest of the house for accomplices.

The place looked like a war scene, with gun smoke and bodies lying on the floor. The woman was still crying and embracing her injured husband as the task force members nodded at one another, the anxiety-driven adrenaline subsiding in each one of them. They had functioned like a well-oiled machine that had just saved two innocent lives. All lives matter. Do they not?

# 04: Inside the Federal Building

"GENTS—AND LADY, if I can abuse the term,"—there was laughter at this—"please be seated."

Special Agent Mo "Dogface" Miner was not a happy camper. He just had his butt chewed by the SAC.

"Why the fuck are you letting our cartel-jihadist allies get captured by the locals? You are supposed to know where every local LEA is all of the time, and give these people clear passage. This is a presidential priority. One more screw-up, and you are headed for Alaska."

Dogface looked around the table—every person in the room was a 34th degree "Bubba" with a lifetime of service to the cause, and each was in one of the top three positions of their respective agencies for the Southwestern FEMA District VI territory.

"Come to order. We only have thirty minutes off the clock. The room has been swept.

"POTUS has sent me a secure message. He has one thousand more invited 'guests,' as the local sheriff calls them, coming over the border in the next month, and he is counting on us to give them free passage.

"I know it's tough with all the OTMs and every federal, state, and local agency trying to bag as many illegal aliens as possible, but this is how we earn our Cayman Island end-of-year bonuses, so I need for each of you to double-down.

"Next month we're going to try something new. I've arranged for a National Guard unit commanded by one of us—another 34th—to schedule a drill that will clear all LEAs from a five-mile-wide open border. Another 34th commanding a Mexican military unit is going to do the same thing on their side, mirroring our control and creating a corridor.

"We are going to jam five hundred jihadists up America's ass in one night. The hard part is going to be distributing them in the few hours of darkness that we will have left.

"FEMA, this is where your private train comes in. I want to load all five hundred on your train, which will be announced as rapid deployment test and evaluation, and then have you distribute twenty-five at a time from here to Ithica, New York. You will have one boxcar isolated from the larger group, and that will be how we transport the radioactive material and explosives that will be dropped in Phoenix, with 36th a part of the special team.

"An FBI 34th will meet the train at each stop—I'll give you the locations and the timing through our encrypted channel that NSA cannot see, much less read—and my counterpart will ensure that a shielded school bus takes each twenty-five off your hands and to various drop off points, including bus depots.

"Each jihadist will be armed and have one backpack with shielded communications, money, water, and food for three days. They are not to be searched and nothing is to be taken from them. These people will kill you if you break protocol, and we don't want any incidents. Make sure your 34ths are on the train and at each stop, and make sure all of the unwitting personnel have very clear instructions—the cover story is that these are crisis actors on their way to a major exercise, everything in their possession is GFE and not to be inspected or interfered with in any way.

"Now, any questions? Tom?"

"Sir, we've detected communications between Mexican intelligence and the police chiefs in major US cities. The Mexicans are on to us, and they seem to have decided it is in their interests to help US police stop and expel the OTMs, including our jihadists. Any thoughts on this potential threat to the operation?"

"Thank you, Tom. POTUS is aware of this new Mexican campaign, he is mobilizing the 34ths through the 36ers on the Mexican side to try to redirect their official resources to the Yucatan, where our CIA counterparts are assassinating a few landowners and generally making their usual mess. I understand that the 'Free Republic of the Yucatan' will make news the week before we jam our five hundred.

"Separately the secretary of Homeland Security, who was always a 36er, is in the process of hand-picking new chiefs of police, and the mayors, many of them 35ers, are being offered substantial financial incentives to switch out the few remaining chiefs that are not part of our movement.

"One last thing. The White Hats within the CIA are starting to piss me off. They have been running undeclared drone operations in our territory, and I am concerned that they and some of the military White Hats might be planning to intervene to stop our program.

"There is also a US marshal in Phoenix who has been asking too many questions and, of course, the goddamned tribal police taking down some of our people in the desert. I've assigned our Whitewater Enterprises contractor the mission of terminating these annoying assholes.

"Those of you in a position to do so, when they end up dead, make sure the investigation is slow-rolled the way we have slow-rolled all of our executions of high-profile people."

# 05: MEN IN BLACK ON A DESERT ROAD

IT WAS 11:15 at night when they arrived with their prisoners at task force headquarters, where they placed the three of them in separate rooms. Murphy asked if he could have a go at one of them. John thought for a moment, then said, "Settle down. We need to wait for the boss before we start asking questions. These guys were over their heads, quickly, and that's puzzling to a poor Indian like me. What do you think, Bellamy?"

"Don't know. They're up here to do something, but what that is . . . can't say, yet. But I think we just might find out at some point. Do ya think?" He looked at John when he spoke to the group.

Armando Grant walked briskly through the door and asked for the whole story. "Talk fast, John, the feds are on their way here, and they said they want to take the case over as soon as they arrive. You have any idea why they would want to do that?"

"They ain't taking no freaking case over, boss. Come on . . . we almost got a couple of us killed grabbing these assholes . . . and these other assholes with fed badges think they're swooping in and taking over?"

"I'll make that call, John. Let's see what they have and hear what they got to say. I'll do the talking . . . keep that in mind. Okay?" He was no one to try to push around, and that made John calm down some. But he wasn't kicking in to whatever crap they were bringing.

"Let me talk with this one." Bellamy pointed at the one in the first interview room. He was inked all along his neck with gang symbols that told him even though this was a relatively young man, he had been "inside." He looked to be maybe twenty-three years old at most.

John said, "Okay, I'll take the one in the middle room. Noche, you get with the guy on the end."

Bellamy walked in and was met with a defiant glare from Outlaw Number One. He watched the lawman sit down. A sneer came to his face as he said, "What'chu looking at, *pendejo*?"

"You." Bellamy was measuring this man and not engaging him yet.

"You lookin' at me like you like me. You got me hooked up here, man. I can't do nothin'. If you take these cuffs off, I'll give you a lesson in what you get when you piss people like me off."

Bellamy didn't say a word. He just sat quietly staring at the outlaw, who was staring right back at him.

"Come on, asshole, you got somethin' to say. Come on, say it." He was pushing hard but getting nowhere with Bellamy.

The lawman got up slowly from his chair and backed out of the room, never changing the expression on his face or breaking eye contact with the manacled man glaring at him.

Bellamy walked down the hall and tapped on the door of the room where Outlaw Number Two was being held. John opened the door as Bellamy waved his head toward the room that he had just left and said, "He's giving up his compadres. He's ready to make a deal."

"That's bullshit, man. Come on . . . what'chu you think you got here?" Outlaw Number Two chuckled dismissively and leaned back in his chair, a confident smile on his face.

"We got you . . . that's what we got." Murphy was sitting in the shadows directly behind him as he leaned forward and tapped him on the back of his head. "And before you know it, your girlfriend in the other room is gonna make a deal. Then we'll really be telling you that we got you . . . for a long, long time."

"Fuck you, asshole." He looked hardened, with short, cropped hair. His Mandarin-style mustache was full and somewhat complimented by the teardrop tattoo under his left eye. A prison gang identifier. Like the other two, he was no older than his mid-twenties, but his eyes held an old intensity that made Bellamy glad he was cuffed.

John stepped outside the room and asked Bellamy, "You get anywhere with yours?"

"No, but he is psyched . . . pissed-off psyched." He made a face and smiled with confidence. "He'll be more talkative as time goes by."

"What's he got for ink?" John had all three figured for prison gang members, which made them more likely to have nothing to lose.

"Let's go see what's up with Noche." John nodded his head toward door number three. He knocked, and Deanne opened the door. Noche was sitting with his head close to Outlaw Number Three's, smoking a cigarette with him, one of Noche's assets when trying to gain another's confidence.

"Yeah, man." The bearded man, handcuffed in front, was having a good conversation with Noche. He exhaled a big cloud of smoke. "These dudes ain't Chicano or anything like that. They look like us, but they don't act like us."

Bonnie asked him, "Where are they from?" She was expecting to hear him say they were from some other Latin American country.

"Pakistan . . . but they speak Spanish like they come from Spain when they speak slow. But when they get excited, they sound like they're gargling or somethin'."

"I don't get that, Paco." Noche was speaking in his normal laid-back voice that was so disarming even desperados like Number Three were comfortable around him. Everybody liked Noche, everyone except his former wife. She did not like him, even a little bit.

Before John could speak, the task force commander opened the door and beckoned John out into the hall. Standing there was a group of four federal agents, including a tall, thin, middle-aged man wearing dark glasses, a black suit, white shirt, and power tie. In an instant, John did not like the vibe he got from him.

Armando announced John and Bellamy to the group. They acknowledged one another except for the one in the dark glasses. After a moment, he said, "We'll take over from here."

"Like hell, you will," was John's instant response. "These three belong to us until we say they don't."

"Not anymore. We got warrants . . . federal warrants." He waved some papers at John, indicating that he was holding the warrants in his hand.

"You can stick them up your ass. We're not done talking with these guys. When we are, we'll let you know." John was right in Sunglasses' face as he spoke.

"Back off, John. That's an order." Armando pointed at the big man. "We'll sort this out in my office." The task force commander turned and led the way to the front of the building.

John told Bellamy to get back to his prisoner and have Bonnie sit in with him.

As soon as the door to Armando's office closed, John looked at his boss and the so-far-unnamed federal agent with the sunglasses and asked, "What's going on here? I'm wondering how you guys got here so fast. And what gives you the balls to think that we're just going to turn these guys over to you?"

Sunglasses made a face, let out a frustrated breath, and looked at Armando. "Please explain reality to your boy here."

Armando lost his cool for a moment. "He's not a 'boy,' and if I were you, I'd apologize damn quick for that remark before he stuffs you in that top desk drawer over there." Armando looked at his desk. "I think John's right . . . uh, 'Agent' . . . ? Haven't heard your name yet. Haven't seen a badge or ID either." He looked at the man in the sunglasses like he expected an answer and nothing was going to happen beyond that moment.

After another frustrated breath, he produced a badge with the initials CSS emblazoned boldly on it, showed the "creds" inside the badge case, and said, "I'm Special Agent Wilson. Not difficult to check me out, and after you do . . . we'll be on our way with our prisoners."

"Like I said, *Special Agent* Wilson, you can be on your way now, but like I keep telling you, those guys ain't going anywhere until we say they are." John spoke quietly but his voice chilled the room. He looked at his boss and asked if he could get back to business with the interviews.

Armando nodded his approval, and John left the room after giving Wilson a look he had learned from his Chinese internal martial arts teacher. Something that was known as "Iron Face." It was completely void of emotion—empty, an abyss that no one would ever want to fall into.

In an instant, John Gode was gone, and Wilson knew he was not going to prevail over this shadowy man who passed through him like a heavy wind passes through a forest.

Noche was in the hall, waiting for his Shadow Wolf brother. "John, there is something going on with these guys that is not regular business." He was referring to the desperado he was holding and what he had just gotten out of him.

John walked him down the hall and out the side door so they were out of earshot of the feds. "What is it, Noche?"

"He's spewing his views about how lame we are with the way we treat his fellow countrymen through our 'immigration shit,' when he says something about Arabs and that they are going to be coming into Arizona. Then he gets to crowing that 'they are going to make the illegal Mexicans look like people we will welcome when they get done with us.' Then as suddenly as he started giving up what he knew, he stops . . . Like in mid sentence, with an 'oh crap' expression on his face and he clams up." Noche looked deeply concerned as he stared at his law enforcement brother-in-arms.

"He give up any specifics?"

"Nothing at first."

"At first, Noche?"

"It's what I said. He made a mistake that helped me move him to a better place . . . more open to sharing what he really knows."

"What did you do?" John knew how skilled Noche was at getting into people's heads, but his getting to this guy so quickly surprised even him.

"He made the mistake of mentioning how bad he thought he was because even snakes don't scare him."

"Really? He said that?" John liked this story now. "And I bet you showed him how wrong he was for blurting those oh-so-very unwise words . . . and out of the clear blue, I bet." He waited patiently for Noche to continue. "And what did you do?"

"I put a snake at his feet." Noche looked like he was very happy with himself as he almost burst through his cheeks, and a gleeful look filled his dark eyes.

"No, you didn't do that." John had to laugh at the thought. "Did you do that? I thought I was the only one with the 'snake spirit' here."

"Yeah, and I'm the one with the blanket that I dropped on a big fat rattler sitting near my truck, eyeing a mouse that was running toward this building. Pissed that snake off . . . Man, did I do that, and he came out of that old blanket ready to put his anger on the first living creature he met. So I left him alone with my man in there." He paused, watching for a reaction to the story from John.

"You telling me the snake bit him?" John wasn't sure he liked what he was hearing anymore.

"No . . . didn't even get close to that. No . . . he started singing like a night bird as the snake coiled and shook his rattles. I dropped the blanket back on him as that slithering son of a bitch began his move. Right at that moment . . . and that did it. The boy was ours."

"Okay. The suspense is killing me," John said in mock frustration. "What did he give up?"

"Just that the Arab guys enjoy partying on the graves of those they kill. And they are partying on our turf . . . right here in old AZ. You suppose they put some people in the ground right here under our noses?"

"You already know that the Border Patrol found the heads of some poor bastards who were probably their victims. They are known for separating the head from the rest of the body . . . no?" John stated the obvious to Noche.

"He said that these 'parties' have some people, although he doesn't know exactly who they are, he gets a feeling that they are Americanos . . . important Americanos!"

"Did he say what makes him think that?"

Noche was loving this. "I asked him that very same question. Do you see how much alike we think, Gode?"

"But I'm smarter and better lookin' than you . . . asshole."

"Yeah, Gode . . . I was kinda thinking about that." Noche looked toward the agents and said quietly, "They got you scared yet?" He laughed quietly, knowing that John didn't fear many people or things.

John responded with, "Maybe. You never know what they can do." He thought for a moment. "Noche, you gotta try to find out more about this. The OTMs may be what the traffic is all about." His mind raced as things started falling into place. He recalled his conversation with Sweet Tooth about his older brother. The part about lining up hashish and women for after-parties with some high rollers moved around his head. "Maybe, just maybe, this is just a small part of what's going on in the remote part of the desert south of Phoenix," he thought.

Noche noticed that John Gode was in deep thought. He had to ask, "What's running around that shaman head of yours? I ain't seen that look in your eyes for quite some time."

"You think there's more than he's telling you?" John was staring at the wall but not seeing it. "You think that maybe they are doing this here to rub our noses in it someday down the line? Or do you think this is some sort of a jumping off point for getting sleeper cells in place?"

"You really believe this is that deep, John?"

"Sleeper cells of Muslim terrorists?" The big lawman was almost thinking out loud. "Why would high rollers come through this godforsaken part of the state? Why wouldn't they do this in Mexico, where they wouldn't have risk of being caught? Especially if there are *Mexicano importantes* protecting them. Doesn't add up." John was pulling all this apart in his mind and putting the pieces back together, as was his custom.

They went back inside the building and returned to their prisoners as the feds stood by, watching them.

Noche winked at John, nodding at the suit in the sunglasses. He whispered, "Is that guy a spook?"

"Maybe. Keep that in mind, my brother," John whispered.

Walking back into the room, he was greeted by a sneering smile from his outlaw, who asked, "What'chu got, Tonto?"

"I got you, asshole . . . and now that your buddies have put a finger on you . . . it kinda looks like I got you for quite a while." He sat down, folded his arms and stared at the man cuffed and now sitting straight up and staring right back at him.

"Come on, man, you really think I believe that?" the wiry young man spat out in response.

John did not move an inch—just sat there, looking directly in his eyes.

In another interview room, Noche was talking in a low voice, saying to his prisoner, *"Chico, mire chico . . . esta es muy malo . . . por usted."* The Native American nodded his head and pulled his chair closer to the silent man. "Come on . . . let me help you, man. Don't do this to yourself . . . to your family."

"I ain't got no family. What I do got is friends . . . that I can count on. They're my blood. I'm their blood. You got that?"

"Yeah, I have it. Can't figure why you would want to put yourself in jail for guys who are fingering you so that they don't go there."

Both men fell silent as Noche continued his dance, trying to make this desperado do something stupid, like believe him.

The desperado's mind went back in time to a small town in Mexico twelve years before, where he first met his two cohorts when they were thrown together by a tragic set of circumstances. Their parents had been gunned down by a cartel who was at war with a competing cartel for control of the area, which was a pathway to the American border near Nogales, Arizona. All three had been shepherded to a local mission where they were being cared for by the Franciscans, who were becoming overwhelmed by the growing number of children left homeless due to the rampant killings by the warring cartels . . .

The room was quiet as he sat back in his chair, staring but not seeing, as he sank into his memories.

# 06: The Cartel—A Good Boy Learns to Murder

IT WAS TWELVE years earlier in a small Mexican village when an eleven-year-old boy stood silently watching a middle-aged man, hands bound behind his back, on his knees pleading for mercy. Standing over him was an olive-skinned, thin man in his mid-thirties, holding a gun to the terrified man's head.

"Please, please don't kill me. I never did nothing bad to you. I'm not crazy, I know what you do to people who screw with you. I swear on my mother's heart I am with you, Cinco." He closed his eyes, sobbing loudly.

The man holding the gun tapped the pleading man on the top of his head. He smiled and said, "Hey, man, I'm not going to do you. I just wanted to scare you. What kind of an asshole do you think I am?" He twirled the gun on his finger as the kneeling man thanked him profusely, promising him unending dedication and service.

The man with the gun walked over to a boy who was standing nearby. He looked up at the man named Cinco but said nothing. Cinco whispered to the boy, "You want a job, Joven?"

"Sure," the boy answered cautiously, tempered with anxiety pushed by the need to survive. "What do you want, señor?" He had no idea what he was going to be asked to do.

The man smiled, pointed at the kneeling man, and made a sign with his hand to shoot him in the head. The boy backed away when

Cinco offered him the handgun. He looked at him and said, "I don't know how to use one of these."

He whispered, "Oh, it's not hard. You point it at something and pull the trigger. And that's it." He put his arm around the trembling boy's shoulders and handed him the weapon.

The boy cautiously walked up behind the kneeling man and pointed the gun at his head. With his hand shaking so badly, he had to drop it to his side as he said, "I . . . I . . . can't do this. I'm sorry, and I need a job, but I can't do this."

"Pussy!" said one of the other boys who was watching from behind them. He was a little older than the boy holding the gun, and he walked determinedly to him, took the gun from his hand and aimed it at the head of the hysterical man kneeling before him. Without a second's delay, he fired twice. The bullets exploded into the man's head, knocking him backward as he fell to the ground, motionless for all time to come.

"Here, *jefe*. What else do you need?" he asked, expressionless.

The sociopath smiled at him. "You're on, Chico."

"What about the pussy here?" the second boy asked.

"Hey, what about me?" came a question from a third boy, who was also standing nearby. "I have the balls to do what he just did. Just give me a gun and I'll show you."

"*Hijos*, where do you live?" Cinco asked each of the boys.

All three answered almost at once, "Here."

"Where here?"

"By the church sometimes. And in the street, sometimes," said the boy who had shot the kneeling man. "The same for the pussy here, and him over there," he said, pointing at the third boy.

Cinco stared intently at the one now nicknamed "Pussy" and said, "I gave you a chance and you didn't take it. Some things are made so you can't refuse them. They are called opportunities. You get that, kid? Well, this here was one of those . . . opportunities." He took strange delight in criticizing him and continued with, "Now, look. You didn't have the balls to kill that poor son of a bitch." He pointed at the lifeless form bleeding out on the dusty street. "So, what happens now? You got no job, and you been given a nickname by your friend. Ain't that true, Pussy?"

"Can I have another chance, Mister? Just one more chance," the boy begged like he had seen the man on his knees do earlier.

"One more chance to do what?" He laughed cruelly.

"To do what you tell me to do. I can do it." The light of survival was suddenly lit in his head.

Cinco did not respond immediately. He paused for a few moments and then bent down and lifted the boy's face with his fingertip. He looked him coldly in the eye before he spoke. "I'm gonna give you another chance. If you don't do what I tell you to do next time, I got no reason to keep you around. You understand that?"

"Yes. I can do what I'm told. Just let me do it."

"Okay. The three of you get in that wagon over there." He pointed at a jeep that was parked on the street a short way from them. "And, Pussy . . . how about it, we change your name? I'm gonna call you, let me see now . . . okay . . . gonna call you Jaime. I like that name, and you better not make me sorry for doing that."

"You won't be. I promise."

The three boys ran over to the jeep and jumped in as Cinco walked slowly behind, smiling broadly, knowing that he had just recruited three of his cartel's newest members.

# 07: The Feds and the Cartel—What's the Difference?

JOHN KNEW HE was going to lose control of his prisoners to the feds before long, so he took a gamble after hearing what Noche had cooked up with the one he was working. He went back to Armando's office and asked Sunglasses to come with him to talk.

"I got something from one of these *pendejos* that might lead us somewhere."

"Somewhere . . . somewhere, where?" the CSS special agent asked sarcastically.

"You know, asshole, if you would just climb down off that white stallion you're sitting on for a minute or two, I might be able to help you rise to the position in your agency that you think you live in. You know, the one where you have a dick?" John was really trying not to knock this guy on his ass.

Wilson thought for a moment, then thought better of how he was conducting himself. After all, maybe this enigmatic Indian could wind up being an asset to him. Worth a listen, anyway. "Okay, what's your idea?"

John took a long breath, looking intently at the agent as he explained, "One of my guys has gotten a rap with the bad guy he's working. This bad guy has dropped some information about a possible major terrorist attack that may be heading our way soon. He's been offered a deal by us, and if what he tells us is true—and don't even ask me why or how I think it may be true—we will bring you in. This will make your career. You will be the king of your agency. All you gotta do, Special Agent, is leave him in our hands for a few days, and this

43

may pay off . . . big time." John watched the agent as he pondered the possible rewards and repercussions that could come out of a decision on this.

"I need more than just your hunch. Maybe if I talk with him?" Agent Wilson was stalling for time.

"Talk with him about what?" John knew that this guy looked down on him, but that was nothing new, especially when dealing in this area. He had witnessed many lost opportunities because of bad moves by the feds in their gun investigations and stings. Case in point, "Fast and Furious."

Wilson answered, "About what we can do for him if he cooperates."

"You think that he's gonna trust a 'suit'? Come on man . . . really?" John stared at him with a growing fire in his eyes.

"Okay. I'll give you that. Maybe that's not such a great idea. How long do you want to hang on to him?"

"I think we have to hang on to all three of them. If he feels that he's being singled out in front of his compadres, it ain't gonna work."

"So we go home empty?"

"You go home empty." John was emphatic with just a sprinkle of sarcasm.

Wilson shrugged his shoulders. "I have to make a phone call on this. Give me a minute." He turned and walked to the other end of the building where he used his phone. He eyed John closely while he ran things by his superior. When the call ended, he moved back down the hallway to where John was waiting. He shrugged his shoulders and made a gesture indicating his frustration with what he was about to say. "Don't know who you know or if you know . . . but somehow, someway . . . " He paused with a semi-puzzled expression on his face. "They are good with you hanging on to these guys."

"For how long?" John pressed him.

"That's the part that I didn't expect." Agent Wilson looked at the ground and then raised his eyes, slowly saying, "I am here to tell you that 'the powers that be' said for you to keep them as long as they are giving you something." He looked back and forth between John and Armando. "But they want in on everything you get from them. Understood?"

44

John was stunned by that but wasted no time in getting back to his quest. "Thanks," he said quietly as he walked away thinking, "Yeah, I'll just do that, asshole."

Wilson turned to Armando Grant and grunted, "What a sweetheart that guy must be to work with."

"You better not let him hear you call him a sweetheart." Armando chuckled before continuing, "I'd say that you would feel no different about him ten years from today than you do now."

"And why is that?" Wilson asked.

"Your inability to understand where he comes from. That's all." Armando patted him on the back lightly. "Good-bye."

"This is not good-bye, my friend. Think of it more as 'see you soon.' Because you will . . . see me soon. Trust me," warned the head agent.

Armando thought, "This guy takes himself way too seriously. The sign of a true narcissistic prick."

John reassembled his team and brought them up to date on where they were at that moment. He asked for suggestions based on what they were getting from their bad guys.

"I got something real interesting out of the one I'm working," Scotty said, pointing to the room he had just left.

"Like what?" John focused on him and what he was saying.

"I don't know for sure, but my sense of him is he isn't one hundred percent on board with how things are done by these cartels." He pointed at Bonnie and said, "She might have a better way to put this. Care to run this up the pole, Bonnie?"

Bonnie Simms made a face of indecision as she released a light breath and shook her head a bit. "I got that feeling too. We were asking him about what he does for the cartel, and he was not giving us anything. Then Scotty asks him about what he does with the people he brings over the border, and his whole persona changes."

"In what way?" John asked.

"He seemed to lose his cool." She continued, "He gets pissed, real pissed and starts telling us to 'stay out of his shit' about his people." She looked at Scotty, waiting for him to jump back in. He didn't.

Bonnie continued, "He is probably conflicted. That tells me his 'cartel conditioning' might be wearing off. He got real emotional, real quick. He—"

Scotty interjected suddenly with, "I push him . . . He looks at me with this furious pain in his eyes and spits out something about 'him having no choice about doing what he does.' "

"That's what I'm saying, John. I think this guy can be flipped, big time." Bonnie nodded, supporting her comment. "Unless he's a good actor, I think something dark is living in his head."

John went into deep thought for a moment and said, "I think we have something here, folks. My feeling is . . . we might have the opportunity to crack all three of these guys, and if we do, there's no telling where we can go from there. What we do with this is play mind games with all three . . . but we do it one at a time." He was pushing his team.

Noche said, "John Gode, remember what you're dealing with. This ain't something we can handle on our own. I know you know that already, but when we get in the way of Big Brother, we may find Hellfire missiles descending on us from eight different directions."

"Only eight?" John responded quickly. "This could be interesting." He rubbed his chin as he returned to running what was happening through his mind. After a quick moment, he looked at the group and said, "I have to ask you this, my brothers and sisters, are you ready for what could be lying in wait for us a little way down the road?" He looked at them with the greatest intensity any of them had ever seen him express before. It was clear to everyone at that moment that the big lawman knew more about all this than most of them had even dreamed.

Bellamy looked at the group for support before saying, "I want to know what we're up against, John. I think we all want to know that. We're with you with whatever it might be, but it's only fair to let us know what you know . . . if there is anything else to know." He looked around again and saw a few heads nodding in agreement and a few that weren't. "What are we going on, Big John?"

"My gut."

"So, what you're telling us is this is just something you're sensing, not something you know?" Bellamy pressed him.

46

"No. I'm not saying that." John's face was empty but his eyes weren't. He stood there in cold silence, leaving the question unanswered and up for their individual interpretation. But he did know far more than he was saying. Far more. And it was, for the first time in his memory, something that brought a deep fear to his core, something he had to keep hidden until he could determine who he could trust absolutely and without doubt.

"Take your time with this, folks." John was somber. "I mean that! Because I don't know if there is a realistic understanding of how big and how long the reach of the cartels is. I know—believe me, I know—how you all feel about this. But none of us in this room have even scratched the surface of what could be going on here, in DC, and most of all, in Mexico."

"What are you saying, John?" Armando Grant's question came from behind him. The task force commander had walked quietly into the room, his arms folded and a look of concern on his face.

John turned toward his boss and answered, "This is growing, boss. These guys are starting to roll and kinda quick. The feds come swooping in from out of nowhere, trying to grab them from us. Then that shithead agent gets talked out of taking them?" He shook his head and smiled knowingly. "I think we got us way more than drug-running, people-smuggling desperados."

Grant didn't respond. Noche chimed in. "I think we need to get back to talking with these guys and then we need to be finding a safe place to keep them."

"What's wrong with the Pinal County Jail?" Armando seemed puzzled by Noche's statement.

"Nothing . . . if you're talking about regular people. With the way all this is working, I'd say there may be something our bad boys might be in on. Something that maybe we ain't supposed to know," John continued.

Armando said, "You all are playing with yourselves if you think these desperados are gonna crack easy. John, you have to know that. Come on."

"Maybe. Maybe not. I have a feeling about it."

"What kind of feeling, John?" Bellamy piped in.

"Just a feeling."

"Where do we go from here?" Bellamy asked quickly.

"Not sure, but I know where we can put them. Let's keep this rolling," John said quietly as they all dispersed back to their assignments.

# 08: The Mexican Intelligence Perspective

*"Carajo! Gran carajo."*

Jose Maria Gutierrez de Porras, the top counterintelligence officer in Mexico who reported directly to the president of Mexico, was pissed. Seriously pissed.

"People, I need some ideas. The Deep State to the north is on the move. We are seeing one thousand jihadists a month going north, and they seem to have almost miraculous powers both here in Mexico and once across the border—as if they were on diplomatic passports all expenses paid.

"The president is sick and tired of hearing about a wall that is not needed to keep Mexicans out—we already own the fucking USA. The OTMs are giving us a bad name, whether they're Central American baby gangsters or Asian gangsters, I don't care.

"Here is what I need: I need to identify and arrest the Bubbas that are facilitating the movement of OTMs toward the USA, and I particularly want to stop every ISIS soldier trying to cross our territory into the USA.

"It is crystal clear to all of us that the USG is completely penetrated, and this trafficking of human jihadists is approved by the president himself and being protected by rogue elements of the CIA, FBI, and DEA—the same rogue elements that have been smuggling drugs, guns, gold, cash, and small children for the American elite ever since Allen Dulles and J. Edgar Hoover first created the secret state within a state.

"I have no idea what they are planning, but a violent American Spring funded by Constantine Loros and augmented by a wave of false flag attacks absolutely comes to mind.

"Our president is adamant. The USA is half Latino now; we have recovered all the land stolen from us through the Mexcan-American War started on the basis of many lies—yellow journalism—and we need to protect our investment.

"Our counterintelligence in the USA, that now has offices in every Home Station across the country, is on full alert. We have placed observers at every train station and every bus station, and we are seeing the jihadists being dropped off by school buses escorted by the standard FBI SUV.

"Effective immediately, all leaves are cancelled and we are going to twenty-four-hour operations. We have received strong indications that a Mexican army unit led by a 34th degree Bubba is going to clear a corridor for the transport of five hundred jihadists into the USA next week.

"The president has placed his Presidential Guard—a full regiment—and the Presidential Air Unit—on one hour stand-by. Our mission is to capture the five hundred jihadists while they are still on Mexican territory, to capture the Mexican officials who are helping American traitors, and to put on a massive media display prior to the Fourth of July.

"We will show the American people we care as much about the integrity of their Constitution and their Republic as they do."

# 09: Cartel Prisoners

JOHN STEPPED OUTSIDE the task force headquarters building and stared out into the night. His thoughts went back to a small cabin on the reservation he grew up on and the woman who lived there alone these days. His mother's face came before him as he recalled the time when he had come home from an extended assignment, hoping to pleasantly surprise his mother and his deeply troubled younger brother. What he had found that night was his mother lying in bed, sobbing profusely. John rushed to her side, trying to comfort her.

"What's wrong, Amma? What happened?" Just then, he heard the sound of a bottle smash against the door outside the cabin. Whirling around, he moved quickly toward the door and thrust it open. Standing there, wobbling, was his extremely drunk brother, smiling at him with eyes as empty as a cold rainy night. He swayed, holding a half-full bottle of tequila. "What's up, big brother?"

"Adam. Come here." John opened his arms, inviting his brother to come and hug him hello.

He was stupefied by drink. "Hey, man, it's good to see you. Where you been, big brother?" he slurred.

John felt a rush of guilt overwhelm him suddenly as the reality of what his mother and brother were living in hit him hard. "Come on inside, and we can visit. We can talk. Long time, man," was all John could muster, with the thought hitting him that he had not spent any time with his brother Adam for quite a while. John, being ten years older than Adam, had assumed the role of father when their dad left one day, never to return.

51

Adam smiled as he stared at his older brother and waved his open hand in a slow pattern in front of his unsteady body. He extended his bottle of liquor toward John, saying, "I think it's time for you to have a drink . . . Here, I want you to have some of this."

John reached for it to take it away from his inebriated sibling, but before he could grab it, Adam lost his balance and fell backward, laughing as he did.

Adam said, "You know, Mama and I are thinking that you're getting too big to want to hang out with us." He looked at his mother, who shook her head in disagreement with his statement.

"Adam, you know that your brother is busy with his job. It's a good job, and it takes a lot of his time." She tried to intervene, placating her younger son while trying to defend the elder one.

"No. That's not it, Amma. You know that's not it." Adam stumbled, almost losing his balance as he wagged a finger at his brother. "I needed you to help me."

"Help you with what, Adam?" John asked gently.

"With Mama." He thrashed around wildly with anger. "Help me . . . with me! I needed help. I needed your help, John. You've been like a father to me since I was two years old. I looked up to you. I was proud of you. You were my big brother, always there for me. Then one day, I looked around, and you weren't there. You weren't anywhere. You didn't have time for me, your little brother. You didn't have time for our mother, for us. You were too fuckin' busy, hanging out with the 'white eyes.' You were too busy being used by them. And you fell right in with them. You didn't give a shit about us. Not a shit, Big John."

His words echoed in John's mind as clear as if Adam were standing in front of him, confronting him once again.

He talked Adam into settling down and got him into his room, where he collapsed into a heavy sleep across his bed. Amma assured John that she was okay and that Adam wouldn't remember anything about the ugly scene he had just caused. John visited for a while until he was sure that Adam would stay asleep. Before leaving, he promised Amma he would be back soon to check on them. He kissed her on her forehead. "You have the patience of the true Mohawk that you are. If you had Apache blood in your veins, you might not be as patient." He smiled at her with great warmth in his heart.

"I have the blood of a mother of two boys, who are now men, flowing in my veins, John. That brings patience, no matter what tribe I'm from." She hugged him. "Come back soon, my son."

The next time John saw his brother was when he found his body hanging from his belt, attached to a rafter in the shed behind Amma's house two weeks later. A moment that would never leave his mind from then on.

John Nan Tan Gode felt the loss of his brother and the anguish and despair of his mother come rushing back to him as he stood staring into the blackness of the Arizona desert night. He felt as empty as a hollow cave where nothing dwelt, ever. He chanted quietly, praying for the spirit of his dead brother and the peace he wanted for his still-grieving mother.

He remembered the days of his youth when he and Adam would spend their summer evenings sitting with their grandfather, listening to his stories about how the Nation had come to "this place" and why they lived on the land, caring for it and the many creatures that shared it with them. "As my grandfather told my father and me, I will tell you— you must respect this land. You must respect its critters," he would say every time he spoke about the old ways. They would sit near his house under a tree that had been planted by the old man and nourished by him until that very day. He referred to it as the "grandfather tree" and said that whenever he wanted to talk with his grandfather, he would stand under it, speak, and wait for responses that sometimes came lightly on the wind. Those words stayed fresh in John's mind ever since he heard them.

He loved and respected his grandfather and always stayed close to him, physically and spiritually. One day, when he was thirteen, the elder man took John aside and told him, "It's time you learn the old ways."

"What are the old ways, Grandfather?" young John asked.

"They are ways that will help you throughout your life. They are the ways of seeing without looking. And hearing without listening. They are the way of the Spirit." He spoke with a voice that had spirit music deep within. Even at a young age, John recognized his grandfather's uniqueness and high level of understanding. The spiritual power of his grandfather was apparent to him even then, and it was that power which transferred to the tribal police officer he became when the old man had passed. John faithfully practiced the methods taught to him and used them over and over in his work. His tracking ability was uncanny, as was his talent for learning things that pertained to his internal self, like the ancient Chinese art of Bagua and the Japanese art of Aikido. He called them "life arts," not just because they were studied throughout one's life but because, as in his case, they had saved his life on several occasions.

He heard his name being called from inside the building, and as he began to turn from his thoughts and the desert night, he caught sight of a tall, thin man standing where the light and darkness met. He was taken aback because for a moment he thought he saw his beloved grandfather. He waved at the man and the man waved back, then he was gone into the night.

John stood frozen in place, wondering who or what he had just seen. The door suddenly opened behind him as Noche came looking for him. "John, I have an idea that we are getting to the other two," he said with some conviction. "I think we can work them and maybe get something good."

"Yeah, I was thinking that too," John said with a slight smile.

Noche studied his Shadow Wolf brother before saying, "I'm wondering what you're doing out here, big guy. Talking to yourself again?"

John looked at him and shook his head slightly. "I have more interesting conversations that way. No offense, amigo."

"None taken, Brother Gode." He laughed as he held the door open for his close friend and Shadow Wolf brother.

"Where you at now with this?" John asked as they reentered the building.

"We got the other two believing that my guy made a deal with us, and we're telling my guy that we're telling the other two just that." Noche paused for a minute, enjoying what he had just told John. "Your guy is looking pretty pissed right now. You glad?" he asked mischievously.

"I'll let you know when I find out if I have a reason to be glad," the big lawman stated. He returned to the room where his cartel member was sitting with a dismissive look in his eyes. "You feeling good, man?"

John asked as he took his place directly across from the desperado. Looking him in the eyes, he said nothing else.

The silence was broken as the coyote spat out, "You think you're hot shit, don't you? It's easy when you're up against someone who can't do anything to you, Tonto." He looked down at his knees as his frustration came through in his words.

John leaned back in his chair and said, "I'm hearing that word coming from you, and I'm thinking, does this guy really think that I ride with the Lone Ranger? Or does this guy think that I'm just a fool? Ain't that what Tonto means in Spanish? 'Fool'? Fool."

"No, man, I'm thinking that you ride with the Lone Ranger . . . and you got some kind of special relationship with him. You know, like the Village People." He laughed, pleased with himself.

"Now you think that you're gonna piss me off so bad that I'm going to unhook you and then we can go at it, man-to-man, so you can show me what a badass you are. Hey, you think I want to take a chance like that? No . . . not me. No way. That's why the cuffs have to stay on you. You scare me, man. You got a mean eye," John said in a serious manner.

"You really feel that way? I wouldn't give you pain, man. I don't beat up girls. You're safe," the coyote bragged.

John looked at him and let out a breath of relief. "Thanks, I feel a whole lot better now. But I'm sorry to have to be the one to tell you that you're gonna be wearing those things for a long time to come." He leaned toward the cartel member. "Your compadre is singing his skinny ass off about you and your other amigo, and that ain't a good thing for you. You get me?"

"You think I'm gonna swallow that bullshit, *ese*?"

"*Ese*? So now you're calling me 'home boy'? Why you doing that, man?" John asked.

"Because, you know, I know when I'm being played." He laughed.

John didn't say a word more. He got up and left the room.

He was gone for about twenty minutes, and when he returned he announced, "You and your other friend next door are heading to the jail for 'play time,' *ese*."

"What do you mean, my other friend?" he asked in a surly voice.

"That's what I said—your other friend. What do you want me to call him? Your girlfriend?"

The coyote cartel member did not look happy, but he kept his mouth shut as he was moved out of the room and toward the door. The second one was brought over beside him. They were both re-cuffed with their hands behind their backs before they were loaded into the SUV for transport to the Maricopa County Jail.

"We're missing someone," said John's desperado as he looked around for his missing compadre.

"Get used to it," commented Noche. "You gonna miss him for a long time."

"Kiss my ass. You really think I'm buying this bullshit? Really man? He ain't turning. We got too much history." His anger was stirring in his voice.

"Yeah . . . and that's your problem, amigo. You got history," John said quietly. "Let's go."

# 10: Death Sign

THE NEXT MORNING, John tried to reach the woman reporter, Maria, again but he got her voice mail again. He had no way of knowing at that time what had happened the night before.

––––––––––

She had been preparing to go out to get something to eat when she answered a knock on her hotel room door. She was immediately knocked unconscious by one of the three men who rushed into her room. Her hands were quickly tied behind her back and her head covered by a plastic bag. She violently gasped for air that never came, and within minutes, she was dead.

One of the men rifled through her luggage while another went through the drawers of the mahogany bureau that was only a foot or so from her dead body. Finding nothing, he turned to her purse, rifling through it quickly but thoroughly. He said with a smile, "What have we here?" Holding her phone in his hand, he shook his head and chuckled at what he saw on the caller ID. "Looks like we got to her just in time." His smug comment came with the confidence of a fool who sees only what is right before him and misses everything else. He missed what was in the bathroom, hidden in the coffee maker.

They put the limp body in a large, black suitcase that sat on four wheels. One of the three asked the other two, "Where do we do the cutting?"

"In the desert."

"It'll be really dark," one commented.

"That's why we have flashlights," the lead man said dryly. "That meddling, Indian, pain in the ass," he said quietly, almost to himself as he examined the cellphone.

"What's up, boss?" asked one of the men as he righted the suitcase containing the body.

"It's that native cop . . . Goooo-day . . . He's poking around places he shouldn't even know about." Shaking his head as he read the names in the dead woman's phone contact list, he said, "Looks like we may have a problem that we don't need to be having. It may be time to do what needs to be done with him." He placed the phone in his jacket pocket. "This needs to be thought through."

The suitcase rolled smoothly down the hall to the elevator that took them to the crowded hotel lobby, where a busload of senior citizens had just disembarked from their tour bus and were wandering aimlessly throughout the lobby, looking for their suitcases that had been brought to the check-in desk.

"Hey . . . stop him!" one of the older women in the group shouted as she pointed toward a man running out of the lobby with her purse clutched in his hand. He passed right by the men wheeling their dead body–laden suitcase through the crowded lobby.

The confusion helped the men to leave almost unnoticed. They rolled it out the door and down the sloped sidewalk to their waiting van. They had inadvertently timed their departure well.

They drove to a deserted community center parking lot southeast of Phoenix where the small group was met by a fourth man in a dark Humvee. They transferred the suitcase from the van to that vehicle and exchanged drivers as the three rode to a remote area in the desert south of Phoenix.

The dirt road was dusty and uneven, but in the Humvee it was comfortable and not as bouncy as it would have been in most other vehicles. They pulled off the dirt road and drove into a brushy area where they parked the vehicle and unloaded the suitcase.

"How deep do we bury her?" one of the younger men asked the older man.

"Deep enough so the grave doesn't get noticed, but not so deep the coyotes can't get at her. They gotta eat too, ya know." He laughed sadistically. "Cut her hands and feet off and pull all of her teeth out."

"Whoa, padre . . . This ain't what I signed on for. I'm no dentist or surgeon." He was not happy with what he had been told to do.

"You have pliers and you have a machete. What fucking else do you need?" the older man said, showing his loss of patience with his underling.

"I need to know what the deal is before I get asked to do this kind of bullshit. Understand?" he said somewhat menacingly, as he leaned toward the older man's face.

"Calm down, cowboy," the third man suggested with a grin. "I'll do the cutting and the pulling. You hold the light, okay?" He tried to knock back the tension.

"You see how things work out, Phil?" the older man said to his angry cohort, who did indeed calm down almost as quickly as he got upset. The lead man took note of Phil's state of mind, wondering what had set him off and knowing that his temperament could be a problem at some point.

---

Back at the hotel room where the now dead reporter had been staying, there was a knock on the door that went unanswered. Outside the door were two wiry, thin, olive-skinned young men, one of them looking nervously up and down the hallway as they waited for a response. When none came, the one named Jimmy said to his brother, "I think it's time we got outta here. Let's move." They turned and went toward the elevator, but Jimmy thought better of it and chose to use the stairs to get to the lobby. They went out to Jimmy's car, parked in the hotel lot, and sat pondering their next move. Jimmy Begaye felt vulnerable at that moment because of the risk he was taking by even being in the same city as the reporter who occupied the room behind the door he had just knocked on. His mind raced as he wondered if she was setting him up. Was this a test, orchestrated by the cartel bosses? Why was she not there, especially after he had spoken with her a few hours earlier, and she had told him on the phone that she would be waiting for him to arrive?

This whole idea of him agreeing to talk with this reporter was now something he thought was really dumb. Why did he allow himself to get into a position that could get him killed if anyone were to find out about this? Where was this woman? Why had she not been there as she had promised? Why did she insist on him calling her only on her hotel room phone and not her cell phone? He didn't know that she only gave her cell phone number to very few people and only when it suited her purpose. His stomach was sinking like the first car on the steep downward side of a tall roller coaster as he thought of what might now be lying in wait for him down the road as a result of his horny curiosity. Jimmy Begaye was getting worried to the point of panic and with good reason. He was well aware of how deep and widespread the intelligence system for the Sinaloa cartel was. Why did he do this? He knew the answer to that question but still had to ask it of himself.

His mind reeled as he searched for a possible answer to a terrible question asked by barbarous people. He landed on one that might work but would still cause him problems and maybe not get him killed. He was more concerned for his mother and brother, Sweet Tooth, than himself, although he was quite concerned for his own survival. What he would say is that he had been approached by this woman reporter about his connections, and he simply went to find out who she was and whom she was working for. Then he surmised the next question would be, "Why did you keep this to yourself?" Good question.

The excuse he would use would be that he liked the way she looked, and he was hoping to feed her a line of shit that would maybe get him into her pants. Then make the bosses aware of her and what she was trying to learn. Yeah, that would work . . . maybe. He dialed his phone and when it was answered he said, "I need to talk with *Jefe*. I got something he needs to know." He could hear the man who answered the phone saying to someone, "It's for you . . . It's Jimmy B . . . He's got something he wants to tell you."

Jimmy waited, wondering if he was doing the smart thing by calling his boss. A heavy voice came on the other end saying, "Keep this simple, *chico. Entiendo?*"

"Yeah . . . sure, I understand. I got to tell you that I got something you need to know, but now I'm thinking, maybe it should've waited until I'm back there." He sounded unsure of himself.

His boss picked up on that. "You got some trouble?"

"I don't know. Could be . . . that's why I'm calling."

"You understand that I don't like phones. Right?" his *jefe* said in a cautioning way that bordered on threatening.

"I know. It can wait, I think," Jimmy stuttered.

"Make sure you talk to me as soon as you get back. You don't talk to no one else. You understand, *chico*?"

"Sure, boss. Okay." Jimmy felt this was going to turn into something really bad really quick. He thought he screwed up, and he began running a plan through his head as he started the car.

"Who was that on the phone, Jimmy?" Sweet Tooth asked as he sat next to his brother in the car.

"Nothin' . . . It wasn't nothin'." Jimmy was distracted, and his brother was concerned.

"Why are we here, man? Who were you supposed to meet?" Sweet Tooth fired questions his brother wasn't prepared to answer.

"Uh, there was this hot chick who wanted me to come here to see her."

"Why'd you bring me if you had a date?" Sweet Tooth was confused.

"I guess I wanted you to see how the other half lives." He chuckled before starting the car and driving back toward their home. "You hadda see this woman. She is so freakin' hot. Makes me lose my cool." He paused and then caught himself with, "In a good way, little brother."

"What'd she do? Stand you up or somethin'?"

"Chicks that look as good as she does can do that. Even to guys as good-looking as me." He smiled.

"Don't make it right, though," Sweet Tooth said, feeling a bit offended for his brother but admiring Jimmy's bravado just the same.

"Listen to me, Tooth. You don't say nothin' to no one about me coming here and getting stood up. You got that?" Jimmy was adamant.

"Yeah, I got that. You don't want me telling anyone about the time some chick shot you down and I was there to see it." He liked the fact that his big brother was made to look the fool, and his big brother wasn't taking it too well. Sweet Tooth scanned the grounds of the luxurious hotel as they drove off, headed for the other side of the reservation. This side was like another planet, so lush and green. He always liked looking at it. One of the wonders the "white eyes' " gambling habits had brought to his people. A bit ironic.

# 11: THE CARTEL AND THE JIHADISTS

JOHN SAT PENSIVELY staring into the night as Noche drove with the young cartel member in handcuffs in the back seat.

"Where are we going?" the young gangster asked with anger in his tone.

"We're gonna take you somewhere that you might get to like," John said quietly.

"I like my 'hood,' hombre. That's the only place I like right now." He mocked, "You taking me *there*?"

"Uh, maybe you'll change your mind. Maybe this will give you a chance to get in touch with your inner self," John commented.

"My inner self? Where do you think I'm gonna find that place?" he asked in a softer tone.

John turned around in his seat and stared the young cartel member directly in the eyes. "Something about you tells me that you don't like what they make you do to your own people."

There was no response, but he sat defiantly staring right back at John.

The big man continued, "Something tells me that you are feeling real bad about the way those 'homies' are treated by your bosses . . . and by you too."

"And something tells me that you are full of shit, man." The words flew out of the prisoner's mouth like frightened birds from a bush. "Where are you getting this? Why should I feel bad about doing my job?" He paused for a moment and then went on. "It's a job, Tonto. Only a job. Like your job. You're stopping them from getting into this country. From getting a chance to get a taste a' what you got and they don't got. You like your job, don't you?" His inner conflict was starting to show through as he dropped his head.

John said, "I look at it like this. What happens if there are a thousand people trying to get on a boat that only holds, say, five, six hundred? What happens? Think about it," he spoke quietly, studying the young man as he did.

"What do you want me to say, man?" He was irritated by the question.

"I want to hear you say what you think. That's all. What . . . you . . . think." John's voice rose a bit.

"What do I think? It's a loaded question . . . The boat sinks." He shrugged his shoulders, indicating the answer was obvious.

"And?" John did not let up.

"And? What?" the gang member asked as an answer.

"And? I'll keep asking until you have the rationale to answer the question." John's eyes were like frozen fire as he looked at his prisoner.

"What does 'rationale' mean?"

John replied with measured words. "It means lack of stupidity."

"So now you're calling me stupid. Nobody calls me stupid and walks away. You got that, man?" He was practically coming out his skin but not out of the irons on his restrained wrists.

"Don't get me wrong, kid. I don't think you're stupid. I think what you are doing is stupid and wrong for your very own." John never broke his glance.

"My very own what?" Anger was all over the gang member's voice.

"People . . . asshole. Your very own people," John persisted.

The young man started to reply, his jaws so tight they almost jerked out of place as his thoughts turned to words. "Fuck you, asshole."

Gode now knew he had him where he wanted him.

"Your place empty, Noche?" John asked in a near whisper.

"It's always empty when I ain't there." He laughed at his attempt at a witticism. John didn't see the humor.

"Let's head that way," he said, looking straight ahead, his face expressionless.

"After we drop him off, right?" Noche wondered why John wanted to go to his small ranch near Casa Grande, which was about twenty-five miles away from where they were.

"No, we need to talk with him some more before he goes into the system," John said while running some thoughts through his head. "He needs to be able to speak his mind. This is gonna be an important moment for him. He just doesn't understand that yet." The big man looked back at the gangster who was now hunched over in the back seat. "Ain't that true?" he asked. John knew he was getting this guy close to a breaking point, and he decided to keep pushing in that direction.

The desperado just grumbled in response, expressing his displeasure with that question.

Noche was not comfortable with this, but he knew John well enough to know that he could trust his judgment. He turned the vehicle around and started toward Casa Grande. "You know what you're doing, right?" he asked quietly.

"I know exactly what I'm doing. Relax, my brother. Are we not all God's children, after all?"

"You sound like you been on the road to Damascus, John Gode," Noche said, laughing again at his own jest.

"Maybe I have. I'm seeing something that I haven't ever seen before." He turned and looked back at the coyote drug smuggler who might be having a similar experience. "Talk to me, man. I may be your only way back to being human." John paused for a moment. "I want to know your real name. What is it?" he spat out quickly. He got nothing.

"So, tell me what it is that makes you do what you do? Something tells me that you ain't as bad as you want people to believe you are," Gode said almost casually.

The gangster sat back up in the seat and looked at John intensely before taking the subject where he wanted to go, which was justifying his life's work to the big man. "Ain't no way I can tell you how good I live because of what I do." He looked down, chuckled slightly and looked back up at John as he shook his head.

"And that makes you feel good?" John made a Marlon Brando "Godfather" face as he spoke. "Don't shit me, man. You know that I know what is going on in your head."

"Let me tell you, I was on the street by the time I was ten. The bosses took me in and gave me a life after my family was killed. They was all snuffed by one of the other cartels because they was robbing their marijuana crops and got caught. That day I wasn't with them because I was sick."

"You're making me feel bad, man. Real bad. You trying to do that on purpose?" John responded. He looked over at Noche and asked, "You feeling bad?"

Noche just shrugged.

"You see how you're making my friend here feel. He's getting with you on this. I'm not so sure I am, though." John was stoic, sitting motionless. "Where are you at with this, badass? How can you do to helpless people what some assholes did to your own family? I don't get it, kid. Makes me feel confused. And I don't like feeling confused. You understand that. Right?"

The prisoner sat, now silent, looking out the window at the rolling darkness.

"I think you need to be thinking about what you should be doing . . . you could be doing right now. You can undo all this shit," John said quietly.

"What does that mean?" The young man moved around somewhat in the seat. "How can you do that? And not get me killed?" he asked nervously, but the wheels were turning in his head.

Noche looked at John as he returned the look without the prisoner seeing the exchange.

"So you gonna cut me a deal? Is that where you're going?"

"It all depends," John said, shrugging his shoulders.

"All depends on what? We doing a *little dance* now? I don't dance, *jefe*. Not the kind of dance you're talking about." John was moving him along "head-wise," but he said something that was surprising, in the sense that it indicated how much he actually knew. "You think that all that's going on is about *Mexicanos*. Don't you, boss?"

"No, I don't. I know about the jihadists you guys are bringing in," John responded as Noche listened intently to the new turn in the conversation.

"Jihadists? What the fuck?"

They rolled up the dusty dirt road that was about five miles east of Casa Grande, heading toward the secluded property Noche liked to call his *rancho pequeno,* or small ranch. They were kicking up some serious dust as they made their way on the five miles of bad road.

"What's your name, asshole?" John asked suddenly.

"Asshole. Like you said. Where are we going, man?" the desperado asked, sounding concerned.

"A place much nicer than the jail you would be in otherwise. We got some talking to do," John stated resolutely.

John turned around and covered his prisoner's head with a pillowcase that he kept handy in the vehicle for just such occasions as this.

It took Noche another fifteen minutes to get them to his ranch house.

"You got anything to eat or drink?" The prisoner started to express his discomfort, going from defiance to neediness. "I really need to take a piss too."

After parking in front of the house, they moved him out of the back seat, and John kept hold of his arm as Noche led the way to the wooden deck, where he turned on the porch light. He spun his keys before opening the door.

"I need to take a piss really bad," the young gangster mumbled.

Noche removed the pillowcase hood and unhooked him, allowing him to rub his wrists before taking care of business. The Shadow Wolf stood in the bathroom doorway, making sure he didn't go out the window.

He was hooked back up by Noche after he was done. John pointed to the chair he wanted the young gangster to sit in. The big lawman sat immediately opposite him.

"Look, I think you guys think that I got some kinda choice here. If I don't do what they want me to do, everything changes for me." "Asshole" looked from John to Noche, who was over in the kitchen, for understanding.

"That could be over, *ese,*" John said, exhaling as he did. "You could change all that. If you wanted."

"You don't understand. You . . . just . . . don't . . . understand. Those guys are . . . they're like a machine, man. They take you out without even grunting."

"Where did you learn to speak English?" John asked.

"East LA. I lived there on and off for about five years."

"How come?" Noche asked.

"You really gotta ask me that?"

"Yeah, I really do. Why were you living in LA?" Noche inquired in a serious tone.

Looking at John and then half turning toward Noche, he said, "I was a . . . how do you say . . . coordinator? Yeah, I was a coordinator."

"Hell, I thought you were gonna say you were a community organizer. Like Obama was in Chicago." John laughed.

"Yeah—I was just like him."

"That's real good. Never heard anyone give what you did a job description," John responded.

"You know, I did do some sweet organizing there." He thought for a moment. "I was good at doing that, but that's not what they called it."

"Who are 'they'?" John asked.

"The other bosses."

"The cartel guys?" Noche asked from the kitchen.

"No . . . these guys were not *Mexicano*. They sorta looked like us but didn't act like us."

"How so?" John asked.

"Well, you know, like . . . they didn't never think like us. They paid me good, but they had weird ideas."

"Like?"

"Like they told me to get people who weren't afraid of anything. 'Warriors . . . bring us warriors,' they would say to me. 'Bring us people who don't have nothin' and got nothin' to lose.' "

"How many did you find for them?" Noche asked.

"Enough to make a difference."

"How many is that?" John asked as he leaned into the gangster's face. "Exactly how many are we talking about here?"

"I don't know . . . maybe twenty . . . yeah, that was about it. Those bosses gave me a bonus when I got to *número veinte*. Then they gave me something else to do." He sat farther back in his chair, trying to put a little distance between him and the lawman.

"What was that?" Noche asked.

"I said that I was working with this guy from Norte. He's one of your people. At least, he claims to be one of you . . . " His voice trailed off as he began to realize that he had gotten played into saying too much.

"Name?" John asked quickly.

"How the fuck should I know?"

"What part of Norte is he from?"

"I don't know . . . Around here somewhere. Why?" he asked suspiciously.

"I'm doing the asking, Asshole, or whatever your name really is. My question is, where are your recruits from? I would think that East LA would have plenty of interested guys. But exactly what is it they were interested in doing?" John stood up and started pacing up and down.

"Like I told you, *ese*, I was organizing the community. Like Obama did before he organized the country."

"What did the guys you organized do?"

No response. Just a cold glance and total silence.

"So, what's the story with these 'bosses' that look like you but don't act like you?" John asked.

He thought for a minute, then said, "I think they told me that they are starting a landscaping business in the Baja. Then they're expanding north. Here in Arizona and over in California."

"I'm gonna make sure that they know how much you helped us."

"And how are you gonna do that?"

"It's already done."

The gangster realized that the mouse he was playing with turned out to actually be a cat. A big one that had stripes and wasn't playing back. He was beginning to realize that he was screwed, and maybe it was time for him to try to help himself.

John's phone rang. It was Armando Grant, wanting to know where they were.

"We're just talking, boss. Stopped to get our boy something to eat."

"When are you going to hit the jail?" The task force commander seemed concerned that they weren't there yet.

"Not sure." John got up and walked outside where he continued the conversation. "We're learning a few new things and want to keep this going. You okay with that?"

"I guess so. Just don't do anything crazy."

"Relax, boss . . . It's all good," John reassured him.

"I got these feds climbing all over me, over these desperados, and I don't need any more heat on this whole subject and our unit. You get that, John. I know you do."

"Why are they so hot on these guys, boss?"

"Who knows? I got no idea what they're thinking, and this guy Wilson is strange. I'll give you that."

"Are they checking at the jail to see if we dropped these guys?" John was getting bothered by the pressure he was sensing in Armando's voice. "Why don't you just tell these assholes to screw off and let us do our job?"

"Yeah, why don't I?" Armando responded with a frustrated tone in his voice.

John steered the conversation down the path he wanted to go. "I'm thinking that there is way more going on with these guys . . . " He had picked up on something during his interrogation that brought him to a place of great concern. There was something going on that involved this group, that had a possible far-reaching effect on the basic security of the entire country. He would sort it out or sweat it out in the coming days.

"What guys? The feds or the assholes?" Armando pressed him.

"I think of them all as assholes, but the bad guys are who I'm talking about right now. I think we might have a shot at flipping this guy."

John listened closely to what his boss was saying. "Really. You're telling me that you got him to this point already?" Armando sounded like he didn't believe the big man.

"He's been saying some things that lead me to believe we can work him up enough to get him to a point that could get us through a dark door to what may be actually going on south of the border these days." He tried to keep the conversation steered toward the cartels, avoiding the rest of the story going on in his head.

69

"Like what?"

"A lot of things that I don't want to talk about on the phone," John cautioned. "And I humbly suggest that you don't talk with anyone about this. Nobody. Until I can get my arms around the tree, this guy is climbing. You never know what new and evil things those boys are getting into."

Armando didn't respond immediately. Then, "Okay, we'll talk."

"So you're good with this?"

"Good with what?" Armando sounded a bit confused.

"With what we're talking about."

"At the moment, John, I have no idea what we're talking about."

"Okay, gotcha, boss. Will keep you in the loop." John ended the call with Armando exactly where he wanted him and started back into the house.

Suddenly, he caught sight of a man standing off the shadows. He turned toward him and then broke into a dead run, right at him, gun at the ready. Arriving at the spot where the man had been standing, he found no one there. The big lawman checked the bushes and the ground for footprints, but there was nothing indicating that anyone had been standing there. This unsettled him for a moment until he thought about the man he had seen earlier standing in the shadows outside of the task force headquarters. He thought that man looked something like his dead grandfather. He realized that this man looked pretty much the same but from a greater distance away. He chanted a short prayer for the dead and moved on with an awareness of a spirit presence beginning to surround him. It was a good feeling.

"We're taking you to the jail. If your compadres ask you where you've been and you have some smarts, you will say this, and only this—that we took you to get something to eat, and while there, you got a case of the shits, and you had to use the bathroom for quite a while." He stared at the silent desperado. "If you want to get clear of this, you need to stop acting like your name, and talk to me. I know what is going on, *chico*, and even though you think that you got to have the world by the balls . . . You keep playing with these guys, you won't have any balls when they decide that you have insulted the Prophet."

It caused a look of bewilderment on the prisoner's face when those words came out of John Gode's mouth. He could almost hear the words rolling through the desperado's head. "He knows. He knows. They were right about him."

———————

Not another word was spoken until they reached the jail. John asked him, "I need to know your name before we go in there, or I'm gonna book you as 'Asshole.' Now, you may think that's funny . . . and it is to me too. But you ain't gonna be thinking it's funny once the word gets around the community that's your name. Some of the guys in there are gonna come around and see if you live up to your name, and that, my friend, can be quite painful. Awfully painful. So what's it gonna be? You got a name, or not?"

The gangster stared long and hard and then let out a breath as he uttered, "*Jaime, me nombre es Jaime.*"

"Jaime . . . what?"

"Jaime Gomez."

"Aka, Asshole?" Noche said with a smile.

"Jaime. Just call me that."

"Let's go, Jaime." John and Noche walked him into the jail.

# 12: THE BORDER PROJECT

GENERAL CLAP, CALLED "VD" behind his back, was pensive. Forty years of national service, evenly divided between protecting the Constitution and dishonoring the Constitution. He never thought he would see the day that swearing fealty, or allegiance, to a powerful family who were more than just part of the Deep State would make him feel like a third-rate whore on a New York street corner. At the time, he had thought only of the one hundred million dollars in offshore money. Now he understood the price of that one hundred million. Time to retire.

"I'm too old for this shit," he thought. Then he continued, "Let's go, people. I have fifteen minutes to tell you what you need to be doing for the next week. POTUS has accelerated his timeline for Operation Paperclip II. We have one thousand jihadists coming in next month; they all need to be in position and ready to go for the second wave of violence across America that kicks off on Two July."

Like many of the senior servant class in the USG, General Clap—he preferred to be called Director Clap in keeping with his cosmetic role as the nominal director of the national intelligence community—was a 34th degree Bubba. Everyone in the room was also a 34th.

"FBI—beginning immediately you will prepare to receive twenty-five jihadists from a FEMA train that will start in El Paso and run up through Oklahoma, Missouri, Indiana, Ohio, and into New York, ending in Ithica, New York. We're going to show fly-over country what terrorism looks like up close and personal.

"NSA—I am very pleased with your intercepts against Mexican intelligence showing them tipping off our police chiefs. I had already heard of this from the 34ths that are in key police leadership positions, but you identified the rest.

"CIA—you will immediately order every judge that is a 34th or under our blackmail and bribery protocols to start creating a world of pain for every police chief trying to do their job and defense of the Republic. This is our country to do with as we please, not theirs to defend. If you need to kill one as a lesson to the others, go for it. Make it an obvious assassination—that kid who worked for the DNC was not obvious enough—I want the next assassination to scream 'Deep State Hit.' Let's ensure these people know that we own them and their lives are ours to give or take.

"CIA—I also want you to divert at least six drones from your assassination operations. Give me twenty-four-seven coverage of our corridor on both the Mexican and the American sides, and have Whitewater Enterprises put a full company's worth of hit teams on all sides of the corridor. We've ordered all local LEAs away from the corridor, anyone found in the corridor will be assassinated. Make it look like a cartel hit.

"Any questions? None? Good. Get your asses out of my building."

General Clap did not understand the way of the ancient warrior. However, the Shadow Wolves did.

# 13: DEEP STATE SHOOTOUT

JOHN TURNED THE engine of his vehicle off and stretched and yawned before exiting it. He walked slowly through the pitch darkness of the desert night to the door of his home. He checked his surroundings visually and then stood in silence, listening to the rhythm of the night expressed by the desert creatures that lived mostly hidden all around him. He pulled his keys from his pocket and instinctually placed the house key in the lock without looking. He heard a door close in the back of the house as he walked in. Pulling his weapon, he ducked down and moved stealthily with the speed of an ocelot toward the noise. But when he arrived, he found nothing that could have caused it. He searched the area and then turned on a light before holstering his weapon.

He walked into his bedroom and was stunned for the moment at the sight of Alicia lying across his bed with one of his shirts on—and that was about it.

"Hey, did I scare you, little boy?" She threw her head back, released her long, black hair, and gave a sultry laugh as she devoured him with her eyes. She waved him to her.

"Hey, baby. Nice surprise. Almost got you killed, though." He smiled as he moved to her and sat down on the bed, slowly kicking off his boots. "How did you get in?"

"Did you forget the key you leave in the hole under the porch railing?" She kissed his cheek. "I didn't."

"I have trained attack scorpions there." He laughed.

"You didn't train them well enough, Johnny Boy," she commented smugly but in a cute way. She was his lady and a tribal police officer who was also attached to the task force. She had been away on another assignment.

The ringing of his phone broke the moment. "John, you need to get back to the jail and pull your guy out right now." It was Nero Agave, a jail deputy who was a brother Shadow Wolf. "He saw someone in population who has him freaked out, and he is begging me to get you to get him out of here."

"I'm confused. How could he know that you know me?"

"I don't think he does. I just happened to be walking him to a cell when he saw someone who made him piss his pants," Nero responded.

"On my way. Can you pull him into the medical unit until I get there?" John sensed danger and opportunity at the same time.

He told Alicia what was going on, and she wanted to go with him to make the pickup. John agreed to that, and they were in his vehicle heading to the Maricopa County Jail within five minutes. John drove as Alicia put her gear in order. He explained the deal with Jaime to her as they rode. She took it all in and immediately started processing it in her mind. She had a knack for cutting through the minutia on her way to the underlying facts.

"What do you have for weaponry, woman?" John asked, nodding toward Alicia's black canvas bag that she had placed on the floor in front of her before she jumped in the front seat next to him.

"I'm 'mama grizzly bear' ready, m'love," she assured him.

"I would prefer 'mama grizzly bare-ass' ready, but for now we'll go with what you got." He smiled, knowing his lady was way more than just a lady. She was fierce in any situation that required it. No question about that. She was a Shadow Wolf in every sense of the word.

They entered the jail and asked for Nero. He came within a couple of minutes and hustled them to the medical unit where Jaime was sitting propped against a wall, a wild look in his eyes. "Why did you put me in this place? Are you nuts? Freakin' loco, man. If you got any chance of getting me to work with you, Ton—"

John interrupted him. "Don't call me Tonto, okay? You got that? Remember, Tonto always rode away with the Lone Ranger, and you don't want me riding away right now. Do you, asshole?"

The big man looked over at Nero before asking him, "You have any idea who or what set this bird off?"

"Yeah. He was looking at an inmate who was brought in an hour or so before him." Nero was being cautious with what he said in front of Jaime. "His name is Raphael Agente. We turned him over to ICE for deportation about two weeks ago. And true to form, he's right back home with us once again."

"What do you know about him?" John pressed him for as much information as he could get before making a decision on what to do next.

"He's muscle for some of the local gangs in South Phoenix. Quite a head-buster here in population too."

"Who arrested him this time?" John saw this coming together in a bad way.

"Looked like Phoenix PD. He was charged with assault and battery. Story was that somebody pinched his girlfriend's ass in a bar. And here he is." The jail deputy left out the "ta-da" before finishing his story.

"He's cartel, man. I've seen him do people like they was animals in a slaughterhouse. He's got no soul, and he flashed me a cartel sign when he learned I knew him." Jaime interjected, "He's here to get me."

"Maybe this could be your tipping point." John looked at Jaime as he spoke.

"What's that mean? What's a 'tipping point'?"

"Your ticket to ride, Jaime," the big man responded quickly.

"My ticket to ride where?" he asked sarcastically.

"We'll see . . . won't we?" John said, sensing the change that was occurring at that particular moment. He dialed on his phone, and when Armando Grant answered, he explained what had just happened and asked permission to take Jaime out of that jail.

"Where will you put him, John?" Armando sounded concerned.

"Not sure, but we got to get him gone from here," he assured his boss.

"Okay, then take him. But keep me in the loop on every bit of this. Understood?"

"Sure, of course I understand. I'm going to play this by ear." He had turned away from the group as he continued the conversation. "I think we got something really big here, Armando. And we need to take it all the way."

"All the way to where?"

"I don't know," John lied. "But wherever it is now, looks to me to be only the tip."

"Of the *iceberg*?" the task force commander queried.

"No . . . of the *spear*. It's the 'tip of the spear,' boss. And I have a strong feeling that I'm right."

Armando just grunted in agreement.

"I'll be in touch." John ended the call.

"Wrap him up, Nero. We're leaving." John took Alicia aside and briefed her on what they would do when they left the jail. They would head for the reservation and a place to safely stash their apparent convert.

They put Jaime in the back of the SUV with his hands cuffed in front. "If you screw with me, Jaime," John said, indicating his choice to handcuff him in front rather than behind as usual, "my girlfriend here will pull your throat out and hand it to you before you realize you're dead. *Entiendes?*"

"Yeah, I understand, Ton—" Jaime was once again interrupted before saying the name, by John's finger waving "no, no," a sinister smile on his face.

They rolled out of the sheriff's compound and headed toward the reservation. A black SUV pulled out a short way behind them and began following.

Alicia sat sideways in her seat, looking back at the road. "Make a quick right turn on the next street."

He wheeled right, then gunned the engine, racing down the empty street. "What do you see?" he asked.

"I thought we had company, but maybe I was wrong."

John made a left and another left at the next corner, and before long he was back on the street to the reservation.

They entered Indian land some ten minutes later and drove toward the task force HQ, but were suddenly aware of two SUVs now moving up on them, rapidly firing shots that took out the rear window.

Alicia yelled to Jaime, "Stay down!" She opened up with her M4, firing through the now vacant rear window, and took out the windshield on the lead vehicle following them. She strafed again and took out the headlights on both sides. A loud thud and uncontrollable swerving told John they had lost a rear tire. He turned the vehicle suddenly, and it screeched to a halt sideways on the empty road. John opened the rear door and dragged Jaime out and put him on the ground, warning him to stay there as five rounds, aimed at them, whizzed through the night.

The big man went to the front end of the vehicle, and Alicia took the rear as they both opened up on the eight SWAT-clad individuals who were firing back. Two of them ran along a ditch toward John's position, firing furiously. He lit them both up and then just shook his head, wondering why they pulled such a dumb move. It wasn't long before his question was answered. Four others rushed Alicia's position, pouring round after round as they did. Alicia wasn't there, though, as they soon found out when she appeared out of the darkness behind them and took all four out with strafing headshots. There were now two left to deal with, but they chose to disengage and head back out the way they came. John fired at the retreating vehicle, not knowing if he hit anyone or even landed a round on the SUV.

"You okay, Alicia?" John asked loudly.

"I'm good. You?"

"I'm good. Jaime, how about you?"

No response.

"Jaime." John looked down at the motionless body at his feet. He was lying in a pool of blood.

"Damn," was all John could say. He felt bad that he couldn't save this kid. "Damn," he repeated.

Alicia was on the phone calling in the incident to 911. John knelt down by the young man's body and chanted the spirit song that he hoped would help guide him on the path of the dead and maybe the peace he had yet to know. The lawman had seen others die, but this one hit him in a different place, and he had a hard time with it. Maybe it was because it took him back to when he found his brother's body. There was something similar between Jaime and Adam. He felt there was a chance this kid could have been turned around, but now, it was not going to be.

Flashing lights and sirens broke the silence and darkness of the desert night as police and EMT vehicles rolled onto the scene. Bodies strewn about and the two shot-out vehicles sitting in the road resembled a scene from the war in Iraq. The smell of gunpowder was in the air, and smoke rose from the engine compartments of both vehicles.

John called Armando to report what had happened. Grant wasn't happy with it, as expected, but said, "I'm thankful that you two are okay. That kid getting killed is going to bring some major heat from the feds. I know that's not something that surprises you. Right?"

"Yeah, I know what a fan of mine Wilson has become. Right now I'm not the least bit concerned about it, boss. I'm trying to figure out why an assault team jumped our ass out here and how they knew what we were doing and where we were doing it. You got any ideas?" John knew he would not be answered by the task force commander or anyone else he could ask at that moment in time.

John briefed the responding supervisory officers as to how everything went down, and after it was determined that the area was secured, the forensics began. The bodies of the dead were without IDs. Three of them had tattoos that indicated they were part of jail gangs, but that was it.

Armando pulled up a half hour later and jumped right into the middle of the activity. He walked the entire scene, taking in the dead bodies and the two destroyed vehicles. "Did he get capped during the firefight or before it began?" Armando asked, pointing at Jaime's corpse.

John thought that was a strange question. "What do you mean, Armando?" John's feelings showed in his voice.

"Uh, did he get hit in the beginning of the shootout or during it?" Armando repeated.

Alicia asked, "What difference does that make, Chief?"

John looked annoyed. "I pulled him out of this vehicle when we ducked and started shooting back." He patted the hood of his vehicle as he spoke, which was his way of emphasizing the point.

"So he bought it during the shootout." Armando's voice was almost inaudible. He seemed preoccupied with whatever was rolling through his head.

"Yeah, would have to have been when it happened. He was alive when I pulled him from the car. And I didn't see him acting like he had been hit," John responded, indicating the obviousness of his answer.

79

"I'm wondering who they were after?" said the seemingly uncomfortable task force commander.

"My guess, boss, is they were after the kid and John Gode," said Alicia, who was shaking her long, black hair free of the debris she had picked up when she had circled through the cacti to come around behind the four bad guys she had capped.

"Who killed who?" Armando asked, pointing at the SWAT-clad bodies.

"I got these two." John nodded at the two bodies to his right.

"I got these four." Alicia pointed proudly to the rest.

"Impressive. Out-numbered and from the look of it, obviously out-gunned . . . And yet, you're still standing and they ain't. Why am I not surprised?" He looked again at the bodies. "And relieved," he added quickly.

"Yeah, we surrounded them." Alicia gave a tight-lipped smile and looked at her boss with a bit of coyness showing through in her demeanor, waiting for his response.

"So, two of you surrounded six of them. You gotta tell me how you did that."

"That's a secret technique taught to me by a great internal martial arts teacher." John was stone-faced as he spoke.

"You haven't told me how it works." Armando was curious.

"And I'm not going to."

"Why?"

"Big secret in China. Only shown to Chinese and Native Americans. Bound to silence, boss." John looked over at Alicia, who was eating this up. John took the conversation back to the seriousness of the situation. "What do you think about this, Armando? What the hell is going on?" John turned around with the swiftness of a tiger and the intensity of a charging bear and went right into the face of the man who was rocked by the words flying out of the Shadow Wolf's mouth.

"Settle down, John. We get nowhere if we start lashing out at one another. Something like this is bad enough. Don't make it worse." He sat on the ground and invited Alicia and John to do the same.

"What are we gonna do now? Have a powwow?" John was extremely upset.

"Come on, sit and talk," Armando coaxed them.

"That's the dumbest thing I ever saw you do, Armando. Why would we want to sit on the ground here in the middle of a road, surrounded by seven dead people?" John glared at his boss.

Alicia took her man by his arm and tried to bring him to a calmer state of mind. "Come on, baby. Sitting down anywhere is okay if it gets you somewhere." She smiled. "We are Native Americans, we sit on mother earth always for anything we need."

John looked at her with great warmth in his eyes before he said, "Where'd that come from? You turning into a sage on me?" He chuckled as his frame of mind softened a bit. He sat down across from Armando and next to his woman.

Armando started the conversation. "I think we need to clear the air here, up front and right now."

John sat and stared silently at his boss.

Alicia leaned in toward Armando and asked, "What are we talking about?"

John continued in stone silence.

"I'm talking about the vibe I'm getting from him." Armando nodded at John who was squatting in what for most would be an uncomfortable position.

"Vibes? What are we, hippies now?" John broke his momentary silence with a fierce whisper. "No need to go counter-culture here. No need to believe I'm harboring anything about you, Chief. Why don't you say what it is that has you feeling this unhappy with me. Now that we are so close to mother earth, maybe she will provide the energy for you to be able to speak clearly."

"Wow . . . this is going down a path I wasn't expecting." Armando began shaking his head as he explained himself. "When I got here, you were looking at me with a strange expression—it was in your eyes, John Gode. I have not been on the receiving end of one of those looks from you before, and it made me feel several different emotions. One was anger. Another was fear. Then confusion. After an incident like this, where we are seeing dead bodies everywhere we look, it causes all kinds of stress . . . for everyone."

"I want to know how the fuck did these guys know what we were doing? When we were doing it? And who we were doing it with? How could they be waiting for us, probably even before we got to the jail to pick up that kid? How did that happen?" John was breathing fire.

"Who did you mention this to?" Armando asked.

John paused for a long moment. "You." He pointed in Armando's face.

"Get that finger out of my face." Armando frowned angrily.

John sat silently once again, but this time he had an expression on his face like he was waiting to hear something he needed to hear.

Armando asked, "Who else did you tell?"

"You were the only one," came John's response.

"Then it must have been that they were trailing you, or more likely, they were scanning our conversation. Those are the only possibilities."

"Only possibilities?" John rolled onto his knees. He looked down at the ground as he said, "If they have that kind of technology, we are badly outta luck. No chance against them."

"From what I see, they were the ones with no chance." Armando was trying to lighten the mood with what he considered humor.

"I don't know. Right now, my jury's out on just about everything and everyone." John looked back up at his boss. "We might need to go back to code talking, as the Navajo did back when."

Armando gave a relieved laugh at John's words, thinking he was jesting.

"I'm serious. Think about this for a minute. If they have that kind of technology, I want to know how and where they got it. Then I want to know who is playing here." The big man stood up and invited Armando and Alicia to do the same. When they did, he continued, "Unless we can figure that out, we are all on borrowed time."

"Let's not get too crazy here. You know as well as I that the cartels have more money than the Mexican government, and that kind of wealth can buy you anything you want. I'm surprised they don't have drones," Armando commented.

"What makes you think they don't?" John interjected.

"You think so?" Alicia hadn't thought about that possibility, and it immediately intrigued her.

As he ended the conversation, Armando looked from Alicia to John and asked, "Are we good here?"

"Good with what?" John asked quickly.

"With having a working, trustful relationship."

"John doesn't trust many people these days, Chief. You want that he should make an exception for you?" Alicia asked lightly.

"All I know right now is if we want to keep this unit together, we have to find some way that we can trust one another . . . totally." The task force commander was pulling his leadership persona out of his shirt pocket.

Just then, a forensic specialist approached, saying, "No IDs on any of the attack team bodies. We're rolling prints for some ID possibilities. Also, we ran a look on their vehicle, and it already came back as no record."

"You'll keep going with that look, right?" Armando ordered.

"Roger that. Lots to learn," the young man uttered as he walked away.

"Looks like we might be dealing with *ghosts*," John opined quietly.

"A haunting, gentlemen. We have an actual haunting," was Alicia's way of stating the obvious.

"We'd better get to the shack and file the reports on this. That 'Agent' Wilson will be all over this . . . and very soon." Armando sounded worried as he suggested heading to the task force headquarters.

"You don't work for him. Do you?" Alicia spoke as she picked up her gear.

"And you should care . . . why?" John doubled down, unrelenting in this treatment of his superior.

They piled into Armando's vehicle and headed to task force headquarters, locked in discussion about how best to handle this with the feds. Armando did not respond.

# 14: Exit Strategy

SWEET TOOTH THOUGHT about the time when he and his brother Jimmy were mulling over the best way to hide the money he was bringing home and when it would be safe to start putting it to use to make their mom's life better than it had been in years. This had to be done without drawing attention to their sudden change of fortune.

"Have you said anything to anybody about me and what I'm doing?" Jimmy asked.

"No. I'm saving that for a hot-looking newspaper reporter. Want to get something good for that information." He laughed. "Hey, speaking of that, are you gonna take another shot at hooking up with the reporter babe you were supposed to meet last night?"

"Man, I'm so tempted, but it's too stupid for me to do that. Gotta watch my ass big time these days. Money's too good, and the people I get it from are too dangerous for me to mess up." He smiled as he spoke, but his brother noticed it was not a happy or even a confident smile.

"Jimmy, you sure that all this ain't gonna get you killed someday?"

"Everybody dies, Tooth. It's all just a matter of how long it can be delayed." Jimmy looked down as the realization of his own mortality seemed to hit him hard suddenly at that moment. "Why did you bring that up, kid brother?" He was bothered more than he felt comfortable with. He did not like that question.

"There's other ways to make money, 'mano," Sweet Tooth advised the person he looked up to most in this world. "What about getting a gig as a long-distance truck driver? We could both get our CDLs and team drive all over the friggin' country."

"Then who's here for Mom?" came Jimmy's sobering question.

"Yeah, I guess you're right." Sweet Tooth was deflated. Then he perked up again. "Maybe we could start a business together. Get Mom involved."

"What kind of business?"

"I don't know." Tooth thought for a moment. "Maybe a food truck. We could sell food and cake and maybe even fruit smoothies."

Jimmy paused for a moment, then said, "I like the way you're thinking, kid. Maybe we could do that. Maybe even do it somewhere else." He was thinking. "I just need to build us a nest egg so we'll have plenty of bucks to fall back on." Jimmy patted his brother's shoulder and smiled. "Not bad, kid. Keep running this stuff through your head, and maybe we'll find something that will makes us rich."

"Don't you think we got enough money now?" Sweet Tooth asked innocently.

"No." Jimmy laughed. "We don't got anywhere near that, but what is coming our way real soon could get me to the place where we do have enough to jump into something that can do it for all of us." Jimmy was packing his bag, getting ready to roll. "I should be able to get back here in a couple a' weeks. Until then, here's my new number. Put it in your phone, but put it under a made-up name. Can't be too careful with this shit."

"What's with the made-up name? I don't like what's starting to happen here. You may be getting into this too deep, and you know what I'm saying." Sweet Tooth had a problem. "I'm hoping that you got things under control. You do . . . don't you, Jimmy?"

"You got it, bro. I have things under control." Jimmy hugged his brother good-bye. "I'll stop by the casino on the way out so I can say bye to Mom." Their mom worked there as cleaning lady.

When he parked at the casino a half hour later, Jimmy had no idea that he was being watched and filmed by a shadowy man with a heart as empty as a cave. He was parked near the front of the building in a nondescript white van with the logo of an electrical contractor's firm, "Busy Bee Electric." Jimmy looked left and right before entering the building and then upon entering the slot area in the main room, he caught sight of his mother wiping down the gaming machines.

Menta Begaye was a good mother, who although had just reached fifty years of age, looked like a person in her sixties. She smiled as her son Jimmy approached her. He hugged her, and she kissed his cheek in response. "What a nice surprise, Jimmy. You dropped by Mama's workplace." She chuckled.

"Yeah, Mama. Thought I could sneak up on you." He chuckled as he looked lovingly at the woman who raised him and his brother without her husband, who was killed in an auto accident when they were barely out of diapers. "Maybe someday soon you won't have to do this stuff anymore." He swept his hand around, indicating the entire casino.

"Oh, it's not all that bad, honey. I got lots of friends here, and we take care of one another." She nodded. "Don't worry about me. Worry about you. Be careful of who you run with."

That statement caused Jimmy Begaye to wonder if she knew what he was really doing these days. "What do you mean, Mama? I'm doing okay, and as soon as I get a promotion, I'll have enough money to help you out . . . Maybe even good to the point of you retiring."

She laughed. "I wouldn't know what to do with myself if I had nothing to do. Watch game shows all day? Naw, that's not me. I'd probably wind up fat and lazy. You wanna do that to your mother?"

"I'm thinking that maybe you, me, and Sweet Tooth can go into business together. You know . . . like a family thing. Like maybe get a food truck going." He wanted so much for her to let him provide for her, but she was too set in her ways of being the family provider to even listen to his suggestion.

"We'll see, Son. We'll see." She thought for a moment and asked, "How come you're here?"

"I came to tell you I have to go back on the road with my business."

"Your travel business, Jimmy?" She gave him a skeptical glance as she resumed wiping down the slot machine she had been cleaning when he arrived.

"Come on, Mama. You know how I feel about talking about my business. Just keep in mind that I'm doing good and finally getting somewhere," he said proudly.

"Somewhere, where?" she asked. "I would like to know who you are working for. Are they in Mexico or around here?" She made a face when she spoke. The face of a curious parent when they don't believe their child.

"It's complicated, Mom. That's all I can say right now." He hugged her good-bye, and she hugged him back.

"When will you be back, Jimmy?"

"In a couple a' weeks. Keep an eye on Sweet Tooth in the meantime. Okay?" He turned and began walking away.

Menta Begaye watched her son stroll through the big room and out the door. She shook her head and said a silent prayer asking for his protection. Knowing that it might be some time before she saw him again.

# 15: THE ENEMY WITHIN

MEANWHILE, JOHN GODE had convened a Shadow Wolf–only lunch meeting at Sonny's Restaurant on the reservation. Alicia, Noche, Chico, and Keno were gathered around a table with him. John had spoken with Armando Grant a half hour earlier and had been alerted by him that CSS Special Agent Wilson was on his way there to ask him some questions about the shootout the night before. He had no sooner ended the call when Wilson and two other men in suits came through the door, just as the group's food was brought to the table.

Wilson walked up to John and glared at him. "You want to explain to me how you got one of my prisoners killed last night?"

John looked up at the red-faced federal agent and replied with a simple, "No."

"What the fuck kind of an answer is that? Maybe that nonsense flies with the retards you work with, but it goes nowhere with us." He looked at his two compadres. "You start explaining, and you better tell me something that means something to me about this mess you caused."

"Or?" John asked casually as he sat perfectly relaxed.

"Or? Or?" Wilson looked like he was about to come out of his skin. "Or I'll lock your ass up. You got that, Geronimo? You won't see the light of day again until I say you do." He leaned menacingly into John's face.

"Let me tell you something, 'Oh Great White Father.' If you don't stop disrespecting the name of a fierce warrior chief and start acting like you believe that me and my friends here are actually human beings, I'm going to go Billy Jack on your ass." John took a slow bite of his sandwich as he stared back at the furious CSS special agent. "Billy Jack was a fictional character who kicked dumb shits—uh, like you—in the nuts. He did that a lot in the movies."

"I suppose that's a threat, Geronimo? You got me crapping in my pants. Can't you see me shaking and shitting?" He looked at his fellow agents, who were laughing loudly until John stood up slowly. He was several inches taller than Wilson, who was by now looking up at him.

"I'll tell you what I'm gonna do. Just like Billy Jack did in the movie when he was dealing with his asshole antagonists." John went Tiger Face, a martial arts method of draining all expression from one's face. "I'm going to take this foot here"—he pointed at his left foot—"and I'm going to place it right there, and there's nothing you can do to stop me." He pointed at Wilson's right temple. "Then we can all watch you shit your pants for real."

"Take all this kung fu garbage and stick it up your ass, Geronimo." He pushed hard on John's chest and was astonished when he felt nothing there, as the big man had moved completely out of his way like a cloud riding the evening wind. Losing his balance, the agent stumbled slightly, making him feel stupid and angry at the same time. A dangerous combination, because the next thing he did was come upward, throwing an upper cut at John, catching him with a glancing blow on his chin. Wilson then threw a punch with furious energy, catching John in the ribs but hurting the furious agent's hand far more than it hurt John. Wilson pulled an expandable baton from his pocket, whipped it open to its sixteen-inch length, and launched at John, viciously swinging it, aiming for his collarbone and after he missed that, for the big man's shins.

John evaded that strike easily. It was then that the cat-like, big man lit him up with an open-handed strike to the ribs that doubled him over and then to the floor, where he spit up half his lunch. The other two CSS agents started for John, but Alicia hit one with a wrist strike (Monkey Wrist) that snapped his head back. As he lost his balance, she swung her leg behind him and took him down, where he landed hard on the wooden floor.

The third agent set up in a Praying Mantis kung fu fighting position and threw a double punch at John, just missing his face. John realized that this guy was a trained martial artist just by his movements. The agent threw a crescent kick that turned into a straight kick. Again, John wasn't where his assailant thought he would be, and it threw him completely off. The big lawman hit him three times within a second, laying him out across the table.

"You've really done it now," was all Wilson could muster as he gasped for his breath and rose slowly from the floor. He tried to get to his two cohorts as they got to their feet slowly. "You're under arrest!" he yelled as he went for his weapon.

But John laughed at him. "No, asshole, you're under arrest. For assaulting a police officer."

"I'm a federal agent, and I call the shots here," he said angrily.

"And I'm a tribal police officer, and you are on tribal land . . . and you just assaulted me." John smiled. "You attacked me, acting like the badass you think you are. That's assaulting a police officer, which is a felony here in our sovereign Indian nation."

"That's not all I'm going to do to you." Wilson sneered.

"Drop your weapons, boys," said Noche as he stood with his nine mil pointed at the three disheveled feds. They were standing silently, staring at one another, waiting for the other shoe to drop. That didn't take long at all.

"We're leaving, and what are you gonna do about it?" Wilson said as he turned toward the door. "I'll be back with warrants for all of you." Their weapons were still holstered.

"Won't hold, tough guy," John taunted.

"Of course it will. We're the high law. Want me to spell that out for you?" Wilson bragged smugly.

"Yeah, and the 'high law' enforcement officers just attacked a few dopey Indians." John stared Wilson down.

"That's bullshit, Gode, and you know what's gonna happen next?"

"To you or to me?"

"To all of ya. I'm coming back with an army if I have to, but you ain't walking on this."

"Well, Agent Wilson—or is that Special Agent Wilson? We got way more witnesses than you got." John pointed to the twenty or so other people in the restaurant who were standing frozen in their places, watching this all unfold. And they were all tribe members. "So get your chicken asses out of here, and stay gone or you'll be facing a tribal judge, who I hear actually is the great-great grandson of Geronimo." All the Wolves laughed again as the three agents dragged themselves out of the restaurant with Wilson mumbling as he led the way.

John watched them go with the sinking feeling that this was leading nowhere good. It was never productive to screw with the feds because of their long reach. But what he had going for him was that being Native American, they could not violate their political correctness position. Especially when screwing with the Indians didn't fly in DC these days. Didn't look too good when raised at presidential press conferences. He liked those thoughts, even though he despised the misplaced rationale of the "do-gooders" who blindly followed like lemmings in the march to the cliffs of national disaster.

Wilson clutched his injured ribs as he walked toward his car, saying to himself, "This son of a bitch needs a 'girls' night out.' And now he's going to get one."

# 16: The Coffee Pot

JOHN'S PHONE BUZZED. It was his Shadow Wolf brother Sunday, longtime mentor and beloved guardian, who worked in security at the casino while actually being a deep undercover DEA agent. "I need to see you."

"What's up?" John was surprised by the serious tone in Sunday's voice.

"Come by. We'll talk."

"Coming." John was on his way.

Twenty minutes later as he wheeled into the parking lot, he noticed a van sitting in a spot facing the entrance to the hotel. It was one he had seen before, and when he saw cars or people more than once in a short while, he became aware of them. "Busy Bee Electric," he said to himself. He made a note of the signage on the side of the vehicle, and memorizing the license plate, walked into the hotel lobby that was also the entrance to the casino.

Sunday was sitting at a slot machine, pretending to be surveilling a player when he was actually playing the slots. Pushing the play button on the machine, Sunday did not look at the big lawman as John straddled the stool next to his Shadow Wolf brother. He put a ten-dollar bill in the machine and waited for Sunday to start talking.

"Strange goings on here last night, Gode." Sunday had an accent similar to the late character actor Chief Dan George. He had a dry sense of humor that came through if you paid close attention to his words.

"What's that?" John asked quietly.

"We got a call from a newspaper in New York asking us to look in on a lady who checked in a couple a' days ago. Seems she disappeared, and they wanted us to look for her before they called the police."

"You got anything on it?" John continued playing his machine.

"Got her name. Maria Alvarez." Sunday kept his eyes on the dancing lights of the machine he was playing. "She's a hotshot investigative reporter. I checked her room and didn't see anything unusual. 'Cept she hasn't been there since sometime yesterday." Sunday looked over his shoulder at the man he was supposedly checking on.

"So she's still checked in?"

"Yep. You want ta' look?"

John replied, "I got nothing better to do at the moment."

"Meet me by the elevators in a minute." He got up and walked away.

John faked being frustrated with his machine and closed out his play. He stood up and looked around the area, acting like he was seeking a friendlier game. He walked over to the coffee shop, and seeing a bit of a line there, he decided to forego a much-desired cup of coffee. He instead went through the casino toward the elevator bank, where he boarded the one with Sunday holding the doors open. Within a moment, they arrived on the second floor and moved quickly down the hallway to where Sunday used his security entry key, and they were in. John handed a pair of latex gloves to Sunday before putting on his pair. "I'll take this end. You start there." He pointed toward the bathroom end of the suite.

Both men knew how to track and wasted no time trying to find a trail that might lead them to "a place of understanding," as John's grandfather would describe that moment where people find answers to big questions.

"She's probably a neat freak," Sunday commented stoically. "Not usual to see rooms in hotels kept this orderly. Like she never did nothing here, and yet she was here for two days and refused maid service on both of them. Quite a gal."

"Sounds like you admire her." John laughed as he searched under the bed.

"No . . . those kind make me uncomfortable."

"Too tidy?" Again John laughed.

"Too rigid. Breakable. You need to be able to bend in today's world," Sunday said resignedly.

"Like the government when they say BOHICA?"

"What do you mean, Gode?" Sunday was puzzled.

"Bend Over, Here It Comes Again. BOHICA, my friend." John chuckled slightly.

"Yeah. I guess that's another way to look at this."

John sat down on the bed and thought for a moment before saying, "I'm not picking up anything. You?"

"Can't say for sure. The spirit in this room seems to be unsettled. Like something bad happened . . . but it's hard to tell when it was." The Shadow Wolves all had a heightened spiritual and energy sensitivity. He was speaking to the man he had seen grow spiritually into a powerful shaman, starting from a young man being guided by his grandfather, who himself had been an incredible storytelling shaman, respected by all who ever knew him.

Looking at the coffeepot, John asked, "I need a cup of coffee. Do you suppose . . . ?"

"Help yourself, Big John." Sunday pointed toward the coffeepot.

"You want one?" the big man asked.

"No . . . I drink only green tea these days. I'm civilized now, you know."

"Smart man," John remarked as he went to the sink and filled the coffeepot with water. Then he pulled the basket out so he could put the coffee package in place and was surprised by what he saw. "What have we here?" There, sitting in the basket, was a flash drive. "Look at this, Sunday."

"Leave it to you, Gode," the older man said as he examined what John had discovered. "Nice find. Probably hers. Anyone else's and it would either be water-damaged or gone. I like the way she thinks," he praised.

John flipped it in his fingers as he thought for a moment. "Can I get a laptop quick? Real quick."

Sunday said, "Come with me." He opened the door and looked up and down the hallway before exiting the room. "I'll get hold of the video surveillance and take a look at what was happening in the lobby over the past day or so."

"Good idea." John thought for a moment, then said, "We should take a look for something that doesn't fit the traffic in this place. Can you get me somewhere I can view it?"

"You thinking what I'm thinking?" Sunday asked.

"What's that?"

"This was probably done by pros, John. The room's too clean."

"Except for this." The big lawman held up the flash drive. "How do we do this without drawing attention?"

"I know people," Sunday said quietly.

"We have to keep this between us. No one else, Sunday. No. One. Else!"

"What do you think is going on here?"

"Something very big and very bad." John's face went void of expression as he spoke, and it triggered concern in Sunday.

"Come on, what is it that you think is going on?"

"I can't put it in words yet, my brother. It's . . . "

"It's what? You're really starting to worry me out with the way you're acting. This ain't you. What's driving this, John?"

"My gut."

"That's it? Your gut?" Sunday knew John's instincts were incredibly sharp, and when he said "my gut," that meant it could practically be taken as fact.

"How do we get somewhere I can open this flash drive alone? Can we do that now?"

"Like I said, I know people. Follow me."

He led the way to an empty room full of video screens recording the activity in the casino and the hotel lobby. Sunday suggested John pull up a chair and sit in front of a screen.

"Here's my laptop," he said as he handed it to the big man, who flipped it open quickly and plugged in the flash drive. Sunday, standing opposite him, watched Gode's eyes as they flashed back and forth, devouring what he was seeing. Then he heard a woman's voice.

"There are tens of thousands, and they're already here. They've been arriving over the past seven years, known to and protected by highly placed officials in our government. My brother was one of their earliest victims . . . that's why I started my probe. I got nowhere with the authorities in DC, and soon after meeting with some of them I sensed I was being followed. The Islamic terrorists that are here are supported by sympathetic lawyers, doctors, judges, and CEOs, all woven into our society, funding the soldiers of their caliphate as they prepare to become active and begin the process of taking down what they call us—the Great Satan. They plan to make America the front line in their campaign of terror. I know of a man who might be able to help stop this or at least work with those who can help to stop this, because the kick-off of this plan is in Arizona with the help of the neighboring cartels. I plan to contact him while I'm here and compare information. He is part of and a leader in a network that stretches across this country of little-known blood brothers and sisters who have special abilities. I also know that he is addicted to coffee." She chuckled slyly before ending the message with, "And he can lead me to the man who probably has all the answers I need before I move on this."

John looked up at Sunday and asked, "Do you believe this could actually be happening here?"

"There is very little that would surprise me these days, Big John. These are times that are not like anything we've seen before . . . so yes, I tend to feel I should believe it."

John took the flash drive out of the computer port and thought for a moment before putting it in his pocket. He took a deep breath and said, "Let's look at the lobby videos, Sunday."

He sat watching the screens, eyes darting to and fro, as he searched the dual images in view—one, the casino and the other, the lobby.

"I'm going to get you a cup of coffee. How do you want it?" Sunday asked.

"Hot and black."

"Like your women?"

"That was once true, if the opportunity presented itself," John responded but remained laser-focused on the screen.

"Sugar?"

"Not from you."

Sunday nodded at John's comment and was somewhat relieved by the big man's sense of humor returning. "Maybe the mood change is caused by the prospect of a cup of coffee. Or maybe it is something else quite different," he thought. Returning with the coffee, he found John still intently staring at the screen.

Waving Sunday to him, the big lawman pointed at three men who were on the video, cautiously wheeling a large suitcase through a crowd of seniors in the lobby waiting to check in. Their faces were not clearly visible because they were all wearing hats and sunglasses. Two had beards and one a heavy mustache. They kept their heads down, initially making it difficult to get a make on them.

"They look like hippies in suits, with fake facial hair," Sunday commented flatly. "That one there looks like an older guy trying to look like a younger guy. No fool like an old fool. Eh?"

The video showed them moving through the crowd, and one of them was rocked by a younger man who came out of the crowd after snatching a senior lady's purse, knocking him out of his escape path as he ran away.

"There, Sunday! I need stills of these guys in the lobby, right there, with this guy's face . . . right there." John pointed at what he needed.

"Can do . . . John Gode," Sunday said assuredly.

"Something's going on here that makes me think that what we're seeing is a body being moved." John's wheels were turning.

"That suitcase looks like it's got something pretty heavy in it." John looked at Sunday, who seemed lost in thought for a moment. "You see it, Sunday?"

He thought Sunday wasn't comprehending what was going on or was distracted by something he wasn't aware of. The older Native American caught himself and looked somewhat embarrassed by his momentary lapse.

"You okay?" John was surprised and concerned by Sunday's demeanor.

"Yeah, I'm okay. I'm okay." He looked down and away from John as he spoke.

"Where are your thoughts, Sunday?"

The response was a shrug of the shoulders and a shake of the head. But Sunday didn't say anything.

Gode kept still for a few seconds, still assessing his mentor. "Can you get me copies of these stills?"

Sunday rose and went to the computer keyboard. "Here, let's pull them off the surveillance video, and we'll store them in your phone right now." Sunday isolated the stills and forwarded them. "Does that work, Big John?"

Gode kept staring at Sunday, wondering what was on his mind that made his whole manner shift so dramatically. He didn't push his concern any further than he already had, but he was uneasy as he left the casino, hoping that his mentor wasn't getting ill or having some kind of mental issue. He had known this man all his life and couldn't recall ever seeing him come off this way. Something was wrong here.

He said so long to Sunday who replied, "John, I . . . I . . . " Then stopped without going any further.

"What is it, Sunday?" John stared at the older tribesman, waiting for some kind of response. None came with the exception of him raising his hand in good-bye.

Pulling out onto the main road pointing north toward Phoenix, he got a call. It was Sunday. "John Gode, I need to talk with you again. Come on back, right now."

He spun a quick U-turn and raced back to the casino.

Sunday was waiting in the video surveillance room as John came roaring through the door, ready for anything that might be waiting for him. But he wasn't quite ready for what he was about to hear. "What the hell is going on with you?" he asked his mentor.

"Here, sit down. I've got something to say to you, and it makes my heart heavy to lay this all on you, but . . . I have nowhere else to go with this. Sit down, John Gode."

"Give it up, Sunday. Come on. You are acting strange, man."

"You're probably gonna think that I've gone completely insane with what I'm going to tell you, but I have to do this." He watched John closely as he said, "Truth is, I am far more imbedded with national intelligence than anyone could ever know. Whatever you think I have been doing in the DEA, I haven't actually been doing."

John stared, totally focused as he urged him on. "Okay. Come on, man, what is going on with you? Talk to me."

Sunday took a deep breath and was somber. "Okay, here it is." He breathed deeply again. "Our POTUS has personally filtered in and protected over five hundred operatives and useful fools into the

Department of Justice, the Department of State, FEMA, EPA, FBI, DEA, Secret Service, NSA, CIA, and ATF. They are so hidden in those departments and branches that it would take an army to find and remove them before the 'takedown' begins."

"Takedown? What takedown?"

"It's something already begun, John Gode." The older man repositioned himself in his chair and leaned in toward the tribal policeman. He spoke quietly. "I know that you have already figured out some of this, and you think what you've found is really bad, but it's nothing compared to what I'm about to tell you. And you might think that I'm hallucinating to the point of being crazy. I wish that was all it was, son. Believe me." He patted John on the arm. "There is the Deep State, that is in full operation, being funded by international bankers in and outside of this country. Their money is the main reason this POTUS got elected and re-elected. He is arm-in-arm with them and the Islamic terrorists, as they have begun taking this country apart. Step by step and there is nothing I know of that can stop it. The leaders are so sophisticated that most of their people don't even know who they are working for or what will be the result of what they are doing, and that makes it practically impossible to find and neutralize them. Many of these people do not have any idea that they are being used by the Deep State so insidiously, and if they knew, I'm sure they would be pissed and probably wouldn't be part of what is going on."

"And you're telling me that this goes up to the White House?" John asked grimly.

"Yeah, I'm telling you that. To the White House. There are around fifty members of the Muslim Brotherhood, Hezbollah, and possibly even ISIS that were brought in by POTUS, and they are there for the long haul, even after he is gone. That should tell you everything. But there's more. I know you picked up on it when he negotiated with the terrorists on the release of the soldier who deserted his unit in Afghanistan, wandered into their camp, and was captured by them."

"Yeah. Of course I remember that."

"Then you also remember that POTUS traded four high-ranking commanders of ISIS and the Taliban, who are back on the battlefield and trying to kill our guys, in a trade for him. Doesn't that tell you something?"

"I'd have to have been living under a rock to miss that one."

Sunday continued. "Why does this POTUS spend millions of dollars to hide his history? No college records. There doesn't seem to be anyone who knew him, even in law school. No wedding pictures of him and his wife. How was he able to keep this all private when everyone else who ever occupied the White House had to give up everything, including the color of their underwear and everyone they ever knew? Not him. He is the one and only exception to this. The one and only. Why?"

John shrugged his shoulders. "I wish I knew." This conversation was setting in and deeply disturbing him.

"Money can do powerful things, John Gode. What I'm talking about is what is called by some a cabal. An alliance of the bankers, the media, the terrorists, and the do-gooders who are the useful fools of everyone I just mentioned. And this is the scariest part of what has gone on. POTUS walked into the NSA and ordered them to delete an entire section, thousands of files, on the Muslim Brotherhood, Hezbollah, and even ISIS. All that intel and tracking tools, gone. Poof. Up in smoke. Done."

"Are you certain about what you're telling me, Sunday?"

"Absolutely positive, and you know what? Nobody would believe this, and I'm at a point where I have to do something, but there isn't anyone in government that I can trust with this. The corruption is spreading like the plague."

"Why did you wait so long to tell me?"

"I didn't want to get you killed."

"But now it's okay to get me killed? Come on, Sunday, tell me the whole story," John demanded with irony in his voice.

"We have reached a tipping point, and if we don't somehow, someway get this out to the people, there is nothing any of us will be able to do. We could very probably be there already. If anything happens to me, you are going to be screwed because you will then be one of the few left who know about this. You better know that if they get wind you know this, your life won't be worth a shit."

"So what prompted you to finally tell me all this?"

"The news gal," Sunday answered without pause.

"You talked with her?"

"No. Sure wish I had. What brought me to this point was when I realized that she was somehow aware of me and what I know but didn't have my identity. She knew only where I am but that was it. And that's why she was here at this hotel." Sunday's face was expressionless, but his eyes were filled with fire as he continued. "Someone figured that out, John, and I think she paid the price. And now that path is closed as an avenue to get the existence and identities of these hidden Deep State assholes out to the public," Sunday said quietly.

"Would you have done that? Would you have gone to the press?"

"Yeah, I would have. If it was someone who I could trust."

"How do you know you could trust her?"

"She's dead. She was killed by the people who are going to try to kill us, John Gode. You know that, right?"

"So it's your gut that makes you think she could have been trusted?"

"Yeah. Sound familiar?"

"Yeah, maybe, but we had better get our shit together and start watching our backs."

"Again, trust only Shadow Wolves. We are bound by blood, and that is our greatest tool."

# 17: Girls' Night Out

NOCHE WAS SITTING at his desk in the task force squad room, watching John, who was intensely focused on a phone conversation he was immersed in. He looked stressed as he spoke into the phone. After the conversation ended, he said, "Hey, what do you say we grab us a couple a cold ones over at the Flats, Big John?"

He thought for a moment. "Yeah, that sounds good, Noche. But only one for me . . . been a long day, my brother. Got a lot on my mind that I didn't have this morning."

They drove the seven miles to the Tortilla Flats Café out on a well-traveled but dusty trail on the reservation, discussing what John heard during the phone conversation. The sun was setting, and the air was beginning to be cooled by the rolling desert evening breeze.

"What'cha got on your mind, John? You sure look like something's bothering the living shit outta you."

"I'm tying to find a way to let you know just what that is, without violating my protocol and compromising yours."

"Do whatever works for you, big guy. I know the drill and that means I know I don't have to know what you can't talk about. I'm good with that."

"But it's not that simple, Noche. Not at all. Fact is, you do need to know about this. To keep you breathing."

"Okay . . . there's no one here but you and me. So . . . ?"

"I'm being informed about shit that is going on between some people in government all the way up to the White House that could rain hell down on this country."

Noche watched John closely. "I'm hearing you."

"I just got a heads up that because of something I did there's a hit coming at us."

"Us? You and me?"

"Us . . . meaning me and anyone close to me." John said with deep concern in his voice.

"What exactly is it that you did?"

"I found a body in the desert."

"Yeah, I know that, John."

"I also found a tooth. One that I believed came from that toothless body, and I withheld from declaring it as evidence."

"What made you do that?"

"My gut."

"Why did I even ask a dumb-ass question like that?" Noche muttered.

"It seems that as it turns out, the tooth belonged to someone who was investigating major corruption in several areas of the federal government and getting close to proving it."

"How does this bring you . . . us into the mix?"

"What I just got in that conversation is that her killers found my name on her list of people who she could trust with this information, and they believe that I may have enough to blow this whole thing wide open."

"Do you?"

"What I think is, with all this shit going on around us, I think we got our hands full."

"And you think we don't have our hands full, John?"

"No . . . actually, what I think is that what we've seen so far is just the tip of the spear." The big lawman paused for a moment. "My brother, we are quite possibly in the middle of a major shit storm. Bigger than any of us have ever experienced before."

"John Gode, I gotta admit, there have been times when I had the thought that partnering with you would get me into some bad shit. But man oh man, this is beyond anything I ever figured on. What do we do?"

"Have a beer and chill for a bit. Come on, I'm buying."

The parking lot had quite a few cars parked in it. John commented, "Looks like some other people had the same urge for a beer. Great minds think alike, amigo." He nudged him with a friendly elbow poke to his ribs as he let out a quiet laugh.

They parked out back in the lot because they were in a task force vehicle and didn't want their emergency equipment, like the grill lights, to be too obvious to the public.

The café was dimly lit, and overhead fans brought a slight breeze to their faces as they found a table and sat down.

Noche held up two fingers for the bartender, who knew them both well enough to know their brand of beer, which he had sitting in front of them within the next two minutes. "Thanks, Frankie," Noche said as he tipped the longneck bottle toward the bartender, who in turn acknowledged them with a slight bow of the head.

"I like this, Noche. Feels like 'Cheers,' where everybody knows your name." He lifted the beer to his mouth as Noche chuckled.

"Everyone on that show 'Cheers' knew one another's names because they all lived at that bar. You, however, live in the desert, where no one knows your name, and when it gets dark they can't even see you," Noche said just before being interrupted by a very attractive lady who came over to the table and sat down with them.

"And who are you, my lovely?" Noche asked with pleasant surprise tingeing his voice.

"Name's Sheila." She sat right across from John, staring intently into his eyes. She was tall, slender, and looked like she was about twenty, with long dark hair flowing over her shoulders. "What's yours?"

"Just call me Noche."

"Not asking you . . . I'm asking him." She nodded her head toward John.

"Here we go again. You suck up all the oxygen in the room, Gode. No one's got a chance when you're around. How could I have forgotten that? What a dumb-ass." He laughed as he good-naturedly slapped the table.

"So the name is Gode? That's it?" She leaned forward, exposing her ample breasts to John as her blouse fell away from her body far enough to bring them into his view.

The big lawman remained expressionless as he stared back at her, forcing her to drop her eyes for a second. This gave John the opportunity to take control of the moment and direct the focus from him back onto her.

"Even though I'm enjoying the view, Sheila, I'm having trouble with why you're showing it to me," John said almost in a whisper, which caused her to lean in closer.

Sheila didn't respond. She just stared at him intently.

"My name's John. So nice to meet you." He nodded with a smile as he responded with an air of confidence that seemed to stall her approach. "What can I do for you?"

"I'd like to buy you a drink. I want to see how long it takes for that drink to go from your lips to your brain." She chuckled suggestively.

"To my brain? Not my stomach first?" John asked lightly.

"To your blood, actually." She smiled. "After it gets there, the rest is academic."

"Academic? Interesting." John was impressed by her choice of words.

"So . . . what'll you have?"

"Too late, lovely lady. I already have this beer, and that's my limit when I'm driving."

"Why not let your buddy here drive?" She looked at Noche as she spoke.

"He doesn't like to drive at night, so I can't quite rely on that." John smiled and leaned back in his chair. "I hate to turn down an offer like this from such a beauty, but I have to do that. Thanks for stopping by."

"Okay, I'll have to take that for a no. You know you might regret this, Tall Man."

"Regret? In what way?"

She shrugged and answered, "Nobody on their deathbed ever regrets what they did in life . . . they regret what they didn't do. And you," she said emphatically, "will regret not doing me." She rose slowly with her eyes fixed on John, then turned and walked away, swaying her hips in slow and sexy manner as she went.

Noche said loud enough for her to hear, "So what about giving me a try, gorgeous?"

"You're not tall enough," she answered stoically. And she was gone.

"John Gode . . . what is this?" Noche sat with his hands out in front of him, palms up, questioning. "The best-looking woman I have ever seen around here tries to flat out pick your ass up, and you friggin' turn her down . . . cold? What is it? You need Viagra? I have Viagra right here in my wallet. Not that I need it."

"Then why do you carry it?" John laughed.

"Just in case. But let me tell you, with something that looks like that . . . in no way would I need any help."

John just sat looking at his close friend with a knowing grin, arms folded. He chuckled. "You still don't get it. Do you?"

"Get what, John?"

"That chick was on a mission."

"What kind of a mission?"

"She walks up to me in a bar full of people, like she was waiting for me. Then she treats you like dog shit as she tries to attract me. And to do what? I don't know."

"But what mission, John?"

He shrugged. "Not sure. Maybe it's Alicia trying to test my fidelity. Or maybe she's just a hooker. Who can say?"

"If she's a hooker, then why didn't she take me on?"

"Like she said, you're not tall enough."

John went over to the bar, paid their tab, and returned. "Come on, Brother Noche. Time to go."

John was strangely silent as they approached their vehicle. Noche asked, "What's wrong? You giving up talking all of a sudden?"

"I don't know. I feel like something's wrong."

"What kind of wrong?"

As John unlocked the doors with his fob, several gunshots exploded into the night, breaking the glass on the front driver's side. "That kind of wrong," he blurted quickly as they both dove for cover.

The air was filled with the sound of bullets flying and coming at them from three directions. They both lay still, trying to somehow blend with the darkness of the area where they were parked.

Light, approaching footsteps that were suddenly interrupted caused John to focus his attention on the top of a car that was parked less than twenty feet away. A bullet ricocheted six inches from his head.

He rolled to his right, firing. As he did, he was surprised to hear what sounded like a woman's voice cry out as his rounds found their mark.

"You hear that, John?"

"That's one," he whispered as he scanned the area around them, searching the night.

They were fired upon again, this time from two directions.

John crouched, poised, ready to change his position. He waited until Noche was ready, then they both moved in opposite directions, crouch-running as shots rang out, tracking their steps. Windows were blown out by the spray of bullets, just missing both men.

Noche found the first shooter's dead body right in front of him. "Shit!" he said loudly as he saw that the body lying in a pool of blood was a woman. A gorgeous woman.

Several rounds flew past Noche's head, taking out the windows of the car parked behind him. People started streaming out of the café as the shooting continued.

"Police! Get back inside," John shouted to the confused group. They all scampered rapidly back into the building.

Rounds were immediately fired at where John had been when he shouted his warning. His gut took him to another part of the parking lot. It was then that he picked up the image of a shooter's head bobbing up and down behind a car only a few feet from him. He threw a stone at the tire of a car parked next to the shooter, who immediately raised up and fired a spray at the sound. That was all John needed. He pumped two rounds into the shooter's head.

Noche's hair was covered with broken glass as another volley of shots rang out. He returned fire to where the shots were coming from, but his shots did not find the target. John moved silently toward the same spot when movement to his right caught his attention. A black-clad assailant ran directly at him and leaped into the air, attempting to drive a kick to his head. But it missed, as John parried the action. This was followed by several furiously thrown crescent kicks, followed by another series of straight kicks aimed at his chest, shins, and chin. But the big lawman was not there when they arrived. He threw a punch that landed in the assailant's lower ribs, followed by an open-handed strike to the head that drove "him" to the ground. Only he was actually a she, which John learned as he removed the black ski mask, revealing the face of the woman who tried picking him up in the café. She revived, threw a kick at him, and jumped to her feet, holding her handgun and starting to pull the trigger. John moved to his right and fired his weapon once, killing her instantly. Her round went upward toward the sky as she fell backward with eyes wide open, seeing nothing.

# 18: Jihad in the Desert

It was mid-afternoon the next day when John's cell phone rang, and what he heard got his blood racing. Alicia said she just had received a call from one of her informant "watchers" near Nogales on the immediate north side of the border, saying that a small group of vehicles, SUVs, and Hummers had crossed into US territory and were moving north in the desert at a pretty good speed for off-road travel.

"Get a team together. Load up heavy, and meet me on the dirt road right off of Riggs, and get there quick. Don't bring anyone who isn't Wolf. Keep this under the radar with everyone else. I'll be there in fifteen minutes waiting for you," he whispered into the phone as the reality of what he was learning now set. He kept phone conversations short and as generic as possible because he knew how easily he could be audio monitored. Not to mention there may be a "grabber" on his phone. He was realizing what could be coming at him and anyone close to him. If what he thought it was proved to be more than a figment of an investigative reporter's imagination, he didn't want any of his people to pay the ultimate price because he got sloppy and said more than he should have to any one of them. This had the potential to be the biggest case he had ever come close to getting his hands on, and he knew how devastating the potential outcome could be.

Steering his new ride out of the parking area, he made a quick right and gunned the engine for a quarter of a mile to a stop sign on a crossroad. John scanned the road behind him through the rearview mirror. Nothing. He looked overhead. Nothing. The Apache lawman made another quick right into the farthest end of the parking lot he had just left. He looked around for whatever it was that was bothering him. He saw no one. Yet, his gut was telling him that he was in danger.

He sat in one spot for a few seconds, then abruptly got out of the vehicle and started walking toward a truck parked near a clump of small trees. He spun around when he saw no one inside and ran back to his SUV. He backed it up and reverse J-turned, rolling out of the lot and onto the tribal road on his way to his Shadow Wolf team. The truck did not move.

He arrived at the meeting point twenty minutes later after taking a circuitous route just in case. The team arrived ten minutes after that. They had two SUVs and one Hummer that was an Iraq war surplus vehicle, which they had received along with hi-tech vision equipment and twenty assorted rifles and automatics that gave them the punch of an Army Special Forces unit.

Alicia briefed them on the information she had received, and after she was finished John assigned the six Shadow Wolves their responsibilities. They drove twelve miles and took up positions using the boulders at the foot of a hill for cover while John took a position with a sniper rifle about fifty feet up the hill, near the top. He used his glasses to scan the terrain for telltale dust indicating movement on the trail, one of the thoroughfares that had came to be known to John as being frequently used by the cartels through the rough desert landscape. They did a quick com check using mic clicks so they wouldn't tip off the approaching convoy. Within ten minutes, the big man picked up a dust trail coming their way. He clicked his mic four times, a click for each vehicle as they came within range of his glasses.

"They're getting ballsy and even more ballsy every time I see them," Noche said to Chico, whom he and Lonzo were partnering with. They made a deadly combination to go against. Alicia, Manny, and Arthur made an even deadlier group.

The convoy stopped suddenly. "Uh-oh," John whispered to himself as he watched the drivers of all four vehicles get out and gather together with a heavyset man, who was pointing east and directly opposite of where the lawmen were set up. They conversed for a few minutes, then started back to their vehicles. As the heavyset man was getting back into his car, he stopped and stared at where the Wolves were hiding. Then he got into his vehicle, and they resumed their trek right at them.

John clicked again, and when Noche looked up at him, the big man pointed with two fingers to his eyes and then at the approaching vehicles. He held up fingers indicating three minutes before they got to them.

His estimate was off because they started rolling faster as they got closer. John put his eye on the sniper scope, took a breath, and waited. He didn't have to wait long as the convoy rolled into view. Shots fired from the lead vehicle danced in the dirt in front of Noche's Hummer. The Wolf teams were deployed behind the boulders and opened up on that vehicle as the occupants bailed, all shooting at Noche's team. The second cartel vehicle stopped suddenly as the roof opened, and a .50-caliber-toting man opened fire on their position, blowing pieces of rock everywhere as they all dropped down. John had a fix on the gunner and placed a round in the center of his head, which blew apart as he dropped down into the vehicle with half his head gone. The three vehicles following started racing toward Alicia's team after they caught sight of them.

"Let's rip open these sons of Satan and leave them like piles of coyote shit in the desert." As the heavyset leader yelled into his radio, John put one into his chest and another into his head. He was gone.

Alicia opened up on the tires with her weapon, and both in front were torn to shreds. The two SUVs in the rear started rolling in reverse as both Wolf teams hopped in their vehicles and pursued, stopping them quickly.

John had rapid-fired at both retreating vehicles, and that brought them to a stop and surrender as two men exited each vehicle with their hands in the air. The two who survived from the lead vehicles emerged hands-up. They all simultaneously dropped to their knees, hands folded behind their necks, yelling, "Don't shoot! Don't shoot!"

John ran down the hill toward them as the team pulled up to where they were clustered. Alicia checked the vehicles with a shotgun pointed ahead of her steps. "All clear." She nodded toward the rapidly approaching John.

Noche and Lonzo kept their weapons at the ready and pointed at the group as John and Chico pulled them up one at a time and "tossed" them for weapons. They found one on each of them. They were then handcuffed behind their backs and sat on the ground.

"You speak English?" John said, looking from one to the other. One of them said, "I do." He kept his head down, but it was easy to see he was a little road-worn.

"I'm going to ask you some questions that I want honest answers to." The big man squatted down in front of him and tipped his chin up so they could look one another in the eye. "Now, I already know the answer to many of these questions, and if it looks like you're bullshitting me, I will stop asking you questions and move on to one of your friends here and start asking them. Your lack of cooperation will put you in a bad place with me. You understand me?"

"None of them speak English, so what then?" the bulked-up cartel member asked smugly, looking at John defiantly.

"Doesn't matter, because my friend here"—John nodded toward Noche—"speaks Spanish better than you. So do we have an understanding? Do you want to save yourself from a lot of shit?"

The gangster shrugged with a gesture indicating "what else can I do?"

"Okay. First question. What brings you to my country this fine day?"

"We're just here looking for pussy." He laughed, looking the big lawman in the face.

"Really?" John indicated he did not like that answer at all. "There's only gonna be one more question, and if you don't answer it right, I will move on." John looked at the next "banger," sizing him up, then back at the one he was talking with.

"Why are you here? And . . . why did you shoot at us?"

"We didn't know who you were. We still don't know who you really are. So why take a chance, amigo?"

"Makes sense." John shook his head in mock understanding. "Is that the way you generally treat people who you don't know?"

"Yeah. That's how we do it in my country. Keeps the weird people out of your hair." He half laughed.

"But you're not in your country . . . amigo," John commented as he ended that conversation.

Another of the captured group spoke up. "I speak English, man. Ask me some questions." He sounded like a wiseass too.

John shrugged his shoulders and asked why he was in Arizona.

"It's what we do. Gotta make a livin', you know."

"Dying ain't much of a livin'," John quipped.

"Hey . . . we ain't dead." He laughed uncomfortably.

"Yet," Alicia added.

He took note of her and didn't like her attitude. "You don't do that. American cops don't kill people for nothing." He perked up suddenly, realizing that his belief was based in truth, in an ironic way. "You guys are different than . . . "

"Than what?" Noche asked.

"Than most other cops in the world."

"What makes you think we're American cops?" John asked in passing.

"So we playing games now? Huh?" the buffed gangster asked, trying to stare John down.

The big lawman looked over at the heavyset dead man in the first vehicle. "What's his name?"

"I don't know his real name. We just called him A.B."

"A.B. got a last name?"

"Don't know what that was." The young gang member looked up as he spoke.

"Where was he from?"

"I don't know, man. Don't know nothing about him except that he farted a lot." He thought he had said something funny. But no one laughed.

"So, you come here with this guy and the other guys, and none of you know his name?" John looked around at them. "You open up on us because you don't know who we are? You got to be thinking that we're as big of assholes as you are." John looked the handcuffed gangster in the eye. "You're really not very smart, are you?"

"What'dya mean?"

"Like I just said, you come here working for someone, and you're trying to tell me that you don't even know his name. Then you start shooting at us without knowing who we are. Now . . . you're giving me shit and pissing me off . . . and your life depends on me, at this time. Not smart. Not smart even a little bit."

"What do you think I would do if I was smart? Answer your *pendejo* questions?"

John released a slow breath. "Yeah, and that's because I'm smart," John commented with menacing smile.

"You just look like a big dummy to me."

"Yeah . . . so how come you're on the ground in handcuffs looking at a 'big dummy' and looking at a long time in jail?" John paused for a moment, then said, "I don't think there is any doubt about who's smart, *chico*." He started walking toward his vehicle, and suddenly whipped around and pointed at his prisoner, saying, "*Suhih bukhara*," a quote attributed to Mohammed meaning "war is deceit."

The grounded gangster seemed stunned, then a big smile crossed his face. "Shit! What is this? A test, man?" He had a developing expression of realization on his face as he said, "I know you guys go to big lengths to test us, but you just killed one of your best supporters to prove our loyalty?"

"Yeah, I guess I can trust you. You held tight." It seemed like John had tricked him in a big way with just two Arab words.

"We know how to do this," the man on the ground bragged, as if he were talking with a fellow jihadist. Relaxing, he said, "You guys are real good, but why do you have her with you?" He nodded toward Alicia, who was standing expressionless, watching him with her arms folded.

"She wants to know why they have you with them," John responded quickly. He nodded at the rest of that group and laughed sarcastically. He continued, "How long before the rest come along?"

"We sent them up the second way two hours ago. It was a plan change that came down from Phoenix."

John asked, "How many?"

"How many what?" the gangster responded.

"Soldiers of Allah? Come on, man. How many?"

"The usual. Only this time we used four Hummers. Had to leave one a little north of the border." The gangster seemed to have completely fallen for John's ruse because of the Prophet's quote.

A moment later he seemed to realize his mistake as the rest of the task force arrived and took them into custody.

Bellamy grabbed the muscular wise guy and practically threw him into the back seat of his vehicle.

"Don't break him. He's got a head full of information we can use," John whispered to the task force teammate as he walked him away from the vehicle.

John then returned to Bellamy's vehicle, leaned in, and whispered to the prisoner, "Stay cool. I'll come and get you out of this. Stay strong, soldier of Allah."

The man looked at John but said nothing.

# 19: TRACING WEAPONS

THE NIGHT WAS quiet as John exited his vehicle with a large gear bag filled with weapons confiscated from the desperados his team had taken down earlier that day in the desert south of Phoenix. Alicia and Sunday, carrying the .50-caliber machine gun, made their way into the gun lab run by a forensic private investigator named Arlo Gerber. They were quickly welcomed by the quirky, slender, dark-skinned forensic weapons expert who asked them to lay all the weapons out on a table made of a thick piece of plywood resting on two sawhorses. He immediately honed in on the AK rifles and the .50-caliber machine gun, which was sprinkled with blood spots.

"Looks like somebody died today," Arlo commented quietly. "Guns have a way of making that happen. Don't they?" He looked from face to face for a response. He was several inches shorter than John but moved like a man who knew where he was going . . . and how to get there.

John asked, "My brother, I need a favor from you. As a Shadow Wolf, I know you can be trusted with what I need you to do."

"What favor is that, John Gode?" He took a sip of the coffee he was holding in his left hand and looked curiously at the lawman. "It isn't a favor to do what I can for a brother Shadow Wolf. It is what we do for one another. No?" He glanced again at the array of guns lying before him and asked, "Something about this collection?" He tapped one of the rifles on its stock, then picked it up and made sure it was unloaded before he checked for serial numbers.

"Can you nail exactly where these were bought?" John's eyes were intense, drinking in the variety of weaponry lying before him, knowing what he was asking his Shadow Wolf brother to do—hack into an ATF database—was highly illegal.

"Should be able to, but why don't you just run it up the government IT flagpole?"

"ATF has to be kept out of the loop on this. So does DHS. That's why I need you to run the history of these weapons under the radar. Let's make this Shadow Wolves only, okay, my brother?" John's voice was filled with his intention.

Arlo picked up the handguns one by one, examining them closely. "These are almost new . . . looks like they were worked."

"Worked?" John asked quickly.

"Yeah. Let me have a longer look. Make yourselves comfortable." He was totally into this small gathering of the "pack" as he went about his business. There was a bond among Shadow Wolves, unique to them, that created a wall between them and the outside world.

Alicia walked slowly over to John and cooed, "Hey, big guy, got some time for a lonely and neglected woman?" She rubbed herself softly against his side and smiled coyly, looking up into his eyes.

He looked back at her and ran his finger through her long, black hair as he smiled warmly. "Let's get us a room," he whispered in her ear with a chuckle.

Sunday commented stoically, "Maybe I should close my eyes and plug my ears?"

"I missed you. Please don't go anywhere for a while. Okay?" John asked quietly, then ran his finger under her chin as he lifted her beautiful face.

"Hey, I got something here." Arlo's eyes were glued to his laptop screen as he spoke. "Three of the handguns and two of the rifles were sold out of a shop in Tucson."

"When?" John asked.

"Give me a minute." Arlo was intently scanning what he had before him on the screen. "They were all sold to the same person . . . and it looks like that happened two months ago." He looked up at John, then over at Sunday, who sat staring back. Alicia caught his glance as she moved toward him to view his laptop.

"Buyer's name?" John asked quickly.

"Jimmy Begaye. His address is . . . " He paused for a moment, then continued, "Shit, this guy lives here on the rez." Arlo did not like seeing trouble coming to or from the reservation. "This could be a problem for us," he muttered.

"Beyond the obvious, Arlo, why do you say that?"

Arlo responded, "Not beyond, but right smack in the middle. The cartels are probably using our people to do bad things for them. And most of these bad things are directed at the white man. Not a good development for us." He shook his head.

"What about the rest of them?" Sunday asked.

"I'll need some time to get this all in a bag." He turned toward John and smiled knowingly. "I don't think you and Alicia need to hang around here while I poke around this darkness." He stood up and scratched his head. "Do you want to leave this collection with me? Or should I just record the information that's on them and work with that?"

John thought for a moment. "I think we'd better take them with us for 'chain of custody' concerns down the road. How long do you think it will take you to run the rest of the weapons?"

"Not sure, but I think I can have enough for you by tomorrow afternoon to get some solid leads. What I just found out about the three I ran was because I had been running something else on a data file I already had open when you got here," Arlo explained.

"I think from this point on, no one in this room should even say a three-word sentence about this. Understood?" the big lawman said emphatically.

"Can I tell my girlfriend?" Sunday said with no expression on his face.

"You don't have a girlfriend," John said.

"You ain't met her yet," Sunday responded, looking totally void of emotion, which was his normal demeanor. But that demeanor completely masked the size of his genius intellect. "She is charming and completely civilized. Just like the ladies who run with those *ruling chiefs* in DC. You know . . . the same bunch who know what's best for us all, here on the rez." Sunday was as close to John as his late grandfather had been, although he was younger in years than Grandfather Nan Tan Gode. John owed him big time, along with his shaman grandfather, for

118

keeping him on the "pathway" in his early years, then mentoring him on his way to a career in law enforcement and to "the wisdom," his spirit nature.

"Where the hell did that come from?" John blurted, laughing at Sunday's comment. After thinking a moment, he accepted it as his just being "dry, ol' Sunday." He kept looking at his Shadow Wolf brother and friend, wondering what would be coming out of his mouth next.

An hour later, the weapons went back into the gear bags when Arlo indicated he had all he needed to proceed with his end after he had finished writing down the serial numbers, filming, and checking the status of each of them.

Alicia asked, "What do we do now?"

"We already did the paperwork on the incident and have let Armando know enough of what happened to cover our asses. Let's head home and deal with the rest when we hear back from Arlo." They put the gear in John's vehicle. Sunday hugged both Alicia and John before he drove away, saying, "Behave yourselves, youngins. You never know who is watching." He winked at both of them.

John told Alicia the whole story on his newest contact, Sweet Tooth, during their drive to his cabin. She remarked, "I'm getting the feeling you've adopted another sidekick, Batman. What are you going to save him from?"

John thought for a moment, then answered, "Himself, maybe."

"Hmmm . . . well maybe, just maybe, you're following that internal compass that so magically kicks in when you're on the trail of something." She glanced at him admiringly, knowing her man had something quite unique among others. After all, the man could actually see footprints on rocks, both hypothetically and physically. Footprints that always led somewhere.

"What'cha thinking, woman?" John uttered, looking over at her for a quick second. "And don't tell me 'nothing.' "

"So your new sidekick's brother, one Jimmy Begaye, is doing the business of the cartel here in this country? Or is that the business of the government?"

John looked at her again. "Baby, he could be serving three interests."

"Meaning?"

"My feeling is that the government of Mexico is totally in league with the biggest and richest cartel, the Sinaloas. Think of it this way, the cartels have more money than the Mexican government. Some of those high up in government are probably being propped up by that Mexican mafia who feed them money, and they also get their poorest of the poor out of their country and into this one."

"Makes sense. So, you believe that they are working hand-in-hand solving one another's problems? Getting their problems out of Mexico and into America. Smart . . . really smart," the dark-haired beauty said softly.

John went on with, "That's nowhere near the end of my theory."

"Oh, there's more?"

"What they are doing is preventing a revolution."

"A revolution? John, come on," she replied, doubt in her tone.

"No. Just think about it this way—they're exporting the people who could foment revolution. The poor, the unskilled, the uneducated—which makes for the unhappy. With the cartel money, they can pay off those in this government who could cause them problems. How do you think so many people are flooding into this country?"

"You been telling anyone else about this?" she asked.

"Not yet. Why?"

"Because this is the kind of stuff that can get you killed."

"There's still more to it," he said pensively. "The cartel, my sense leads me to believe, is being paid off by Islamic jihadists to help them get back and forth across the border and into position here in the country. All over the country."

She did not reply. Alicia's mind was working in high gear, and what was running through it gave her an ominous feeling of dread and anticipation. "You think that the Arabs are coming here through the cartel highways? You really think that, John? Are we talking poor Arab families, or are we talking something else?" Alicia had a strong sense of who her man was and that gave her confidence. But what he was talking about now was something that, uncharacteristically, frightened her deeply.

"I wish it were just poor Arabs instead of what is really coming in. You know as well as I do that we've been finding copies of the Koran strewn in many different parts of the desert between here and the border for the past year. What better indicator that Arabs are now coming across in larger numbers—only, not for the same reason the Mexicans are. My feeling is that they're part of a large jihad with big money. Money they are throwing around in Mexico and now, right here in Phoenix and in East LA. They're recruiting for their jihad soldiers in Syria, Iraq, Pakistan, Libya, and many other Islamic states and dropping them into the US under the protective wing of our government."

Alicia was becoming more uneasy by John's take on all this as the road rolled by under them. "Our government? This government? DC?" She shook her head, trying to shake the reality of John's words. "How high up do you think this goes?"

"To the White House," he answered without reservation.

"John, please tell me that you haven't told anyone about this? Where did you come up with it? I can't get my head around it. It's too crazy." Her concerns came rapidly as she worried for the safety of this man, whom she loved as no other.

"If you run this along a clear path of logic, all you gotta do is connect the dots. Over the past seven years, we have had a big increase in mosques in almost every state. Parts of Michigan are now under Sharia law. Sharia law, here in the United States, babe. We, our people, are a sovereign nation, like all our tribes around this country, and we have our courts, but we are still subjugated to the high law of the US. Right?"

"Right."

"How come those who only recently arrived here have been given the freedom to have their own court system not subject to the US government? Here's the answer, and it's not rocket science . . . who's been running this country for the past seven or eight years? Who was raised Muslim? Who apologizes for America to its enemies? Who bows to Muslim kings? Who has a history that no one can know?" John's passion was driven by the deep frustration of watching his country being so easily corrupted and manipulated and led to place from which there could be no return.

"This is mind numbing, but . . . " Alicia looked down as she spoke.

"But what?"

"What do we do? Who can we trust with this?" She was a bit freaked.

"Tell me . . . who would you go to with it?" John asked quietly.

Alicia started to blurt a reply but caught herself before the words came out of her mouth. Then she just shrugged and asked John the same question.

"The only ones I trust right now . . . and I emphasize the words, 'only ones' . . . are our brother and sister Shadow Wolves." John expressed his resolve intensely.

"I want you to be unbelievably cautious with what you say and especially who you say it to. You hear me, John? I heard what you just said about trusting only Shadow Wolves, but, but . . . " Alicia cautioned this man whom she loved above all others in this world without getting all her thoughts out. She was somewhat flabbergasted at that moment. "Listen to me, John . . . listen. You can't say anything about this until we absolutely know who we're talking to. Okay?"

The lawman looked over at his woman and smiled warmly. "Of course I hear you. I'm sitting right next to you. How could I not?"

"Come on, John. The one quirk I find most annoying about you is your selective hearing. Don't try to shit me any more than a minute on this. It's too big for it to not get you hurt if this is real." She looked at him imploringly. "You are my world, John Gode. My whole world, and I'm here with you because I feel that way. I want to catch the bad guys as much as you want to. But this looks like what we are dealing with is worse than anything we've come up against ever before." She paused for a moment, and as John started to speak, she interrupted him, raising her hand to signal "stop" as she went on. "I will give my life for you. I will protect you always and love you beyond always. Do you understand me?" Her eyes were filled with tears as she looked him up and down.

He nodded, deeply touched by her words. He knew what was between them, but she had never before voiced how deeply she cared for him. He felt that she was more than he deserved. Much more.

John tried to calm her fears by taking her mind off what was troubling her as he sat with his hand on her left thigh, high enough up her leg to get a bit of a shiver out of her.

She patted his hand and said lightly, "The dog in you always maintains. Doesn't it, my love?"

"It's the only thing that makes sense to me right now. You want me to sit up and bark?" He was trying to keep the conversation light and away from the ominous cloud that was following them that day. And that cloud was full, big, and mean.

"I don't give a damn about that, John. I give a damn about you staying in one piece and continuing to be my man. And I want my man alive." Alicia sensed the cloud as much as John did.

"Whatever it is that's landed in my lap is maybe a little bit more than I can handle with what we have at hand, but we can gather what we need from the Indian Nations across this country," John remarked confidently.

"What's making you say that, John?"

"My gut."

# 20: The Drive

THE EARLY MORNING sun coming through the bedroom window woke Alicia first. She nuzzled close into John's body as his arm draped across her in a strong embrace.

He came awake saying, "And where did you come from?" He rubbed his eyes and then sat up in bed. Looking around the room, he uttered sleepily, "I guess nobody got in here and killed us last night."

"What's this 'we' stuff?" she muttered sleepily.

He laughed softly in response. "Do you feel that you deserve a cup of coffee?"

"I do."

"And you expect me to make it, don't you?" John chided.

"Uh, yeah? You offered," she said, yawning.

"I simply asked the question." He laughed quietly as he threw his legs over the side of the bed. He put on his pajama pants and a tee shirt and looked back at the woman who gave him a reason to like getting up in the morning. He knew exactly how she liked her coffee.

John's phone rang. It was Sunday, his Shadow Wolf brother, on the other end saying, "I got something to tell you that you ain't gonna like."

"What did the federal asshole do now?" was John's immediate response to Sunday's comment.

"Oh . . . him . . . he is already climbing all over Armando about the shootout yesterday. He's demanding a full report," Sunday said flatly.

"What did Armando tell him?"

"Nothing," replied Sunday.

"What time is it?" John asked, thinking that it must be later than he thought.

"It's early."

"Yeah, I kinda figured that out." John knew better than to take the conversation any farther down that path. Instead he asked, "Tell me more about what's going on with the feds." He busied himself with the single-shot coffee machine on the kitchen counter as he spoke.

"This guy, Wilson, is uncomfortably mysterious," Sunday commented slowly.

"Mysterious? Never quite thought of him that way. More asshole-ish than mysterious." John liked his own description of Wilson far better than Sunday's.

"No . . . you're missing the point, Gode. I checked him with my people, and he came back empty," Sunday said dryly.

"Empty?"

"Empty, as in he doesn't exist. *Empty*—at least, not in the CSS," Sunday intoned stoically. "This is a strange happening. If he is government, he is buried so deep that even my folks can't find him." Sunday wanted to make certain what he was saying was clearly understood. "We have to be careful how far we go because they are always looking out for dogs who come sniffing, and they don't like sniffing, even a little bit."

"You're telling me that he's some kind of a super spook?" John was astonished by what his Shadow Wolf brother had just said. "Who told you this?"

"Another Wolf who works where this information can be had." Sunday seemed a bit annoyed at John's question, and John knew better than to ask about his intelligence sources. Sunday knew things before anybody else knew them and that was because of whom he knew and where they were.

"What's wrong?" Alicia got out of bed and approached John with concern caused by the expression on the big man's face.

"I'll be a son of a bitch. This is what these pricks are capable of." John slammed his left palm onto the dresser he was standing near, expressing his anger and frustration at allowing himself to be taken in by this guy so easily. He had been so intensely focused on his dislike that he had completely disregarded even questioning who he was . . . or wasn't.

"John Gode, listen to me," Sunday demanded in his sage-like manner. "You can't let this toothpaste out of the tube yet. If you do, I'm afraid that they will be able to track my information and that could get us one or two less brothers."

John whispered with his jaws clenched in anger, "How long, Sunday?"

"How long, what?"

"How long do we have to let this guy roam around here before we cap his ass?" John's intensity did not abate.

"Two, maybe three days." Sunday's tone did not change.

"We need to get the four desperados we bagged yesterday out of the county jail and into our holding facility before this guy grabs them. He's probably in bed with them and their bosses, and he needs to keep them quiet or dead." John's wheels were rolling. His innate ability to call the right shots almost instantly was what maintained the confidence of his peers.

He threw on his clothes and so did Alicia. Walking quickly out to his vehicle, he called Noche, told him what was happening, and asked that he call the rest of the Wolves who had been with them at the shootout in the desert and tell them to meet up at the jail.

John's phone rang again. "Hey, it's Jill, from forensics."

"Yeah, hi, Jill. You have something for me?"

"That piece of tooth you dropped off belonged to a woman. Looks like she has tribal blood somewhere in her family."

John thought for a few seconds. "Anything else?"

"Not yet. But I'd be careful if I were you."

"Careful? About what?"

"About whatever it is you are looking at these days. My feeling is this looks like a pro's work."

"What makes you say that?"

"This is a piece of a tooth. Looks to me like it was purposely pieced. That's what people do when they want to make the path of understanding more difficult to follow." She paused for a moment as John continued to listen intently. "I can't discuss this any more than what I'm saying, but I need to tell you when you are marked."

"What are you hearing, Jill?" John got intense.

"That you are causing some folks a lot of heartburn. Folks in high places. Stay awake, John." She ended the call.

"Who was that, John?"

"Forensics, on something I left with them."

"Problem?"

"Maybe."

Although she wanted to know more, Alicia dropped the subject, sensing her man was not ready to talk about it.

They were soon rolling rapidly down the dusty back road from John's cabin toward the paved road.

"What's the plan?" Alicia asked as she watched the road disappearing under their wheels.

"We pick up all four of the Carteleros and take them to the tribal holding station for a little chat."

"For how long? I don't have to say that's not where we can keep prisoners a long time," Alicia said.

"We can hold them for as long as we need to. This shit is going over the edge, and we may be the only ones who know it." John hit the gas pedal and sent the vehicle into a racing speed. They pulled up at the jail just as Noche and Chico arrived.

"I feel like we might have something big going on in this little piece of our desert, folks. And we might have to break some rules in order to smoke it out. You good with that?" He looked at Noche and Chico for opinions, and he saw heads nodding "okay." Noche explained that all he could rouse that quickly was Chico.

"Listen, people, we have got to take these four mutts to the rez and hold them there. And we have got to go now!" John directed the crew as they took custody of the foursome and left the jail grounds, with John and Alicia carrying two prisoners and Noche and Chico carrying the other two.

A half hour later, three SUVs rolled up to the jail, and Wilson led five "agents" into the facility to find that the objects of his quest were no longer there. He shouted at the officer in charge, screaming at him that they had no right to release "his" prisoners to anyone else. "Where were they taken? Under whose authority were they transferred?" He demanded answers.

The jail commander answered cautiously, wondering if he was now in a compromised position by releasing the four to the tribal police. He said slowly, "They were the arresting officers on record, and there is no hold from your agency on file, so it wasn't irregular in any way to release them."

"What kind of a dumb system do you have here, Lieutenant? I know there's a hold on them, because we laid it on them two hours ago." His face was beet-red with rage.

"I don't know where you lodged that hold, but it is not in our system. We check for holds before anyone gets released. Did not see anything on them." He started to stand his ground as he became bothered by Wilson's demeanor.

"Oh, piss off, Abner," Wilson said furiously as he turned and left the building, wheels on fire.

At that moment, John heard from his mentor, Sunday. "Got some more news, John Gode. It's not good."

"Okay, lay it on me."

"There is something going down around you. My Storytellers are saying that you are being targeted by some big honchos from back east," Sunday warned.

"Where back east?"

"DC . . . John Gode . . . DC . . . the land of the Redskins." That was Sunday's way of making a joke in a serious situation by bringing up the politically-correct silliness over the name of that team. "That makes some sense out of that highway ambush. These guys look like they don't play. And now it appears that they are looking to do something to you. How do you spell Deep State?"

"First word begins with a 'B.' I'll call you back as soon as I drop this load. Keep your phone on ring." John couldn't say anything more within earshot of the prisoners. They arrived at the reservation holding facility twenty minutes later and placed the Carteleros in separate interview rooms. John asked Noche and Chico to walk security on the facility. Noche was in the hall and Chico outside the building.

He ran Sunday's words through his head before he called him back. "We need to get a meeting of everyone in this pack. Can you put the word out?" John asked.

"When?" Sunday asked.

"Now . . . as soon as possible," John urged him.

"Okay, big guy. Keep your head down. I'll get moving and let you know as soon as I have it all set."

John assured his brother Wolf that he would be careful.

Sunday added, "Where do you want us to go for the meeting?"

"Get them here to the facility." John ended the call.

"What did he say?" Alicia looked at John, wanting to hear everything he knew.

"Someone's got a hit out on me."

"Why am I not surprised. Who put the hit out?" Alicia's voice rose, indicating her concern.

"Looks like it's coming from DC," John answered, trying to think this through.

"Wilson?"

"I think he's just the tip of the iceberg. This looks to be reaching way above his pay grade."

"Why would the big ones want your head, John? You're just a desert Injun. Why would those so far removed want you dead?" She looked at John questioningly.

"I think that's something we need to find out."

"And fast," Alicia blurted.

John's phone rang. It was Armando Grant. "What the hell did you do now, Gode? What! The! Fuck!" He was definitely not in a good mood.

"What'dya mean, boss? Is that piece of 'dung shit' agent running all over your ass?" John was becoming annoyed with his supervisor's lack of spine when dealing with Wilson.

"I mean, what's going on with the guys you brought in yesterday? Where are they at this moment, John?" Armando was furious and John could feel the pressure he was under from the feds coming through in his boss's voice.

"Can't tell you that over the phone," John said determinedly.

"Why not?" the task force commander demanded.

"National security considerations. We could be hacked."

"What does that mean?"

John responded sarcastically, "My country, 'tis of thee. Sweet land of liberty."

129

"What? You hitting the firewater, Gode?" Armando was beside himself.

"Look . . . I made a decision with *my* prisoners and *my* investigation to talk some more with these boys about the beauty of observing the 'spirit of cooperation' between our two countries," John explained. "I'm trying to develop more of a spirit of cooperation between our two countries. That's all, boss."

"Listen to me . . . and listen to me closely. You bring those prisoners back to the Maricopa County Jail . . . Now!"

"Boss, believe me, that is not something I can do at the moment, and I am not exaggerating about the national security part of this case."

John paused, waiting for Armando to say something, but he didn't. John continued, "These are my team's arrests. We grabbed them in the state of Arizona on reservation land, they have tribal charges for now, and the feds have jurisdiction too, but we have first dibs . . . for now." John again waited for a response, and hearing none, he ended with, "You've gotta trust me on this. I'll do ya proud, I promise."

"You're more 'n likely gonna get me done in, Tall Man. You need to bring those fuckers back to MCSO lockup. Do it now, John, before you take all of us down with this." Armando had never sounded more concerned. But he eventually gave in. "Tell me how long will this take?" he asked with exasperation flowing in his voice.

"As long as it takes," John replied dryly.

"You don't have that long. Get them back by dawn tomorrow. No ifs, ands, or—"

"Buts." John finished the sentence for him. "Okay, boss." That ended the call.

"Armando's pissed," John said dryly as he put the phone back in his pocket, wondering what the feds could actually do to his boss. He made a mental note to call the US marshal for the district of Arizona, Eric Cahn, whom he had come to know over the past few years. He was a marshal who had come up through the ranks and was highly respected by all Arizona law enforcement agencies. John innately felt he could be trusted with some, if not all, of what he had discovered.

"What's the plan?" Noche asked.

"We need to have a heart-to-heart chat with these guys. I'm in a chatty mood. How about you?" John smiled as he asked Noche to call in the "pack" for help with securing the facility. Noche started calling in the Wolves.

Two hours later after a briefing by John, the facility was surrounded by eight Shadow Wolves. They were so hidden in the terrain that they couldn't be seen from ten feet away.

John targeted the Cartelero member who he sensed was most likely to see things his way. "You wanna talk?" he asked as he sat down across the table from the prisoner, who was staring at him coldly but not saying anything. "You might be able to help yourself here."

"That would be a first for me," the handcuffed, brown-skinned man answered sarcastically.

"Where'd you learn English, *ese?*" John asked, surprised by his lack of a Latino accent.

"I get around." He laughed and moved in his chair, straightening his back.

"Around where?" John leaned into him.

He shrugged and said, "Anywhere the wind blows and I can find some 'blow' . . . Poof . . . I'm there."

"You do realize that you are looking at some heavy time here, amigo. Right?" John's eyes flashed as he spoke.

"Yeah . . . and?"

"And . . . come on . . . you're a young guy. You look straight. You look healthy. You're looking at my woman like you're horny." John didn't blink as he went on. "So why would you want to spend a good part of the rest of your life without that kind of 'trim,' man? Holed up with nothing but other guys who smell worse than you?"

The Cartelero grinned before he asked, "You know, I'm wondering now, is this guy a cop? Or is this guy a pimp? What are you saying here?"

"This guy"—John pointed at himself—"could be your ticket to ride." He paused, looking down, shaking his head. "I got you by the balls, and I'm holding all the cards. But you know what? I'm feeling generous today. I feel like making a deal."

"What kinda deal, Geronimo?" He was getting curious but still projected defiance.

"Why are you calling me by the name of my great ancestor?" John asked icily.

"You the red man. You the lawman. I don't know . . . I'm just wondering, I guess, why you're working for 'white eyes' for peanuts when you could be making real money with us."

"Wondering what? If I'm for sale?"

"Wondering if you 'speak with forked tongue' like Geronimo accused your handlers of doing with him."

"How would you know anything Geronimo might have said and who he might have said it to?" John was beginning to loose his cool with this guy.

"Hey, man, I saw that in a movie. Don't get pissed. You know how the white man screws all of us over most of the time. I thought that maybe you bought their bullshit and that's why you got a gun on your hip and you're wearing a badge. That's all."

He was twenty-nine years old. Wiry, about five-foot-eight, with a thin mustache. John thought that he reminded him of someone, but he couldn't recall who that someone was at that moment.

"You want me to help you or not?" John acted as if he were getting ready to walk.

"I'm listening. Talk to me," he blurted, seeming not to want to lose the opportunity to get himself out of this situation. He winked at John, making sure no one else saw him do it. John winked back and mouthed silently, "Allah Akbar."

"Here's the deal, you give me what I want, and I give you the rest of your life back. A chance to get your ass out of this," John stated.

"Why should I trust a cop? What guarantee do I have that you won't get what you want out of me—and I'm sure that's information—then you leave me hanging? You get what I mean?"

"Yeah, I get it. You're gonna have to trust me. I don't give a shit about nailing you or your dumb-ass friends. I want to know what you know about who is sending you here and what you are bringing." John's face went empty and hard to read. "If you give me something big and it turns out to be real, this world of shit could turn into something that smells a lot better for you."

"I don't know much about anything other than hot women. That's my obsession."

"Big word . . . obsession. Surprises me that you know that word. What other words do you know? Maybe words like the names of your bosses in Phoenix. The one who changed the plan for the second group coming in yesterday?"

"You want to get me killed, don't you? If I give up what I know, I'm a dead man walking, Geronimo," he jumped back at John. "You can stop this mess right now."

"How?"

"Letting me go."

John shrugged and said, "I could do that and might do that, but you know what you gotta do to justify my freeing you. Give me the names of the guys who changed the plan yesterday. That's all you gotta do. And if you don't, you either spend a long time behind bars or get your ass killed behind those bars because you know too much."

The lawman was emphatic, and his subject looked like he was thinking hard about what he was hearing, wondering if he was still being tested by the double-agent Indian cop. Or was he being played by one of the smartest cops he had ever come up against?

"Okay . . . so let's say we do a deal. Only saying, at this point. What exactly does that get me?"

"Depends on how honest your answers are."

"I got something good. Some of it is what I know for sure, and some of it is what I think is going on. Which do you want to hear first?" The prisoner was cocky.

John leaned into him. "The name of the Phoenix boss."

"Franky Headcase," he blurted with a laugh.

"He's been dead for three weeks," John said without losing a beat, immediately recognizing the sarcasm.

"He don't exist, and he never did."

"Like I said, you're gonna spend a lot of time behind bars. I'll make sure of that," John said quietly, never breaking his stare.

"Look . . . let's knock off the shit. Either you're not what you say you are, or maybe you got turned in Iraq or Afghanistan?" the prisoner suggested.

"I never had to be turned. I was already there. How about you?"

"I don't know what you're talking about. Turn? What does that mean? Turn what? To shit?" the gangster pontificated.

"What do I call you?" Alicia suddenly joined in the conversation.

"Why do you want to know that? You want me to call you someday, *chica*? You could make me give up something, and I would make you glad you worked me." He winked at her.

"Yeah, I'd like that," she said sarcastically. "Let's start that process with you telling me your name so I'll know it's you when you grace me with your call."

"I'm Gato . . . Most people call me Gato. I like it when I'm called Gato. You got anything to drink, *chica*?"

"Sure . . . beer or whiskey?"

"Both. Okay? One pleases my taste and the other my thirst."

John looked at him. "That's a very profound line. I've got to remember it."

Alicia left the room and returned with a bottle of water. She placed it before Gato.

"Let us proceed." John sat quietly waiting. His eyes pierced through the prisoner.

# 21: Deep State Jihadist Army Revealed

SUNDAY EXITED HIS vehicle and started walking through the parking lot toward the casino. He did not notice the window rolling down on the white van parked two rows over from where he had parked. In a second, a silent bullet found its mark in the enigmatic Shadow Wolf's head. He fell sideways between two parked cars, dead before he hit the ground.

No one noticed Sunday lying lifeless on the ground at first, and as the shooter rolled slowly out of the lot, the world seemed eerily changed by the passing of a spiritual man. Emptiness permeated the air, and John felt the passing in his heart instantly.

"Something just happened," he said to Alicia as they were sitting in the meeting room of the tribal police facility.

Alicia was concerned when she saw the expression on his face. It came from out of nowhere, and she did not know where to go with it. "What do you think happened?" was all she could muster.

"I don't know . . . " He looked up at the ceiling, then at her. "I don't know." He shook his head. They had taken a slight break to talk about where they had gotten to so far with Gato.

She said, "Let's go back in the room and finish the interview with that jerk."

John settled himself and went with her, but as he rounded a corner in the corridor, his eyes went to the rear door of the facility. Daylight shining through the glass prevented him from focusing on the figure standing a foot or so into the building. He instinctively drew his weapon, causing Alicia to do the same. "What's wrong?" she asked, looking in the direction of where John was aiming, but she saw no one there.

John released a breath and said reassuringly to Alicia, "It's good, babe. Sorry." He holstered his weapon.

"Sorry? Sorry about what? What just happened, John?" she asked with growing concern for him.

"I thought I saw someone standing by the door. Now I realize what it was that I saw . . . or think I saw," he explained. "Forget it for now. I'll explain later."

She was shaken by what she had just experienced but maintained her composure.

They entered the room and resumed their conversation with Gato. What they learned from that interview was sobering. Both were seasoned law enforcement officers, but what came out of the Cartelero's mouth made John know that they had been chasing rabbits when they should have been killing snakes. What got their attention were the claims of corruption and treasonous actions of some US Government agents he had seen while doing his business. The corruption, apparently, could be running as deep as claimed—as John had feared and Alicia had sensed. And it wasn't regarding the illegal aliens coming from Mexico and Central America.

"How do you come to know all this, Gato?" John asked, not convinced about his level of knowledge. "Why would the bosses let a guy at your level know all this?"

"How do you know what my level is?" His accent changed slightly, and John picked up on it.

"That's a good point. How do I know what your level is?" John pondered Gato's statement, then told him, "I'm going to get us all some food. Take a break and eat." He stood up, stretched, then continued, "I'm craving some pulled pork. Sound good to you?"

Gato instantly reacted, obviously repulsed by the suggestion. "I don't eat the swine," he spat out but then caught himself and added, "I mean, pork makes me sick. I mean really sick."

"Yeah. I bet it does." They walked him back to the cell block and put him in a cell by himself after tossing him one more time to make sure he had nothing secreted somewhere on him that could help him escape.

Noche came running down the hall toward John, his face distorted in anguish. He stuttered, "John . . . I . . . I don't believe this, John." He shook his head, looking down.

"Don't believe what? What is it?" John's stomach felt like it was dropping as he observed his close friend's anguish.

"Sunday's dead. They nailed him in the casino parking lot a couple of hours ago," Noche said with an air of defeat.

John's head began to spin. "What happened? How did this happen? Who the hell could have gotten to him?" Sunday, a big influence in John's life since he was a kid, was suddenly gone. "This cannot be," John's thoughts thundered through his head. He began shaking.

"Keep control, Big John. Keep control." Noche drew the inner strength to sadly urge in a whisper, knowing how bad this was for all of them but especially for John.

"You know," John said as he dropped his head, "I just thought I saw my grandfather in the hallway near the back door." He nodded his head in the direction of the door. "He probably came to tell me. He knew Sunday for many years. They were both incredible friends and trackers."

"Your dead grandfather, John?" Noche seemed puzzled.

"The only one I ever knew. The only one . . . " John's voice trailed off.

"What are we up against here?" Noche asked, his eyes focused on his Shadow Wolf brother, hoping he was not going over the edge.

"We need to talk. All of us." The tall lawman was now becoming angry as the reality of Sunday's assassination began to take hold of him.

"How far do we reach into the pack, John?"

"As far as we need to go. The only ones who can be trusted are the Wolves. It's got to be a blood trust . . . and nothing else."

"What are we gonna do with these hombres?" Noche asked, nodding his head toward the rooms the other Carteleros were being held.

"We have to protect the one I'm talking with. He could be a Pandora's box in all this."

"What do we do with him?"

"For now, we say that he escaped, and we're holding on to the rest as a way to get him back."

"Do you think Wilson's gonna buy that?" Noche asked.

"Right now, Wilson's not my priority." John was determined. "He's a spook, Noche. Probably a 'spook's spook.' Sunday told me that this guy Wilson doesn't even exist, and now Sunday's dead. Makes me really understand what we're up against. At least that is the beginning of what we might actually be looking at. We need to be very careful about who we can trust outside of the pack."

"What are we talking here, John?" Noche sensed that John knew more than he was saying. "Shouldn't we be reaching out for help outside our community?"

"If we can find that."

Noche looked puzzled. "You're telling me that there's no one we can trust?

"Bingo!"

"No one? Come on, Gode, you gotta be kidding me. There's gotta be—"

"No . . . no gotta be, here, with this."

"Maybe we should talk with Eric Cahn. He could help us." The words came slowly from Noche.

"Bring in the US marshal?" John asked, happily surprised by the suggestion.

"Why not? He's been stand-up on a lot of stuff that has to do with the rez. From what I hear, he's not chicken-shit about breaking balls, even when DC puts pressure on him not to do so," Noche said with the deep sadness still in his voice over Sunday.

"But why would he want to get involved? He's got his hands full with the DOJ assholes who are trying to run him into the ground for opening his mouth about the way ATF handled 'Fast and Furious.' And then how the AG protected them and the president from criminal charges. Shit, man, he'd have to be crazy to even consider working with us." John was hoping that what he was saying was actually wrong. Maybe the marshal would get involved, if it came to that. He could only hope.

Two hours later, a drone was circling over their heads as it viewed the facility. The drone pilot was miles away but might as well have been in the craft as he observed the facility and the area surrounding the building. The eight Shadow Wolves, who had been gathered earlier and placed in protective positions around the building thirty minutes before, were not detectable as they lay still in total blend with the landscape.

"See anything?" Wilson asked the drone pilot on his phone.

"Yeah, there are a few cars in the lot but no one moving around outside the building."

"Keep eyes on that area."

"For how long?" came the drone pilot's question.

"Until I tell you to leave. Got that?"

"Sho' thing, boss," the pilot responded in voice loaded with sarcasm.

One of the Shadow Wolves who was lying prone in the protective circle around the facility quickly picked up on the drone and observed it as it hung in the air. He did not want to give away his position by moving to make a call into John to alert him. He stayed frozen in position as the bird continued to hover.

Within a few minutes, Wilson called the drone pilot back, ordering him to fly his craft in surveillance over the area around John Gode's cabin to see if there was any activity there. "Got the coordinates?"

"Yes," he answered tersely. Wilson had rubbed him the wrong way with his tone and manner.

The drone controller flew the robot craft off, and the Wolf observing it immediately texted John to alert him, hoping there wasn't another one somewhere unseen overhead.

"Keep your eyes open, my brother," John replied as he thought it might be time to move to another location. His sense was that Wilson was figuring out that they were on the reservation and probably right where they were. He wondered how much firepower the opposition had and what they were willing to do with it.

139

Just then, he heard a faint whisper come to his ear. A familiar voice said, "Trust the old ways, Nan Tan. Trust only your brothers and sisters."

"What?" John spun around, startled by what he heard or thought he heard. He saw no one but noticed a white feather in midair, floating to the floor a few feet from where he was standing.

Alicia, who was standing near John, was alerted when she saw him spin around. "What is it?" She stared in the same direction John was looking. Her eyes followed him as he bent down to pick up the feather. "Where did that come from?" she asked, puzzled by its sudden appearance.

"Not sure it wasn't there all along," John said quietly.

"No, I would have seen it if it was. You know me and feathers," she said, referring to her penchant for collecting pretty feathers. Especially large ones like this. "Give it here," she requested as she extended her opened hand.

John shook his head no. "I think I need to hang on to this one." He smiled sadly at her, hoping she would understand his refusal. "It might have come from a special place."

"What?" she asked, somewhat confused by his words.

"We'll talk about it later."

Alicia changed the subject. "I think we need to go at them, John. I mean the SCC. They have some strange people among them. At least the group we met. Whatever they are up to could be hard to undo if we don't do something . . . like go right at them."

"That's exactly what we need to do, but we can't go at them from the direction they think we'll be coming."

"Let's finish the conversation with Gato. My gut tells me he's telling part of what he knows, and the part that he's not telling could spell big trouble for this country and especially for us because of where we're sitting in proximity to the border."

John and Alicia brought him back from the cell into the interview room, and the big man sat down again, across the table from the Cartelero. Alicia sat against the wall, studying Gato intently.

"I need you to tell me how many jihadis are coming across that border." John leaned into him with a new intensity.

"You gonna let me go if I tell you the wrong number? Because I know that you know that number way better than I do."

"How would I know that?" John asked.

He just laughed knowingly as a response.

"I'm gonna hurt you bad if you don't stop playing me. Real bad."

"You can't do that. You're an American cop. You guys don't do that." The gangster leaned back in his chair and smiled confidently.

"I have no limit to what I can do to you right now if I wanted to. You know, all it would take is me dropping to your amigos in there that you flipped on them, and your life won't be worth a nickle." John paused for a minute, giving Gato time to consider his situation. "So what is it gonna be?"

"They won't believe that shit, man. We been 'round each other too long for that to settle in. Come on," he said smugly. But there was something in his eyes that John picked up.

"They won't believe it until I take them back to the jail but hang on to you." John smiled slyly through his words.

The desperado tightened his lips. It seemed to John as if maybe the bad spot Gato was in was finally starting to dawn on him before he spoke. "Look . . . maybe there's a place I can take you to, where they meet with some of your *federales* in the desert, and they party all night, drinking, celebrating, and doing what they want to some hot *mamitas*. Then before the sun comes up, they take some poor bastards out into the brush and they fucking behead them, right in front of the ones they are keeping alive. It keeps the ones watching from running off at the mouth." He looked John square in the eye as he spoke.

"Where in the desert?" John asked quickly.

"Look . . . you need to stop playing this stupid game with me. That is, if you want to get something from me. I know who you are, but you have no idea who I am. Do you?" Gato challenged.

"Maybe I don't know who you are, but I know what you are," John responded.

"What's that, lawman?" Gato's persona suddenly changed completely from Mexican gangster to Other Than Mexican, his accent changing as he did.

"You're a member of the jihad," John said with absolute authority.

Gato paused, looking hard at John. "How'd you figure that out?"

"I offered you pork," John said stoically. "Wasn't too hard after that. When did you turn?"

"When I met Mohammed."

"The prophet?"

"No . . . the guy you know, named Mohammed, who told me about you and what you did for his family," Gato remarked.

"What's he talking about?" Alicia asked John, confused by what she was hearing.

"Long story, from way before I met you." Gato's statement caused John to quickly rethink what was going on.

"Mohammed said I should find you, or have you find me, and tell you that someone close to you is going to take you out. Mohammed says he owes you a debt that he can never repay, but he wants to try by saving your life."

"Explain to me, uh, Gato, is it? How did we get to this point? How did you come to be imbedded with this group that just happened to be taken down by my unit? And how did you come to be singled out by me as your interrogator?" John didn't blink as he spoke. "And what's your friggin' name?"

"It's Gato, and it's got to stay that way for all our sakes." He looked from John to Alicia and back to John. "I'm working within this group as an agent of a foreign power that'll go unnamed for now, and I report to Mohammed. It took a few years to get us in place. That man named A.B., who you thought was the leader of our gang . . . wasn't. He was taking directions, from someone who I was trying to identify, and somehow wound up where we did, when we did. But you took care of that. Didn't you," he needled.

"So the message is—that's why you were imbedded?" John was laser-focused on Gato's words.

"Bingo!"

"You could a' fooled me," the big lawman mumbled.

"No . . . I don't think I could have fooled you . . . at least not for long. That's why we feel you can be an important part of stopping what this group in DC has been doing to this country and part of the world."

"How did you know that I would be who you would be interacting with now? Why would I pick you out of the group?" John pressed him.

"Mohammed said that you are on a spiritual level that would guide you to me. He spoke about 'your gut,' and felt that the Spirit would deliver this outcome. Mohammed throws logic out the window on most decisions, but stays well within the range of Spirit. Seems to work. No?"

"Why the masquerade? Going to this level to get you here in this place, at this time?"

"It was a test . . . and the only way to do it without the presence of prying eyes and curious ears. The corruption of which we speak reaches clear up to the White House and back down to the 'street.' The money involved makes the cartel resources look like chump change. That makes for an environment of double-dealing, low to no trustworthiness, and even the most principled have been known to fall under the spell of oil money. Many a good man has been seduced by the amount of it when it's waved under their noses. Thus making it necessary to test even you."

"Still, what made you so certain that this would work . . . and that this was the only way to me and mine?" John pushed.

"I follow Mohammed. I work for him, and this was his way in."

"How is Mohammed these days?" John instantly changed the mood and the subject with one question. He was starting to believe this story and this man.

"He is blessed but deeply concerned. Now is the time for action, which only you can bring, John Gode. We don't have much time left." He looked at Alicia and said, "You've been vetted by two agencies, Alicia. Unofficially, of course, but thoroughly all the same."

Alicia smiled wryly as she asked, "What did they find?"

"They found that you are quite impressed with John Nan Tan Gode. Should I say more?" Gato was coy. Then he turned to John saying, "There are units of ISIS-trained soldiers, who are crossing the border almost daily. They are being helped by the cartels and by some in this government. The 'Fast and Furious' guns that you thought were going to the cartels were actually going through them to Islamic fighters. They are spread all over this country as part of the arsenals of the sleeper cells who are awaiting their activation on the 'the day of the great jihad in America.' Some of those guns wound up in Europe too, in the hands of the jihadi there. And they have already been used in some of the shootings."

"So how is it that you are laying all this mind-blowing insanity at the feet of a simple Native American tribal police officer?" John was absorbing what he had heard, but that brought more questions.

"You are a leader in the Shadow Wolf communities throughout this country. The Shadow Wolves are as blood-bound to their roots and principles as they are to the old ways. It is the only national group of warriors who can be trusted and who can get what must be done . . . done. There is no other way."

"The only ones, huh." John watched his eyes as they spoke. It was therein that the truth lay.

"Yeah, John Gode. The ones that can be trusted, because the Muslim Brotherhood is all over the White House and mingled into most enforcement and intelligence agencies."

Alicia, who had remained uncharacteristically quiet, finally said, "I am freakin' out here. What . . . what is going on? I mean, what the hell is happening? This is all surreal! I feel like I'm in a movie . . . or a bad nightmare."

"Bad nightmare is the best way to describe it," John opined somberly. "We're going to need the strength of something from 'the other side' to fight this battle."

"The other side of what?" Alicia asked.

"Of everything that is," John answered, taking a long, slow breath.

"I can remain with you from this point on, to help you. My communication with Mohammed is this way . . . he calls me. I do not call him. So, if you believe me and agree to allow me to help you, you will have to go with your gut about whether or not I'm real. Of course, that will be proved by my actions and not by my words."

John decided that he could work with this interesting double agent, but that decision was based on pure instinct alone. "What next?" he asked quietly.

"There's an event going on about forty miles south of where you grabbed us. I don't know if it's tonight or tomorrow night when they'll be 'partying' again," Gato said.

"How often do they do this?" John asked.

"Depends on what is happening in their universe—"

"How do they get the manpower to do their business?" John asked before Gato finished his sentence.

"That's easy. They tell the cartel *jefes* a few days before, and they get the crew moving. That's their pattern. That's how we've been able to pin their moves before they make them—because of their patterns. And we can tell if different bosses are calling the shots by the way they handle the scheduling and the activities," Gato recounted.

"Different bosses?" John came back instantly.

"Yeah . . . for instance, one time they'll bring two pickup trucks. One has the tents and the second has the music equipment, hookahs, and drinks. Then they have a third vehicle, a van, with the poor bastards whose heads are gonna be chopped off and the ones they bring to watch them doing that." He paused without breaking eye contact with John. "The ones they bring to watch will never betray them after watching what happens to those who screwed up." Gato paused for a moment to allow that to set in. "Then on another foray, they go into the desert and run mock raids with the sharpest precision. These guys are so well-trained and dedicated, it makes stopping them here in this country almost impossible. Chalk it all up to political correctness."

"So why even try, if that's where things are?" Alicia asked.

"I said 'almost' impossible. If all we had to depend on to do it was the US government, then we'd all be toast, and you'd wind up wearing a head scarf, if you still had a head, and all the men would be on prayer rugs five times a day."

John went "Iron Face," totally without expression because he was emptying his mind. He remembered his martial arts teacher's words: "Focus on one thing and that is all you will see. Focus on nothing and you will see everything. Go 'no mind,' John Gode. Go into the void." And he did exactly that, becoming a shadow, emitting no emotion or energy. The complete opposite of what he was, just seconds before. This was his way of gathering energy and clearing his mind.

Gato thought for a moment that John had disappeared. He was startled when the big lawman suddenly returned, silent and foreboding. He stared like a hawk just before taking out a snake.

"You need to change." John broke his silence, still without emotion, as he spoke to Gato.

"Change?"

John responded, "Yes. I will report officially that you broke out of our custody and fled into the desert. That will make it plausible that you might not survive your trek. That will be the end of Gato the cartel gangster and the beginning of Gato, the undercover DEA agent. I need you to be able to roll with us on this, and the only way I can do that is to re-identify you as a DEA undercover agent."

John continued, "Now we need to get a read on whether or not there are some people in the federal law enforcement agencies that we can trust. Cartel money is flowing through every level of our government, but I can't get my arms around just how deep it is in the ranks of law enforcement. The politicos are always up for sale, that's the way it is with those in power. But those in our ranks? I'm having trouble believing they have reached many of them. Wilson excepted," he blurted.

"But you agree that the cartels own a big part of the body politic in the good ol' US of A?" Gato asked.

"Not just this country . . . they also own a good part of the Mexican government." The big man emphasized his point. "You know that better than me, Gato. And with corruption so rampant, Mexico is a fat and safe environment for Islamic terrorists to operate freely." John's frustration was floundering on defeatism. "We are being invaded by an enemy that has no standing army, navy, or air force. Just thousands of highly trained ISIS fighters, with their training camps just miles from our border and some of the people they own in the Mexican and American governments. That's all it takes, and they about grab us by the balls."

Gato said, "Yeah, they have a protective cover that reaches all the way through Mexico, across the border, and up into the White House. With the question remaining just how deep in numbers they actually are."

John thought for a moment and said, "The one thing that jumps out at me is how Muslims and Catholics can mix together. It's not something that seems like it would go down too easily."

"It all comes down to money. The jihadists have plenty of it, and the Catholics who are working with them want plenty of it. As long as that's a factor, the whole thing works. The people who are being victimized there are the peons who have to work for these tyrants. But that is where the chink could develop in their armor."

"Who's the big player on the Catholic side of the street?" Alicia asked.

"Antonio Septuan, who operates out of the City of Angels. He is one ruthless and heartless son of a bitch."

"What have you got on him?"

"He is a reptile . . . suspected of wiping out large groups of people just to get his point across," Gato said.

"Where are the murders being committed? Mexico?" John asked quietly.

"Mostly, but there are few in LA. Really brutal stuff. This guy has been tied to the wave of beheadings going on near the border in Mexico too."

"What's the motive for the beheadings?" Alicia asked.

"Trying to get a message across," Gato responded.

"To who?" John questioned.

"To anyone who gets in his way."

"So to summarize, this Septuan is a major player for the cartel, and they're doing business with the OTMs?" the big lawman asked.

"The one but *not* the only," Gato stated knowingly.

"So he's the lynchpin between the OTMs and the cartels? Does that apply to the entire southern border?" John asked.

"He's got California and Arizona. In New Mexico and Texas there's another big boss man named Peppy Costa. He's even worse than Septuan. Probably doesn't even go to confession. They both bow down to someone who goes by the name of Mandrell."

"So that means Septuan is a Catholic too?" John chided. "Is Mandrell a Muslim, by any chance?"

"Have no idea, but can fully attest to the fact that what they are doing here is what they have been doing overseas. What's happening in Europe? They're flooding the place. They're in every country. Hell, they're even a force in Australia. Now ask yourself this question—how did this happen? Answer . . . the power of oil money for the leaders and the power of guilt for the fools who are led."

"And this is *exactly* what we have here. *Exactly!*" John said emphatically.

"I hope you're wrong, John . . . I can't tell you how much I hope you're wrong on this," Alicia said quietly as she stared off into nowhere.

"I'm not wrong. Look at what we have in DC. Since these people have been there, Islamic terrorism is showing up in places in the last five years that it wouldn't have even been thought of before," John said resignedly. "I've been picking up on this but telling myself it couldn't really be happening. Not here. But you know what? I was wrong, and now I'm looking around at a lot of people who are not catching on to this, and that is not good. We've been chasing the lesser dragons."

"Lesser dragons, John?"

"Yeah, lesser dragons. We've been chasing the drugs, distracted by them when we should have been chasing the bigger dragons. Picking up on the guns coming through here."

"The 'bigger dragons'? You mean OTMs?" Alicia was feeling inadequate as this new mindset took over. She asked herself why she hadn't caught on to it, at least a bit sooner.

"Yeah . . . this is what we need to be looking at, maybe with more focus than we have been giving the drugs and people smuggling." John was suddenly feeling a heavy weight smothering him as the reality of what had inordinately slipped by him began to set in.

"What do we do, John?"

"What do we do?" John thought for a moment about Alicia's question and then said, "As a good start, let's get everyone together in the briefing room. Tell the group outside to leave one of them there so we have eyes and the rest to come in." Alicia told Noche what John said, and he immediately went to one of the Wolves who was circling the facility. He passed the word and within five minutes they were all in the big room.

John looked around the group and asked Chico to sit in the doorway so he could observe the hallway to where the prisoners were being held. They were all handcuffed behind their backs, and their feet were shackled, so one pair of eyes on them would be adequate.

The big lawman said, "Look . . . I picked up some intel from my guy in there." He nodded toward the room Gato was in. "It turns out that he is a deep undercover." He looked from face to face to see if anyone had a question. No one did, so he continued, "I need you all to trust me on this guy being one of us. He has been gathering intelligence that started out with drug cartels that brought him to government corruption that reaches pretty high up. A lot happened along the way that brought him to us."

"You sure about that, John Gode?" Chico asked, expressing concern that seemed to be shared with others in the room.

John seized the moment. "Brothers and sisters, like I said, you have to trust me on this. No more. No less."

A murmur went through the room as the pack came together behind their leader.

Noche spoke up. "We trust you, Big John. If you say this guy is real . . . this guy is real." He looked around the room for agreement, which he got, then went on. "What he's telling you ain't nothing new to us. Come on . . . we've been watching what's coming out of Mexico for years, and that could not be happening without their, and our, top government bosses saying it was okay."

"So we got some bad, bad people around what's going on . . . in the desert, not many miles from where we are standing. Shit like I never thought happened around here, ever before." Alicia had deep concern dominating her voice.

"Like I said, corruption from the top down . . . Gotta be," Noche added.

"Yeah, but we're not just talking Mexico here. We're talking the government of these United States of America," John said once again.

A lanky, young Shadow Wolf nicknamed "Perky," who had been part of the outside protective circle, said, "I thought you were gonna tell us something we didn't know." He laughed and was joined in the laughter by the rest of the group.

"I'm not trying to be funny. This is some heavy shit because we don't know who or where the bad guys are. If someone as 'awake' as Sunday could be taken out like he was, there is no telling in which direction the next round might be coming from and under what circumstance."

The room fell silent as the understanding seemed to deepen of how much Sunday's death would impact every one of them from that day on.

"I think we need to do a prayer for our fallen brother." The group remained silent with eyes closed, and John chanted.

# 22: Grandfather's Ghost

WILSON ORDERED A team of four to the cabin of Amma Gode, aging mother of the Native American lawman. "I want you to scoop her up and bring her out to the cave."

"Which one?" Kazi Kamir, the lead man on his team, asked.

"How many caves do you know about, Kazi? Within the area."

"Not sure, so I'll go with the one I believe you're talking about." Kazi felt foolish asking which cave to take her to. He was a cold-hearted killer who didn't like looking dumb, and that's how Wilson had a habit of making him feel. "What do we do if there's resistance?"

"We are talking about a woman in her sixties," Wilson shot back sarcastically. "You afraid she's gonna kick your ass?" He laughed sarcastically as he smirked.

"No, sir, but I am aware of who her son is. That's why I asked." He was well aware of John Gode, and although he thought he would not have trouble taking him, he had a lingering feeling of not wanting to have to try.

"We have eyes on him, and he is not anywhere near her cabin at this time. If we have missed anyone else who might be there, kill them. But bring her to the cave alive."

"Roger that, Your Excellency."

Wilson barked, "I want you to take her to that fuckin' cave. Keep her there until I tell you otherwise."

"When are you gonna be there?" Kazi asked.

"Not sure yet."

"Okay. I'll get my part done." He took a crack team of three with him.

151

Kazi Kamir was nobody's fool. He had been trained in Iran by the Quds and had no qualms about killing anyone who got in his way, especially if they were a Jew or an American. He had a great disdain and distrust for this man, Agent Douglas Wilson, but had no choice but to work with him for what he thought was the greater good, knowing that the mission lying ahead was wrought with a good deal of potential for catastrophe for himself *and* for his handlers in Iran. However, the opportunity here to be part of something so great was too enticing not to risk everything trying to make this work. For if it did, it could rattle America to its core for many years, even more than the World Trade Center coming down.

He gathered his team and briefed them thoroughly on taking Amma Gode. The plan was to set out in two vehicles to the cabin of John Gode's mother. They had sophisticated weaponry, provided to them by the Quds and Wilson. Kazi warned them about the uncanny abilities of John Gode and his Shadow Wolf brothers and sisters. "I've been told that these people can move like actual shadows, hit you from all directions, and then just disappear like they were never there."

"Sounds like bullshit to me," was the first comment from one of the group. "I've seen and heard stuff like this many times. The thing I enjoy most about it is the look in the eyes of these fools right before I take their heads off with one of these." With an insidious smile on his lips, he lifted the small sword from the scabbard on his belt. His name was Kumar. His age was thirty-one. He was brown-skinned, with a heavy beard and a body that reflected someone who was in excellent shape. The same could be said for his two other cohorts.

A half hour later, they rolled slowly up to the cabin of Amma Gode, on alert and at the ready for just about anything. The cabin was quiet with no sign of activity as the sun sent the last glimmers of light across the desert sky before fully setting. Disembarking from their vehicles, Kazi sent two to the back while he and Kumar went to the front. Kumar tried to walk lightly on the weathered wooden planks of the porch before he knocked loudly on the door. There was no response. He knocked again and they heard a woman's voice announce, "I'm coming, I'm coming. Give me just a minute." They readied their weapons in anticipation of someone other than Amma answering the door.

A few seconds later, they heard, "Can I help you?" Amma Gode sleepily stood slightly behind a half-opened door. The half-smile on her face disappeared instantly as she took in the sight of weapons pointed at her. "Oh no!" she yelled as she tried to slam the door. But it was futile, as they rushed through, knocking her down. Kumar stayed with her as Kazi searched the premises. Finding no one, they put her in the back seat of Kazi's vehicle, with Kumar sitting next to her.

---

At that moment, John was struck with a strange feeling. He turned to Alicia. "I think something bad, something very bad, is happening."

"Again? What's making you say that?" Alicia was unsettled by what she heard. She caught the trajectory of John's eyes as he stared into the shadows of an empty building not forty feet away. After leaving Gato in one of the offices with Noche, Alicia accompanied John when he went outside the holding facility to get some "night spirit" and clear his mind. They walked along a path toward several empty buildings a thousand feet or so from the facility.

"Do you see that?" he whispered as he nodded his head toward one of the buildings.

"Do I see what?" she asked, somewhat puzzled.

"Him." John pointed at an area near the doorway of the building.

"I think I see something but can't tell what it is. Looks like someone, or something, standing in a mist," she said, staring intently, hoping to determine what was there.

"It's him. Can't you see him? He's right there." John pointed at the doorway of the empty building.

"Him? Who?" Alicia asked in a whisper as she drew her weapon and pointed it in the direction of where John was looking.

"My grandfather. He's standing right there." John started walking slowly toward the doorway. "Stay put," he whispered. As he got closer, the image of his grandfather faded away. Exasperated, he turned toward Alicia, saying loudly, "I don't like this. He only shows up when something is wrong."

"Does he speak to you?" Alicia asked.

"He doesn't have to. It's the look in his eyes and the energy change he brings when he comes that carries a message."

153

Alicia was concerned that the stress of losing his spiritual mentor, Sunday, might be having a powerfully negative effect on John. He seemed a bit dazed since hearing the news about his trusted friend. It had thrown him off-center, and she had the frightening thought that this could somehow be his undoing. She would stay at his side every second going forward, whether he wanted that or not.

"I have to go and find a bush. Wait for me there. Be right back." He moved to a spot behind the building for privacy, but what he got was much more than that. He came face to face with his dead grandfather, putting him in a semi-stupor. Recovering quickly, he stammered, "Grandfather. Is this really you?"

The misty apparition nodded in the affirmative. His words came as if over a great distance, and yet he was no more than eight feet from his grandson as he spoke.

"Listen closely, John Gode, because this is the only time I'm going to be able to talk with you. The one and only time I'm going to hold your face and lift your face up and tell you something. You must look forward and not backward. If the Great Spirit wanted you to live in the past, He would have given you eyes in the back of your head. Do not allow your heart to be painted with the brush of false division. Find your way in all the dimensions. You are a spirit of the universe. You are a part of everyone. When you understand this, you can walk this earth like I walked it once. I have told you this since you were a baby—you can always judge a man by the way he walks. By the tracks he leaves. Read those tracks, my grandson."

The vision began to fade, and John asked quickly, "What do you mean, I'm looking backwards? Grandfather. What does that mean?" But no answer came as John found himself speaking to the empty air. He was stunned by his grandfather's spirit words.

"Who were you talking with, John?" Alicia asked.

"Probably myself." John shrugged.

"Must have been. I heard only your voice and figured you were on the phone with someone."

"Maybe I was," John said as he stared with empty eyes at the ground and then at the sky, still trying to make sense of what he had just experienced.

John and Alicia drove to the Maricopa County Jail with three of the four prisoners shackled in the back seat. "Where's Gato?" two of them asked a split second apart.

"He'll be along after he gets out of the hospital," John said quietly.

"Why's he in the hospital?" The prisoner sitting in the center had an air of suspicion as he asked.

"He thought he could take me. He found out he was wrong," John answered.

"He still alive?" the desperado asked.

"He is, but . . . I think he wishes he weren't." John smiled as he answered, looking at him in the rearview mirror. The Cartelero stared at the back of John's head, wondering if he was being told the truth. He made a face without realizing that he was doing so. John picked up on it as he watched him in the rearview mirror again.

They pulled up in front of the jail a short time later. Before they got out of the car, John turned in his seat behind the wheel and asked them, "How come you all speak English when you're questioned?"

The one in the middle seat, whose nickname was "Loco," answered sarcastically, "I think it's because you ask questions in English." He smiled at the big lawman.

"Maybe another reason is you all are from El Norte. I'd say, judging from your accents, you hail from East LA." John paused, took a slow breath, and continued. "You know, I'm gonna tell you one more time before we go in there—you can help yourselves in a big way if you want to cooperate with me."

"Yeah, and how long do you think we'd be alive after we do that, Geronimo?" came the reply from Loco.

"Longer than you will in jail. Do you really think your patrons are gonna let you live, knowing what you know?" John said, looking for an opening.

"How do you know what we know?" Loco asked with great interest.

"I'm psychic," John answered with a slight smile. "Yeah, I really am." He looked at Alicia. "Go ahead, tell them." He pointed at all three as he spoke.

"He sure is all that. Why, just this morning he told me where I graduated from high school," she spoke admiringly. "Out of the clear blue, he comes out with that. And I thought, damn, how does he do that? I mean, we're talking about something else, and he stops right in the middle of the conversation and comes out with that."

Acting like he didn't hear a word Alicia said, Loco asked John cautiously, "If we did know something and we did what you are saying we should do, how do we not get . . . " He made a motion toward the man sitting to his left with his head, like it was being separated from his body.

"We can make you all disappear. Like you never existed. It's a big world out there, and we can find you a place where no one can find you, and you'll be living like kings. People will bow down to you," John Gode said, sounding like a philosopher poet, trying to coax an outcome.

The lightness of the moment disappeared abruptly as a cloud came over Loco's face. "You have no idea what you're up against, *ese*," the desperado said somberly as he shook his head and looked down. "What you have coming at you is like nothing you ever saw before. Prepare to shit your pants." He chuckled, catching himself before he continued with the unlikely thought of maybe cooperating with the lawman.

John said, "Last time." He nodded toward the jailhouse. "Once you're in there, I can't help you . . . even though I may want to try."

Nothing more was said, and they were removed from the car and walked into the jail. Alicia did the paperwork necessary to return them as John sought out Billie Rainwater, a brother Shadow Wolf. He showed up two minutes after he was paged on the jail intercom system.

John looked Billie square in the eye. "The time may come, and come very soon, when I will have to ask for all my Shadow Wolf brothers and sisters to stand with me against some evil people. It will be a life and death matter if it comes to pass. How do my words hit you?"

Billie responded, "I'm here because you helped me get here. I remember the time when we got jumped by the wise-asses at that basketball finals game. There were seven of them and two of us when you stood with me. Because of you, we walked away straight up. They didn't. I don't know too many of us who could make that happen." He patted John on the arm, smiled, and went on. "I'll be there when you need me to be there, my brother."

After leaving the building, Alicia sat behind the wheel as John got in on the passenger side, saying, "Let's move, babe."

She sped away, looking in the rearview for any sign of a tail. She didn't see any vehicles, nor did she see the drone that was directly overhead.

———————

Miles away, Wilson was on the phone with the drone pilot, getting a scouting report from him. "What you got?" he asked.

"I got him in the cross hairs with my finger on the trigger."

"You're telling me that you have eyes on John Gode?"

The drone pilot responded with, "Looking down on them right now. Looks like he has his girlfriend with him. Two for the price of one, boss. Is it a go?"

"You don't do anything until I say otherwise. Do you understand me? Not one hair on that prick's head harmed until the word is given from me! Do you understand me?" He paused for a moment and then asked in bit more cordial voice, "Are there any other vehicles with him?"

"Negative."

"Then continue to follow them. And only that . . . *comprendo*?" That call ended and Wilson was running things through his mind as his phone rang again.

"Douglas Wilson?"

"Could be. Who is this?"

"I'm calling for Mandrell, and that's all you need to know. I have a message for you." The voice had an eerie quality and sounded almost hollow.

"What's that?" Wilson's words had an uncharacteristic tone . . . that of uncertainty.

"You've already been told in great detail, Douglas. Do I need to tell our benefactors that you don't remember the terms? Is that what you want me to do?"

"No. That's not necessary," Wilson replied quickly.

"I was hoping you would say that."

"When do we begin?" Wilson asked slowly.

"When the time is right. Have you lined up your route to the camp?"

"The camp or the cave?" Wilson was confused.

"Clean up your issue with Gode first. I believe that will take place soon. Am I right?"

"Yeah," Wilson responded attentively.

"Tighten that situation up and make certain that there is no trail back to the 'event.' Nine-one-one mode. No trail left unburned. Okay?"

"Got that."

"Douglas, if you don't retrieve the device that was passed on to the dead Shadow Wolf, your world will come apart faster than the speed of thought. Mandrell is not at all happy about that slipping through your hands. You do know why, don't you?"

Wilson felt a pressure he did not relish, and he made a mental note to take care of getting back on Mandrell's good side as soon as things settled down. Mandrell was the only part of the whole equation that he could not put a label on. He knew this person was highly placed in the government bureaucracy, but that was all he knew about him, and that did not sit well with Douglas Wilson, agent extraordinaire. Did not sit well indeed.

# 23: Dead Reporter Talks

JOHN AND ALICIA pulled up in front of the tribal reservation holding facility and entered the building quickly. Gathered there were twenty Shadow Wolves. There were seventeen men and three women in all. "How many others can we expect?" John asked as he looked around the group, greeting them with a slight smile.

Noche volunteered, "We have fourteen more on the move."

"Where are they?" Alicia asked.

"Some are driving down from the White Mountains and the others from south of Flagstaff. They're all about an hour to an hour and a half out, last time I checked a few minutes ago."

"Call 'em, and tell them to meet up at your place, Noche, and to stay off the radios. They should not come here." John thought quickly. "We definitely have eyes on us. Maybe more than just a drone or two."

John went to an interview room, alone, to review the flash drive he had found in the reporter's hotel room again. What he saw and heard caused him to revisit his initial evaluation of who and what he was going up against. What had initially begun as a business-as-usual series of arrests in the desert south of Phoenix had turned into the series of events that would have international implications. He invited Gato into the room with Alicia and Noche. Then he went through the flash drive with them. The voice they all heard on it belonged to the woman investigative reporter who gave a rapid account of people coming to the Arizona desert to conduct jihad in the Phoenix area, Las Vegas, Minneapolis, DC, and New York. That part of it blazed in his mind, and her statement that there were many already here preparing for a big attack filled him with dread. He caught a few things he had missed on

159

the first go-round. She identified two people whom she had uncovered as part of the plan. One was Douglas Wilson and the second was a man she didn't name, an attorney high up in the Justice Department who was special counsel to the president. She spoke of collusion with two Mexican cartels and high-ranking Mexican officials. The cartels were doing business with the jihadists that involved gun running and drug smuggling. They were being well paid with Middle Eastern oil money. She named the American and Mexican agents who controlled the distribution of weapons throughout the cartels on both sides of the border. She talked about the corruption that went into the judicial system and thought she could produce the names of some powerful elected officials who were heavily involved in the cocaine business and the resulting vulnerable situation they had placed themselves in to be blackmailed. And blackmailed, she believed, they were, and that enabled the cartels and jihadists to work their way into a place far more dangerous to this country than anything since the Civil War. Before the end of her narrative, she told of continuing her investigation into local law enforcement, her planned meeting with John Gode over the next day or so, and that she was told he could be trusted. And she was praying to God that it was true.

The room was silent for a few moments as Gato, Alicia, and Noche gathered themselves. John was already there and planning the next move as they digested the overwhelming information they had just heard.

Gato broke the silence with, "This is not new to me. We've been in on this from the grunt level of the cartel, but there's far more she claims going on than we uncovered. If what she's gathered is true, then we really have a huge problem with how deep the corruption has settled in throughout the government. At this point in time we can't trust anyone."

Noche and Alicia voiced their opinions on what they had learned. They seemed stunned by the enormity of what could be hanging over the country and was about to land like a crazed hawk on its unsuspecting prey.

Reality sometimes has a funny way of settling into a person's mind, with different results for each person involved. Noche's growing reaction was one of dismay and hoping that John had the ability to do what he did best—take down the bad guys. Subdue the threat. Alicia's thoughts went to believing that where they were heading was a place of existential proportions. She understood that what the Islamic extremists were about was destroying the will of anyone who opposed their ideological march to a world governed by a caliphate. She began to mentally prepare for what could turn out to be Armageddon. John was already prepared.

"What do we do now?" Alicia asked solemnly.

"How do we even begin to fight this?" Noche was unsettled due to what he had just learned and the loss of a dear friend and brother, most likely killed by the very people who were about to try to change his way of life.

John's phone buzzed, and he saw that it was Sweet Tooth calling. He answered. "Talk to me."

"John Gode, I just got a call from my brother Jimmy, all freaked out and everything. He wanted me to call you to give you a heads up that some Arab guys are going to blow up the casino on our rez, and that's where our mom works." He was frantic.

"Did he say when this is supposed to happen?"

"Soon. He said it's gonna happen soon. Can't you do somethin'? I mean, it's my mother, man."

"I need more information on it. Good, tight information. And I'm going to need you and Jimmy to work with me closely. Can you make that happen?" John spoke quickly, understanding immediately what was happening, but Sweet Tooth was silent. John pushed him. "Can you do that? You need to tell me and not try doing something else . . . Tooth?"

"Yeah, I'll do whatever it takes. That goes without saying. I believe you can save my mother, but I'm really worried that you can't help Jimmy."

"I can save his ass but I need him working this from the inside for my unit. And you have to keep your mouth shut. You can't talk about this to anyone." John drew a heavy breath. "I know this is nothing but terrible for you, but if you work with me, I'll keep your brother and your mother alive."

"Sure, I'll do everything I can to help stop this. It goes without saying Jimmy will too." Sweet Tooth sounded resolved and somewhat relieved.

John assured him, "The only people who will know about what you told me are people I would trust with my life and who I will need to help me stop it from happening."

Sweet Tooth said, "Jimmy made me promise that I wouldn't tell my mom. But I think I have to, so she doesn't wind up working her job there when this shit happens." His panic was growing with his fear bouncing between his mom and brother.

"I need you to talk with Jimmy and ask if he knows when the next big party is set for the desert. I need to know where it is going to happen. How many will be there, the amount of weapons, and what sort of weapons. If you can get him to get me that information, I promise you that I can keep your mom safe and prevent them from taking out the casino and maybe half the reservation. Can you do what I ask, Sweet Tooth? I need to know this so I can do what needs to be done."

"I gotta be careful that I don't blow his cover by calling him. The people he works for watch him and a lot of the guys like him, like, real close. They are suspicious people. They're like, all paranoid. That's what Jimmy says, anyway."

"Can you do this?" John pressed him again.

"Yeah, I guess. Let me come up with a good reason for my calling him, then I'll do it. His bosses don't want their people to get a lot of phone calls on anything other than business."

"Stay in close contact with me, Tooth. Okay? You understand?" John was intense.

"I got no reason not to. You're the only person I know I could go to with this. I got no one else." He sounded like someone many years older than his age, with stress making his voice raspy.

"And, listen to me . . . do not . . . say anything about this to anyone . . . not even your mother."

"You really mean that? I can't tell her? Come on, man."

"If you want her, you, and Jimmy to still be breathing when this is over . . . that's exactly what you won't do."

"Shit," he said dejectedly. "Okay, I hear ya. This is hard."

"I know it is, Tooth, but it's gotta be this way. Trust me," John cautioned him.

# 24: Deep State Jihadists Attack

EARLIER THAT DAY in a Sinaloa compound in the Mexican desert, some fifty miles south of Nogales, Arizona, Jimmy Begaye was locked in conversation with a Middle Eastern man named Ali Maloof regarding a plan he had recently been made aware of as a test of his loyalty. "I am having a problem with this, and I know you would have one too. Hey, man, this is my mother I'm talking about, and I don't know how else to say this."

"What is it that you want to say? Why are we talking about this?" Maloof's eyes flared as he stared at the uncomfortable young man. "You knew when you signed on that you would be giving up a lot. Why do you think we pay so well? And now, maybe to you, the outside chance that your mother might get hurt is a chance you're apparently not willing to take?" He studied the young man, watching his reaction.

Jimmy's emotions were coming through strong as he replied cautiously, "I didn't expect this. I don't know how you could think this would be something that any of us would not be worried about. I know that you and me come from different places, but that doesn't mean that we don't think alike on most things . . . does it?" Jimmy was stammering as he spoke. He did not make eye contact with Ali Maloof. His mind was racing, stirred by the terrifying thought that his mother could be killed as a result of actions that he had a hand in.

Ali Maloof was the most brutal of the brutal, dedicated totally to bringing down and destroying the Great Satan, the United States of America. He repeatedly tested anyone near him whom he was forced to use in his "great quest." He had no qualms about taking any action necessary to reach his goals. He walked in blood, unimpeded by the chaos and misery he felt were necessary tools in order to bring down any and all he considered enemies of his way of life, in the service of his god. He drew his weapon and pointed it at Jimmy's head. "I did not think that you would have these concerns, simple as they are, and so very troubling. I do not have time for this and I will ask you a question, which if you don't answer properly, I will kill you."

Jimmy put his hands in front of his face pleading for his life. He was terrified.

Maloof smiled cunningly, looking through eyes that wore the expression like those of a circling shark. "My question to you is this: are you a Christian?"

Jimmy's heart sank into his stomach as he responded with, "No. I haven't been that for a long time."

"Will you renounce this culture and swear your love and service to Allah? Will you prove that love in service to him? Get down on your knees and kneel in surrender to his will. Now, touch your forehead to the ground and praise him. Otherwise, you can tell him in person in just a few seconds," the jihadist said, looking down on the groveling young man.

Without delay, Jimmy obeyed. He knew that what he was doing was violating everything he was raised to believe in, but he had to buy time. The time to make certain his mother and kid brother would be safe. He prayed as he faced east, a prayer he never thought he would say, led by Maloof. His only thought at that moment was for his survival, before asking for forgiveness from the God he had known since he was a child.

The only reason Ali Maloof did not kill him was he needed him. However, that need would be short-lived. When all was said and done, he could at least claim this young man as another convert to Islam. He knew that many of those who were on his payroll were also doomed because they were nothing more than infidels; at least, they were in his mind. The only infidel he did not have a problem working with was the one who saw the world as he did . . . Douglas Wilson. The American agent who believed in, figuratively and literally, dismembering anyone who got in his way. Maloof admired such men, identifying with their, what he called, "strength and power" over the weak. Wilson was now his agent, he had been bought and paid for, ironically by the very money originally sent from America to the Middle East to satisfy its own insatiable thirst for oil. "How just," he thought, "that they are paying us to rid the world of them."

Ali Maloof had a small army at his command. An army that would do anything for the right price. An army that could deliver total devastation to any place his leaders would determine appropriate. It was his greatest achievement in life to have gotten this far, so close to the heart of the Great Satan and now standing poised, with a scepter at the ready, to behead this "supreme evil." Now that they were spread throughout the United States, they could begin the great process of taking it down with so few resources that it brought the "true power" of Allah to the eyes of all men . . . even those that were shut.

As Jimmy returned to his feet, he bowed to Ali Maloof and promised he was ready to do whatever it took "for the will of Allah." Whatever it took. Ali looked at him with fierce intensity. He then dismissed Jimmy with a wave of his hand, without uttering another word. As the young man walked away, Maloof studied his pace and direction before turning back to the task at hand.

A few minutes later, Jimmy's phone rang and Sweet Tooth spoke hurriedly about his conversation with John Gode, without using his name. Jimmy's upset came through clearly to his brother, who again began to panic. The fear of losing his brother and mother was overwhelming. The call ended on a somber note with a promise to one another that they would be careful and say nothing to anyone other than the Native American lawman. "Give it three or four hours before you call anyone. I have to think this through and make sure we don't get burned bad by me turning on these guys."

"Jimmy, we can't play around with this. It's our mother that's at risk here." His head was spinning. "I . . . I know what a bad spot you must be in, but you gotta find a way to keep our mom in one piece and you with your head still on your shoulders."

A shudder went down Jimmy's spine as the reality slammed him. "I'll give you the word on when to call that person. You don't say nothin' to no one. You got that, kid?" He was almost coming apart and he just could not let that happen.

Ali Maloof called Wilson while sitting on the porch of the rambling house he occupied on the Sinaloa compound. "Have you made progress, Douglas?"

"So far, so good," came the response.

"The device of the infidel bitch . . . Do you have it?" Maloof pushed.

"Not yet, but we're close. I know it's in either the hands of the Indian or still in the casino's hotel. No matter, it will not be around much longer. We have John Gode by the balls, and what he does with that is a no-win for him in any way . . . even if he cooperates."

"No-win?"

"That's the only way I can describe it. He is painted into a corner he can't get out of. Whatever direction he goes . . . wham, he's a dead man," Wilson crowed.

"You really got a hard-on for this man," he emphasized after a pause. "Don't let it distort your judgment, Douglas. There is no room for error from this point forward. You don't have the luxury of mucking this up," Maloof cautioned.

"I don't muck up things. I fuck up people. Gode is 'people,' and this is open season on his kind, my friend. Now I must be about our business. Talk soon." The rogue agent ended the call. He turned to the man standing in the shadows behind him and motioned for him to sit down across from him.

Wilson studied a cigar he had taken out of jacket pocket. He rolled it around in his hand and lifted it to his nose, enjoying the aroma.

"What's up?" came the question from the short, balding, middle-aged man as he took a place in a chair directly in front of him, staring intensely after Wilson ended his call.

"I need to know one way or another . . . and I need to know now if you have any idea whether or not Gode has the flash drive we couldn't find in that bitch's room at the casino." Lying on Wilson's mind was how hard Ali Maloof was pushing him, and it caused him to be extra intense.

"I don't understand why you're asking me this question. You were standing right beside me in the room when we realized that it wasn't anywhere we could find it. I have no idea where it is," came the annoyed response.

"Of course I know that, and don't go getting stupid on me now, Walter. I'm asking . . . what does your man know about it? He's in a better position to know, certainly, than any of us are. No? This isn't rocket science here." Wilson didn't tolerate incompetency well and he wanted Walter to know that, in case he had forgotten.

"Our guy says that Gode and the rest of the Indians haven't been around the last few days. He said that your breathing down that task force group's asses has the rest of the guys on the assignment a bit rattled." Walter chuckled after relaying the information.

"So the casino will now be scheduled for demolition as ground zero for the detonation of the dirty bomb, as previously planned. That flash drive has got to be fried before it gets into the wrong hands, shall we say? After a short while it ain't gonna really matter as much, but for the immediate future it cannot be in the hands of anyone but us. Anyone!" he stressed loudly. "What else have you got for me?"

"The reservation is the perfect location for the origination of the radioactive cloud that will spread over the entire southern section of Phoenix, Mesa, Tempe, and Gilbert. If the wind is right, it'll take out thousands."

"The more we take out, the bigger the bonus," Wilson crowed.

"What I'm getting, Wilson, is that you are probably going to be filthy rich when this is all over." He paused, smiling slightly, wondering if there would be a response. Hearing none, he continued, "I assume that you'll be disappearing then?"

"I'm already gone." Wilson sat up straight in his chair, and looking through icy eyes, he asked, "So, you're certain that you have all the fireworks properly placed?"

"The 'packages' are placed in a dumpster that won't be used until next week, according to my people who have been working there as landscape contractors. All we have to do now is get the radioactive material in position, and wham, there goes a good part of the Valley of the Sun . . . and it'll be gone for a long time to come. What a statement. Huh?" He laughed.

"I have another assignment for you." Wilson leaned forward as he spoke. "John Gode."

"Yeah?"

"I want him taken out. But I want him done when he does his shaman bullshit out in the quiet place that he does his chanting."

"Can do. Is this part of the deal we cut?" Walter asked.

"We'll make it that way, but it happens a few days after the big bang. I'll give you the coordinates of Gode's special place in the desert. All takes place as the sun is setting. This time it will be his last sunset."

"You got it," Walter stated emphatically.

"This will be necessary only if the guy in his group fails to drop him first. But you know? After thinking some more about it, I want him to suffer and not have a quick death. That's why I want you to take him out while he's doing his ritual. But I want his last breaths to be of lingering, insidious pain."

"Do I know this person who might take him out before I do?"

"Yes, you do, but I'm not sayin' who that is. Someone who he trusts. It'll be sweet because he'll never see it coming." Wilson winked as he spoke.

"I don't know, Douglas." Walter shook his head. "This guy is one of the spookiest people I've ever seen or heard about. I don't think he'll go easy under any circumstance."

"When we get done with this Geronimo piss-head, I hope he'll be in so many parts he won't be able to be reassembled for burial or burning," Wilson said, looking at nothing as he spoke.

"What is it about him that makes you want to decimate him so bad?" Walter pressed him.

"That's my secret. Do you want to tell me your secrets, Walter?"

"Not a chance."

Agent Wilson returned to looking Walter in the eye with a smug expression on his face, causing a reaction that Walter did not expect from himself. The reaction was of caution because what he was getting from Wilson was a sense of "cowboy" that usually preceded something big and beyond the scope of his normal expectations. He had no idea as to the enormity what was beginning to take shape all around him, no idea at all.

---

It was pitch-black as Kazi and Kumar rolled up to the mouth of the cave where Wilson's men had prepared for what was to come for the mother of John Gode. They drove their vehicle into the interior far enough so that it could not be seen from the sky or ground.

Amma was blindfolded, and her hands were cuffed behind her back. She asked weakly, "What are you going to do with me?"

"Depends on your son. If he behaves, then you can go back to bed, and he can go back to his normal job duties," Kazi answered in a friendly tone.

"What is it that you want him to do?" she asked.

"Just the right thing."

"The right thing?" she repeated his question.

"He has something we want. We want it very badly, and all he has to do is give it to us and . . . the world goes back to normal. For all of us, dear mother," Kazi assured her.

# 25: Cartel Joins the Jihad

ALI MALOOF CALLED the drug lords to his house for a pre-event meeting as the "last days of the Great Satan jihad" began. He offered them strong coffee as they sat around a large table in his spacious living room. There were ten somber-looking men of various ages and sizes assembled in that room with the master jihadist. He greeted them with, "I am pleased to tell you that our great effort begins this moment. We are ready to take your neighbors to the north down a path that will end a part of history, which they have dominated for far too long." He looked around the table to several nodding heads but no smiling faces.

"Where's the money?" asked one of them, who wore the name "Picasso" because of the scars and slight disfigurement of his forty-something-year-old face. His heavy eyebrows gave him a caveman-like look that made Maloof think twice about how he answered the question.

"First things first, Picasso," Maloof answered slowly as he leaned into the table. "First things first."

Picasso laughed slightly. "I come first. If you want us to do what you want us to do, the first thing that happens is the money is in our hands. Right, amigos?" He never broke his gaze from Maloof as he listened to the response of the other nine cohorts.

"That was never in question, gentlemen. But before anything happens, we have to make sure that we all know what is expected of each of us. Can we proceed?" Maloof was being cautious, knowing he was dealing with men almost as ruthless as him. "Your responsibility lies in Arizona. As we planned, Picasso, you and your men will take out the lodge at the Grand Canyon and make sure that 'glass bridge' is shattered." He paused for a moment and then went on. "Everything will be waiting for you when you get there."

Picasso sat staring with the eyes of a dead man, expressionless and empty, not saying a word.

Maloof leaned forward in his large chair. "Are all of you ready for this?"

"Ready?" Picasso asked in a way that indicated a bit of dismay. "Why you asking that? We don't do nothing that we ain't ready for. Who do you think you're dealing with? Camel jockeys from your desert? Bad enough that we have to take orders from your Iranian people." He grunted but did not break his eye contact with Maloof. This was a bit unsettling for the jihadist.

"That's the deal we made, Picasso. They have to be there for this to get the proper effect. What I want to know from you at this moment is, do you have this clear in your head? Are you certain that you can plant the explosives so they take down what we want taken down? Can you accurately fire a handheld missile? Can this all be done at the time we want it to all happen?"

Picasso laughed sarcastically and paused for a few seconds before saying, "Do you really think you need to ask me any of that shit? I am here to get the money. I wouldn't take it if I had any doubts that this job will be done." He continued his sarcastic laugh. "Tell me about this Indian cop." He studied Maloof as he continued, "He has some of my people a little bit shaky."

"What about him?"

"I hear he and his amigos can disappear. I hear he can take people's hats off with his feet. That's what I hear," Picasso said matter-of-factly.

"Maybe he can, maybe he can't, but I can take his hat and his head off at the same time with this." Maloof pointed at the sword leaning against his chair.

Picasso acted like he didn't hear a word Maloof said. "I hear he likes to screw over the American *federales* too. I hear they're afraid of him. Why would it be like that?"

"I'll handle him and his band of disappearing monkeys . . . or, as the weak-minded insist that they be called, 'Native Americans,' so they don't get their feelings hurt by your calling them Indians." He laughed. "What do they call that nonsense, 'political correctness'?"

Several in the group shrugged in response.

"Yes, my friends, and it is that weakness of the American will that allows you to do what you do and for me to set up their destruction so easily."

"We've been doing this a long time, Maloof. Even before it was so easy to do like it is now. But you know it makes me wonder why they are setting themselves up again for you to take them down again. They don't learn good," he said almost to himself, but everyone in the room heard him.

Maloof motioned to one of his men standing in the corner of the room to bring the satchel he was holding in his hand. He did so and laid it at Maloof's feet, who nodded at it and smiled at Picasso while waving his hand toward it, indicting he should come over and pick it up.

Picasso fixed his eyes on it and waved one of his men over to the bag. When the man had it in his hands, he was told, "Count it." He fixed his gaze back on Maloof.

The jihadist spoke slowly. "That's one half. The rest will be there when the job is done. Like we agreed." He stared at Picasso, then moved his eyes around the group. As he did, he was glad that his men were poised at the ready should the Carteleros have a change of heart.

"How do I know that?" Picasso asked with just a bit of doubt showing in his voice.

"Are you questioning my word?"

"Not yet."

Maloof took a deep breath, looked at the Cartelero intently, and said, "I will need your services again, and maybe even again, after this. That's job security, my friend. It will keep everything where it needs to be, for both of us. No?"

The tension in the room at that moment could have been cut with a knife but subsided quickly when Picasso smiled and said, "We're good." He grunted and arose from his chair, then led his group out of the room and the house. He turned and looked at Maloof. "*Adios.*"

Maloof smiled back before saying, "By the time twenty-four hours pass, America's spirit will be so wounded, it will no longer be able to function. You play a smaller but an extremely important symbolic part of this plan."

Picasso and his men were gone and Maloof breathed a sigh of relief.

————————

At that moment, John Gode's phone rang. His stomach almost left his body as he heard his mother say, "John, I need you to do something for me." Because her voice was weak, John thought she was ill or having a heart attack.

Then another voice got on the phone, saying menacingly, "Gode, you have something I want . . . I have something you want. Care to trade?"

John tried to make out the voice unsuccessfully.

"We have your mother here with us, and she's not going anywhere until we get what you are holding."

"Let me talk to her," he said stoically as his head spun with fear for his mother.

"Here she is."

Amma knew that they were both in great danger, but she could not think of a way to protect her son from what she feared was waiting for him if he came to rescue her. She said in Mohawk, "Do not try to come for me—" as the phone was ripped from her hands.

Kazi spit the words at John. "No code-talking, Geronimo. Got that? We speak English. Okay? Leave that stuff to the Navajo, asshole," the man said threateningly.

"What do you want?" John asked, trying to mask his fury.

"You know what that is. Stop asking stupid questions. Deliver it to us, and Mama here can go back home. Don't deliver it, and you won't hear her voice ever again. It's that simple."

"You hurt her in any way, and I will take you apart in ways you never thought possible. You understand me, 'white eyes'?"

"How are you gonna do that when you have no idea who we are? You don't know for sure that I am even a 'white eyes.' Do you?" He chuckled tauntingly.

"I know who to look for . . . and I will find everyone you are in with, then I'll let them watch me peel you," John said tersely. "I have a guide who will lead me to you."

"A guide? Come on, John. If you had a guide, you would have started for us already." His words caused him to start thinking that maybe there was something to what was being said. These guys had something weird going on around them, and he did not want to take them lightly. But he wanted John to think he did.

"Tell Wilson what I just told you," John said in a hoarse whisper.

"I don't know anyone by that name," came the smug response. "What's it gonna be?"

"Where do you want me to go?" John asked with a cold anger.

"I want you to go to hell, but will settle for you dropping that little piece of equipment at the casino. In one hour exactly, go to the 'Wheel of Power' game machine, and put that puppy on top of it, in the middle, right dead center, and walk on. Don't look back to try to eyeball who picks it up. We okay so far?"

"About as okay as you're ever gonna be, asshole. Go on."

"Now, now, Johnny Boy, that does sound like a threat. You're not in a position to keep threatening me right now."

"I'm not talking about right now," John responded abruptly.

"All you have is 'right now,' Geronimo. No one has tomorrow . . . not even you. Get that package delivered, and your mama will be free to go." He was digging himself a deep hole with this exchange, and he had no idea how deep it really was . . . no idea at all.

"So I do that, then where do I find my mother?"

"Oh, that's the part of this that I haven't mentioned yet."

"Then mention it," John demanded.

"If we don't hear or see anything that tells us you made a copy of the digital for forty-eight hours, she'll be calling you from a public phone to pick her up." He paused for a moment. "If there is any indication that you have a copy, then we got a problem . . . no, wait a minute. Then your mother has a problem. A big one. We together on that?"

"So I keep my end and have to trust you to keep yours? Why should I believe you will keep your word?" John's mind was racing, trying to get some sort of clue from this guy as to where he was and where they had his mother. So far, this was not a good deal. He said, "How do you know that I know what you are talking about? I mean, really."

"I know you have it, John. I just know, and nobody here wants to hurt your mother. So, man up and deliver on this, and life goes back to normal for you and her," he said, trying to be convincing.

"How do I contact you after I do what you want me to do? I need more assurance that you will keep your end of the deal. I don't think that's asking too much, do you?"

"Just get your ass to the casino and do your thing, and the world will be beautiful again. That's it." He ended the call.

John thought for a moment, then gathered Alicia and Noche and began explaining to them about the conversation regarding his mother. Alicia gasped at what she heard. Noche did not react openly, but he joined in John's fury.

Alicia put her arm around the big lawman and asked, "What do we do now? These sons of bitches need something serious landing on their heads." She looked up at John with eyes clouded with fury. "There's something wrong with this world, John, something so wrong that no amount of fixin' can make it right again. What the hell are they doing, dragging your mother into this? She must be scared out of her wits."

John handed the flash drive to Alicia. "Can you get a copy of this, fast?"

She nodded and handed it to Tonio, who was a Shadow Wolf tech wiz who carried an emergency tech kit with him as standard gear. He looked it over and half smiled as he headed to the room his laptop was sitting in.

John's phone rang. It was Sweet Tooth, who said in an anxious voice, "John Gode, Jimmy just called me a minute ago. He dropped off some shit at—now get this—a cave, and he saw an old woman who he thinks could be your mom."

"What makes him think it was my mother?" He knew he was probably right on the money with this. It could be a big break. "Thank you, Grandfather," he whispered quietly.

"What did you say about your grandfather?" Sweet Tooth asked.

"Nothing . . . I was just thinking out loud. Why?" John replied quickly, almost wishing he hadn't mentioned his dead grandfather. "People are going to start thinking I'm half-crazy," he thought.

"Because Jimmy said when he unloaded some stuff at this cave, he saw an old man, who looked like one of us, move past him and back into the cave. He almost automatically followed him, and there, a short way in, he saw this woman sitting by herself, looking really disturbed. Her hair was like, all messed up, and she was wearing only a nightgown. She didn't have no shoes on. He knows who your mother is. She's friends with our mom."

"Did he talk with her?" John pressed him.

"No, he didn't get a chance. When one of the guys who was there noticed where he was, he told my brother to 'get gone.' And he did. Then he called me about it." Sweet Tooth waited for John's response.

"Can Jimmy help us find that cave?" John asked desperately.

"Yeah, he can. He told me to tell you that he can meet up with you and lead you there."

"Okay, Tooth. You did good. So did Jimmy. Now tell him to meet me by the Riggs Road exit off I-10 in about an hour and fifteen. Tell him to pull off into the desert and stay out of sight from the highway."

With a concerned tone obvious in his voice, Sweet Tooth commented, "This sounds like some bad shit, John. Some real bad shit is happening."

"What do you mean?" John asked.

"I'll let Jimmy tell you. He's got a crowded head right now. Full of stuff you need to know. But he's got to tell you himself."

"Okay, Tooth. Stay low, but be available in case I need something in a quick minute. You good?" John asked hurriedly.

"Yeah, I'm good."

John smiled as Alicia planted the flash drive back in his hand. She then placed a second one in his pocket and winked as she did. He said, "Let's get everyone in the briefing room. I have a story to tell that's gonna knock everyone on their asses."

The head count of all the Shadow Wolves in the briefing room was thirty-eight, including four women, one of them Alicia. They sat silently, patiently waiting for John's words on what was coming. He explained point by point, bringing them up to the moment. "Any questions?" he asked as he finished talking.

"How do we get the word out to the feds if we don't know which of them we can trust?" asked one of the men sitting in the back of the room.

"I'm gonna go with the US marshal, Eric Cahn. I believe he can be trusted. Beyond him, the only other law enforcement head I trust is the sheriff, but we can't draw him in yet because the DOJ is all over his ass about the way he handles illegals, and he has court-appointed monitors everywhere, crawling all over his department, watching him."

"Lay it out, John, and let's get ready to roll," another Shadow Wolf called out. John smiled broadly back at him, appreciating the suggestion.

"Right now, I need eight of you to get ready to meet up with me in the desert near I-10 and Riggs Road in an hour. The rest of you need to stand ready for what could be a major takedown. I've got to get a better idea of what our first run is going to need." He scanned the room and was thankful when he saw everyone "dressed in the silence," all in black, ready to blend with the night. He head-motioned to Alicia to come with him and they left for the casino.

Twenty minutes later, they were parked in the casino lot and perused it for any sign of who would be picking up the recorder. There was no indication. John departed the car and walked cautiously toward the casino with his Sig Sauer 9mm in his hand, ready to breathe fire at anyone who might be lying in wait for him. Alicia was out of the car and holding her weapon, covering her lover's back. As she saw John enter the casino, she holstered it and reached for her expandable baton, which she whipped to its full extension. She practice swiped it using a pattern she had learned from her Bagua teacher three years before. It had become one of her favorite hand weapons, and she was exceptionally skilled with it. A few practice swipes a day kept her adept when added to the Eight Palm "old form" Bagua movements.

John walked casually through the casino's main room, stopping occasionally at machines, pretending he was checking them out. After a few minutes, he strolled up to the "Wheel of Power" machine and leaned on it with the flash drive clenched in his hand. He placed it on top, in the middle, and after looking around, he backed away from the machine and turned toward the door. He focused on the exit as he left the main room and eventually, the building. His eyes swept the parking lot for movement, and the movement he saw was Alicia getting back out of the car. Although he couldn't see it from the distance he was at, he knew that her weapon was at the ready and protecting him.

Fifteen minutes later when they rolled off the I-10 highway and into the desert, they were quickly waved toward where the Shadow Wolves were parked. Noche was there, leading the group. He said, "Big John, we're ready for bear, but we hope the bear's not nine feet tall." He chuckled, but concern wasn't difficult to hear in his voice despite his attempt at humor.

"Everybody, we're waiting for someone who's coming here, and he has some information we're gonna need this night." As he ended the sentence, a dark car pulled off the road and into the desert driving toward them. Two of the pack leveled their weapons at the car, which raised a good deal of dust as it skidded to a stop. The door opened slowly, and Jimmy Begaye got out with his hands raised.

John said quickly, "Okay, relax, everybody. He's a friendly and who we've been waiting on."

With an uncertain smile, Begaye walked to the group and said, "I'm Jimmy Begaye, and I need to talk with John Gode."

"Let's hear what you got to say, Jimmy." The tall lawman put his arm around the young man's shoulders as a gesture that he was in safe hands, and he could feel free to tell what he knew.

He related the dire plan he had been made aware of by Ali Maloof hours before. Then he went on to talk about seeing the woman who he believed was Amma Gode and where she was being held captive.

"Did she look like she was hurt?" John asked tersely.

Jimmy didn't want to be the bearer of bad news, but there was no reason to lie about it to make John feel better. "She looks like shit, man." He thought about it for a minute and then said, "I don't mean no disrespect, John Gode, and I think that your mother is a pretty lady and all . . . But she don't look too good right now." He looked down after speaking.

John said nothing, but his wheels were turning.

# 26: US Marshals Versus the Deep State

NOCHE LOOKED JIMMY over and thought for a few seconds before asking, "John, with the shit-storm about to blow over this whole country, I'd say we need to talk with somebody to let them know what's about to happen."

"Who do we trust, Noche? Who can we get this to, especially when we're talking the feds? We don't know who's involved with this, and if we tell the wrong person, our asses will be toast, leaving no one doing anything about anything to shut this shit down." John's intensity was growing.

"I say we put our hopes in the US marshal. Like you've already said, you feel he can be trusted," Noche ventured.

"You feel Eric Cahn is that trustworthy? Why? Give me your reasons."

"Gut . . . Big John. You know about that stuff. Gut," Noche said with a slight smile, nudging him a bit.

Not completely comfortable with the thought, recalling his grandfather's words about "a man's tracks as testimony to his character" made John more inclined to do it. He said, "Okay, Noche, I'm feeling the same way about this, but I had to hear your reasons too. I'll reach out to him right now." John went into his phone for the marshal's number and hit it. Marshal Cahn answered on the third ring. He listened in silence to what John had to say, and when the big lawman was done, there was just quiet on the other end before he spoke.

"John, if you'd a' told me this five years ago, I'd a' told you this was pure fantasy, stirred up by the conspiracy theorists running all over the Internet. Nope, that would have been as far as you would have gotten with me back then."

"And how does this hit you now, Marshal?" John asked cautiously.

Cahn let out a breath. "I no longer think that way, and furthermore, I think that believing this stuff can't happen is for the 'liquid brainers' inside that Washington beltway. That's what I think, John." There was silence and then, "I'm asking you, what do you want me to do with this?"

"Pass it on up the line."

"To who, John? This stuff started coming to the surface with the 'Fast and Furious' gun running fiasco, and although there was evidence staring everyone in the face, nothing happened with it. And on top of that, we have cops all over the country being taken out with the very weapons given to the cartels by our own government."

"Yeah . . . we know that, Marshal. My problem is sitting here with this information and not being able to do anything with it. That's why I'm calling you."

"Thank you, John. So now there's at least two of us in the choir pew," came the instant response.

The US marshal is appointed by the president of the party in charge, and although Eric Cahn had been a Democrat appointee, he himself did not belong to any party. He was a bona fide Independent. He was appointed from within the ranks of the US Marshals Service mostly because local law enforcement thought very highly of him. At root, he was a solid patriot who had served in Iraq. He started out as a deputy US marshal in Pennsylvania and over time, wound up with Phoenix as his duty station. He was promoted to chief deputy in Arizona and did an excellent job with keeping the judges happy and safe. When the then marshal decided to retire, it was plain to see who his replacement would be from the phone calls made by the judges to the White House.

"Where are you now, John?"

"Getting ready to take this to the next level," John said quietly.

"I think I'd better join you before you take out all of these bastards before I can get some pokes at 'em. I'm thinking it will be a real good thing for you and your folks to be deputized by me."

"Would definitely be that, Marshal. It will make a big difference going forward with what probably lies ahead of us." John was feeling better about this already. "When do we get deputized?"

"I'll swear you all in when I get to where you are. Which is?"

John gave him directions, and the call ended. He turned to Noche and said, "I sure as all shit hope you got a gut that's at least half as good as mine."

"Yeah. Me too."

John looked at Noche and shook his head in mock frustration with Noche's nonchalance. But at the same time, he believed that his friend's instincts were right on the money. "I think it's time to get the rest of the pack here. Make the call, Noche?"

"You want 'em here immediately?"

"Yeah. Immediately."

Within twenty-five minutes the rest of the crew were pulling up in their caravan of SUVs and hummers. They exited the vehicles and huddled around John. He briefed them thoroughly.

A half hour later Eric Cahn drove up to the group alone, which surprised John. "Marshal, are you doing this without your deputies?" he asked.

"I think that's best. Besides, all of you are now my deputies. Raise your right hands and repeat after me . . . " He administered the oath of office to all of the Shadow Wolves present.

# 27: Shadow Wolves Fight for America's Future

THEY CAME TOGETHER as John explained the strategy he felt would render the best result in rescuing his mother.

Eric Cahn commented, "John, I think that maybe you might have too much of an emotional investment here, and you should run this by a few of us before we agree on which way to go."

"That would be great, Marshal, but we don't have time to hand-wring. We gotta move now!"

"Move . . . sure," Cahn replied. "Move now? Not so sure." He looked around at the group before returning his attention to John. "If we go in shooting, there's a good chance your mom is a casualty," he cautioned.

"We ain't going in shooting, Marshal. We're just going in. We'll be in back of them before they realize what happened," John assured him confidently. All of the pack agreed. Some more than agreed. They were the ones who had done something like this before.

"How so?" Marshal Cahn wasn't buying it, but he was open to stepping back and letting the process continue. "I sorta know something about you all, and from what it is I do know, there is no doubt that a silent way in would be best. But I can't see how that gets done when you're sneaking up on men with heavy weaponry in a cave . . . who are holding a hostage, to boot."

"We're gonna show you how." John knew his people and the old ways. The marshal was not familiar with either.

"Okay, let's go get this done."

Gato had been fairly silent through most of the conversation until he commented, "John, I know how good you guys are, and I especially know that about you, through Mohammed, but you have to keep in mind what you're going against. These are some of the best Special Forces–types in the world." He touched John on the arm to emphasize his concern. "They might sense us coming."

"No, they won't," John assured him abruptly.

"How do you know that for sure?" Gato asked.

"We won't let them. They won't know what hit them until they won't be feeling anything anyway."

Jimmy Begaye rode with John, Alicia, Gato, and Eric Cahn. Noche and the pack followed in their vehicles, all running silent and dark as they moved slowly but directly toward the cave. Jimmy helped by using the coordinates he had in his phone GPS. The night was intensely dark, with a cloud cover enhancing the darkness.

---

At that moment, Ali Maloof, with his men and Picasso leading the Carteleros, had just crossed the porous border west of Nogales. Following a GPS, they started slowly through the desert to their usual location some sixty miles north to one of the most remote areas in that part of Arizona. It was, literally, in the middle of nowhere. The convoy was larger than the previous convoys and with good reason. For this one was indicative of what they had been preparing for since the arrival of the jihadists in Mexico several years earlier. Their weaponry had become more and more sophisticated since the fall of Benghazi, which led to the almost open door cooperation between them and some in high places in the US government, including law enforcement agencies. Confidence within their ranks had grown exponentially as their caliphate grew in Syria and neighboring Iran due to the American retreat, as they saw it. They indeed were the beneficiaries of having friends in high places.

"Have you heard back from the 'cave contingent'?" Maloof asked his top aide, who was driving.

"No. Nothing."

"What about Begaye?"

"Nothing." He did not move his eyes from the direction he was driving.

Although Maloof did not expect to hear anything, he did want an update from someone. But knowing the Americans, he accepted the silence. It was actually his own wish that communications be kept to a minimum and in code.

---

John's group continued moving slowly toward the cave, and when they were less than two miles out, they stopped and gathered in a circle, again discussing the approach. John said, "Remember the snake clusters around this part of the desert. You know how pissed off a snake can get if you interrupt their 'gettin' some.' Step carefully, especially near that cave."

During mating season, hundreds of rattlers gathered in certain parts of the desert, in the most remote places, to mate. Where they were headed was one of those places.

The group did a quiet prayer chant and short war dance in place, quietly chanting. It made for "strong hearts" as they went into battle.

"Use the knives first, if you can. Silent guns second. Alicia . . . you have the baton?" John looked at her for an answer.

"Always have my baton. You know that better than anyone, John." He knew how deadly she was with those sixteen inches of metal . . . so light . . . so fast . . . so deadly.

They checked their weapons one more time and went back to their vehicles. When they reached a point that was less than a mile from the cave, they left the vehicles and fanned out across the desert floor. They blended into the desert night. Their feet made no sound as they lifted their bodies by lifting their energy upward. All part of what made the Shadow Wolves so deadly. Their stealth ability was much like that of the ninja. No one ever sees them coming, but most know when they've been there and gone.

Half the team went to the right of the cave, and John's team went to the left. The marshal, Gato, and Jimmy Begaye remained back with the vehicles at John's request because of the need for surprise, and they had no experience with being as silent in approaching a target as was necessary. They secreted themselves in the brush a short way from the vehicles and waited for a word from someone in the raid party.

John drew to within two hundred feet of the entrance to the cave. He was twice as close as the others in the teams. Alicia started creeping toward John's position with her MAC-10 slung across her back and her Sig Sauer, with silencer, nestled in her right hand.

"Wait," he said, cautioning her. "I see two of them, and they look like they're guarding the entrance in prone positions on both sides, and I'm surprised that they haven't seen us." He looked through his night vision binoculars.

"Me too."

They both dropped to one knee as John said, "I smell a rat here." He looked around.

"What do you mean?" Alicia asked quietly.

"I think that there's a good chance they have night goggles, and that would make us very easy to see at this range." He thought for a moment. "They could have booby traps all around this area, and they might be expecting an interloper to step on one of them. Maybe that's what they're hoping will happen."

"What do we do with that?" she whispered.

"Give me a minute." He stared into his night vision equipment.

John whispered into his headset mic, "Noche, bring your ass and two of the pack with you toward me. We're about two hundred feet from the cave entrance and at one o'clock as you approach. And stay really low. They could be using night vision."

Noche responded immediately. "What would make you think different?"

"Not certain of that. We're waiting for you." He turned to Alicia and asked in a whisper, "Can you see anybody in the cave?"

"Yeah, I'm looking at three men, and they're moving stuff around. Looks like large wooden boxes."

"Any sign of my mother?"

"No."

A few minutes later, Noche and two of the Shadow Wolves crept up on them like ghosts in the night. "How do we take them?" he asked quietly.

John pointed in the direction of the cave. "There are two guards lying on the ground on either side of the entrance, and we need to get to them from behind. But I'm thinking that these assholes might have planted a booby trap near them and the cave." The tall lawman was running a strategy through his head and was interrupted by a suggestion from Noche.

"Jerry here almost got hisself bit by a rattler he damn near stepped on. He threw his hat on the son of a bitch and grabbed it before it could strike. It's in his backpack, all pissed off and ready to do some harm to the next thing it sees." Noche looked approvingly in the direction of the young man. "So we talked about it and decided we might make it a present to those who grabbed your mother."

John said quickly, "I got an even better idea. Let's drop it on one of those boys who are lying on the ground, pulling guard duty."

"How do we do that, John?" Alicia questioned.

"Noche and the two young Wolves can take it in a wide circle to the right and come in behind the mound above the cave. We'll do the same to the left. When we get set in place, he'll drop the snake on the one who is below them, and that should set off all kinds of pandemonium." This felt right to John.

"Might even drive the guys in the cave to come running when they hear him screaming. And scream he will." Jerry was enjoying this. He was Navajo and had the tribal sense of humor.

"That's exactly what I'm thinking." Gode smiled, knowing he was about to do something that could make for a lifetime memory.

They set out, moving cautiously and as silent as the snake they were carrying. One of the men who were inside the cave came out, and his voice carried through the desert air as he asked, "Everything good out here?"

John recognized it immediately as the voice of the man he had talked with on the phone about his mother.

"Yeah. Nothing moving. I like it like that." He laughed.

John thought, "I'm going to like watching you while I shove this snake down your throat."

They fanned out into the desert darkness, moving swiftly and quietly as they went. John tried to get a visual on his mother's position in the cave, but that was not possible from the angle of their approach.

Alicia nudged him and pointed toward the man standing at the mouth of the cave, peering off in their direction, causing them to stop in place and drop to the ground. John readied himself to get at least three silent shots off in rapid succession, hoping to take all three out. Then the man at the mouth of the cave turned and went back inside.

Alicia whispered, "I hope he didn't pick up on us and is now setting up for our arrival." She looked at John, hoping he could dismiss her fear. He did.

"They have no idea that we're here," he assured her.

"How do you know for sure?"

"They all just looked at the light in the cave, and now their eyes are readjusting," he said and resumed moving forward. They swung wide and began doubling back toward the short rise that housed the cave. As they got to the side, John and Alicia moved like spirits, so quietly they would not have alerted anything or anyone in their path.

Noche and his team were there and in place before John and Alicia arrived. "We're ready," came the whispered message from John over the earphone. That sent Jerry into action. He brought the rattler out of the backpack slowly, but the snake was ready and its rattles were buzzing as he tossed it on the guard ten feet below him. As expected, a shrill scream emanated the night as he was bitten twice by the furious reptile.

Two men emerged from the cave, rifles in hand. One asked, "What's happening with you? Why the hell are you screaming?" As he walked toward the injured man, the snake struck again and hit him in his right calf before he was able to shoot a burst, tearing the animal apart.

John jumped the other guard and in a second had slit his throat from ear to ear. Noche and his team finished what the snake had started by capping both of the men on their side of the cave. Two more came running out, shooting off into the night. Alicia took out two of them, and John took out the one who came out with the man who had been bitten by the snake. He moved silently into the cave, looking left and right for his mother. When she did come into view, she was being held upright by Kazi Kamir, his handgun pressed against her head.

"So, Geronimo, we finally meet." He regarded John with caution, focusing intently on him. He felt that because he held the big lawman's mother, the reaction from him would be foolish and emotion-filled, and if he could turn that into a kill, it would leave the rest of them confused and easy targets. He had been well-trained and felt he could easily escape into the night.

"You have no way out, so why don't you make things easy on yourself and let her go," John said cautiously.

"No, that's just not going to happen," he replied confidently.

"Then I guess some more are gonna die here this night." John moved a bit closer as he spoke. "And I prepared something for you in that eventuality."

"Really? What's that?" Kazi maintained his grip on Amma Gode and kept the gun to her head. He was standing so close to her that none of them could chance a shot. Kazi backed up a few feet farther into the darkness. "What have you prepared for me . . . and now your mother . . . as we leave this troubled world?"

"I dipped my rounds in pig's blood and also my knife. Nothing personal. Just making things interesting. You understand, don't you?" John was hoping to somehow cause him an emotional jolt so he would make a mistake, giving John the opening he needed to get between the Persian terrorist and his mother.

Just then, he saw an old man move between him and Kazi. The old man could be seen by both John and the Persian, and it startled both men. But it startled Kazi enough to loosen his grip on Amma as she collapsed out of his arm and fell forward, giving John the opening he needed. He leaped across the distance between Kamir and himself like a panther through the darkness. Kazi dropped his gun but quickly regained his composure, pulling a knife to meet the oncoming Native American lawman.

John saw that this man was nothing less than a well-trained warrior who moved better than most men he had faced before.

He swiped at John with his dagger, holding it with scabbard up and the blade down, resting against his forearm, a clear indication he was a dangerous foe. But the same could be said of John, who had holstered his weapon, not wanting a round to accidently wind up in his mother's body. But he was now holding a blade as well.

The two men circled, facing one another across a distance of five feet. Kazi moved toward John, slicing the air in front of him, but John parried the move as he gauged the Persian terrorist's speed and technique.

Amma Gode called out, "John . . . the old ways. Remember them." She was terrified for her son. So was Alicia, because she was witnessing the first time John was facing another person who appeared to be as good as he was.

Kazi swiped again, and this time he cut into John's jacket. His confidence grew as he proceeded. "Don't worry, Mother Gode. I'll make certain that you follow your son into eternity. You'll be right with him," he said tauntingly while engaging John with two more rapid swipes.

"Pig's blood, asshole," John whispered as he moved around about forty-five degrees to the right side of Kazi. Those words distracted the Persian enough to give John the opening he needed to move in and strike, drawing blood from the top of Kazi's hand when he tried to evade the whirling pattern of the lawman's blade.

Kazi looked down at the huddled body of John's mother lying on the ground a few feet away and threw a jolting kick that landed a glancing blow on her upper arm, just missing her shoulder. He had hoped that move would infuriate John so he would do something stupid and fall prey to his knife.

It almost worked, as John lunged for him. Losing his footing, he fell forward, just under Kazi's stabbing move. Kazi dove on top of the fallen lawman, his blade coming down on John's throat. John rolled to the side, flipping the Persian and exposing Kazi to another cut, this time on his left arm.

"How's that pig blood feel, asshole? Is it starting to course through your veins, maybe even pissing off the Prophet?" John said in hoarse whisper.

Kazi smiled cunningly and announced, "I have a special delivery for you from the Prophet." He lunged again at John's throat with the point of his knife first. John made a ghost move, evading the thrust, and answered with a deep stab into the Persian's throat, killing him instantly. He dropped to the ground, on his way to meet his Allah.

Alicia and John rushed over to Amma's side, asking if she was all right. She responded groggily, "I'm okay. I'm okay." Then she smiled at her son and said, "I saw your grandfather's movements in your actions, John."

He smiled back at his mother, so thankful that she survived the ordeal.

"Why didn't you leave some of these fellas for me to put a hurt on?" The marshal uttered disappointedly as he walked into the cave, gun at the ready.

John looked at him, smiling slightly. "It's just the Indian way, Marshal. Please don't take it personal."

"Looks like this one did." He pointed at the dead Persian lying in a pool of his own blood, staring blankly at the top of the cave.

Jimmy Begaye came into the cave behind the marshal and took a deep breath as he looked around at the bodies lying on the ground inside and outside the cave. "You guys don't play."

No one responded. Nothing needed to be said, and they all understood that.

"What now?" Alicia asked, looking around the cave.

"Jimmy. Do you think the group down south will be up and running by now?" John asked.

"Yeah, I think that they're up by now. Or they're close to it. They are coordinating the attack on the 'Big Satan' at this get-together. If they get this running, they'll do a lot of damage to this country from west to east. Just like that." He snapped his fingers in time with his words.

"Jimmy, tell the marshal and Gato here everything you know about what the Arabs are going to do and where they're going to do it."

Jimmy explained what he knew of the plan and then what he thought they were going to do as part of it. He had made some notes on the specifics, which he wrote in a code he had invented in case he was discovered. "They're gonna blow up the Mall of America near Minneapolis tomorrow during the peak shopping hours, late mornin'. And they're gonna hit the Statue of Liberty a short time after the mall attack. Then they're gonna do somethin' at the Sears building in Chicago. This is heavy shit, man. Way too heavy for me."

"But it wasn't until your mother might be in danger that you came forward with this. Was it, Jimmy?" John said accusingly.

"No . . . I was trying to figure out a way to let you know so we could avoid another nine-eleven. They watched me real close down there in the camp in Mexico. I wasn't sure about using my phone even. I don't think they trusted me. I don't think that they trust anybody without a prayer rug." He produced a crucifix he was wearing under his shirt. "They treat these things like vampires treat them."

Cahn listened intently and then said resolutely, "I have no choice but to trust someone back east to put this fire out before they eventually take down the whole friggin' civilized world. Trouble is, with the folks we have calling the shots back there, we might just be pissing in the wind by letting them know." He thought for a moment and then went on, "Or even worse . . . if we tell the wrong people, they may send a drone down on our asses before they go ahead and blow up this country and our entire culture. I guess I have no choice but to trust someone who can defuse this to the point of stopping it."

"What and who?" John wondered if the attacks could even be stopped because the law enforcement network had been compromised, and who knew who was on the Arabs' payroll? Right on up to the top. Doubt filled his heart.

"We have to clean this mess up before we head out, John," Cahn said, looking around at the bodies.

John said, "I guess he'll have a shit-fit over what's happening, but I think we need to bring Armando Grant into the mix. To handle this." John pointed at two of the bodies. "I think it might be a good thing if you tell him you needed help instantaneously and grabbed us to help you with this conflict."

"Conflict? It looks like a friggin' World War III was fought here," the marshal said loudly.

"I think it actually is the beginning of that," John said, convinced he was right after learning what he had from Jimmy Begaye and Gato.

Gato said, "I think between Jimmy, Marshal Cahn, and me, we can piece together how to deal with what we need to get to the right people. What you're saying is in-line with what I'm thinking."

"Who's this guy?" The marshal nodded toward Gato, becoming aware that he was not what he appeared to be.

"He's good. Long story, Marshal, but he can be trusted," John assured him. "I gotta get my mother taken care of and kept in a safe place until I get back." He looked at Alicia, hoping she would step up and help, and she did.

"I'll take her to the hospital and stay with her there. If they don't keep her, where should we go that will be safe?"

"To my place," Noche interjected quickly. "You should be safe there. These assholes don't know where I live. Hell, sometimes even I can't find it. Here's the key." He tossed it to Alicia.

"Amma, are you okay enough to walk to one of the cars?" Alicia asked softly as she put her arm around the older woman. "Wait a minute, I need to go get it." She realized the vehicle was still parked a bit of a distance out in the desert. "It's going to take me just a few minutes."

Amma sat on a box against the cave wall. She nodded at Alicia, indicating she was feeling well enough to wait those few minutes. Alicia got the key to one of the other vehicles and arranged with those Wolves to ride with Noche. She then took off running into the desert night toward the vehicle.

John kneeled down and put his arm around his mother. "Are you sure you're okay, Mama? Please tell me if you're anything but that." He looked at her face closely and was glad that he killed the man who had injured her. "I've got to finish this, and that's why I—"

Amma stopped him mid-sentence by putting her fingers to her lips. "I know that, John. You go and do what needs to be done, but go carefully. I can't lose you too. Please, John." She looked at him imploringly through watery eyes as he smiled back with a warmth that only she could put in his heart. But that warmth would soon be replaced by cold fury as he made ready for the biggest battle he had ever faced at any time in his life.

He saw a phone lying on the ground a few feet from him, buzzing with an incoming call. He answered it with a short "yeah" because he felt that it probably belonged to the now-dead Kazi. It was Wilson, who said quickly, "We're on our way to meet up with the Mexican contingent. You stand by until I call you to come there. We're getting the grand plan put into action. Your whole world is about to change, so get ready. Got that?"

John responded again with a simple "yeah" and ended the call.

Within minutes, Alicia had the vehicle in front of the mouth of the cave. She and John assisted Amma into the back seat, which was a more comfortable place for her. He watched and waved as they pulled away from where he was standing, heading for what he hoped would be safer ground.

# 28: The Saudi-White House Jihadist Plan

THE CONVOY OF vehicles rolling through the desert from the south moved along under the cover of night with the precision of the military unit it was. A military unit led by a radical jihadist, composed of a mixture of well-trained Islamists and cold-blooded Carteleros. In the lead vehicle, Ali Maloof dialed his phone, trying to reach Wilson, but the reception was so bad, the call did not go through. He decided to wait until they were farther along before trying again. He was on fire with anticipation of the coming events, which he felt would change history itself, bringing down the "Great Satan" and raising the black flag of jihad, ultimately wherever the American flag once flew. What had happened in Iraq, Afghanistan, France, California, and Florida was about to happen throughout the entire United States, dealing a deathblow not only to America but also to western culture itself. He thought, "They have no idea what is coming, and they are totally unprepared for it. For all throughout the United States, the jihad has established people in the professions thanks to a more-than-willing administration in Washington. As this unfolds, ultimately culminating in a pulse bomb attack, the Americans will be fighting one another in the streets for food. Killing one another out of desperation, doing the job for us." He felt an inner smile brought on by a sense of an impending victory on a scale never seen before.

John was outside the cave talking with Marshal Cahn about what they should do to try to prevent the attacks that were already rolling their way. He said, "According to what I'm hearing from Jimmy Begaye, the plan is to attack our cultural icons across this country, suddenly and synchronized. But he has no specific details other than what we got from the reporter's personal notes I told you about. It's along the exact same lines, and what he brings to the table is good information. Gato backs it up from his perspective." He looked closely at the marshal, trying to get a sense of what he was thinking, and was surprised by what he heard him say.

"I don't think we can hand this off to anyone we would ordinarily report it to. At least, not yet," Eric Cahn said with an air of caution.

"Because we don't have enough detail?" John was puzzled.

Cahn replied quickly, "Because we don't know who we can trust."

"I get that, Marshal, but you have to have a network big enough to get something started on this. Do you have that?"

"I can't run it up the flagpole with any of the federal agencies. I don't have a good feeling about just how deep this thing has gone in our ranks. My sense is that there is an awful lot of money being passed around to quite a few people in high places."

"People . . . like who?"

"Everyone this president has brought in. And the other problem, John, I don't have a clue as to who might be on the take here in Arizona."

"But . . . you mean, there's no one you can go to with this?" John was getting hit by something he already knew but didn't want to admit was as real as it was turning out to be. It made him furious.

"That about says it." Marshal Cahn shook his head as he spoke. "Never thought anything like this could happen. It's unbelievable that we are even having this conversation."

Before he could stop himself, John blurted, "I don't know how you can work for these people."

"What people?" Cahn regarded the big lawman, a bit startled by his outburst.

"You know what and who I'm talking about. The president and his hand puppet attorney general. My gut is that all of this comes right back to them. Lying right at their feet." There was fire in his eyes as he unloaded on the marshal. "How does a man like you work for people like them?"

Cahn stood in cold silence, then took a deep breath before saying, "I don't work for them."

"Then who is it you work for, Marshal? I know that you know, probably better than me, who these people in this president's administration are. They have seeded the government with Muslim Brotherhood members who hate our country. This president has opened the borders and everybody and his uncle have flooded in. We don't know who or where they are. We've lost control, and that's exactly what he wanted." John couldn't stop his tirade. "This great, half-white father who lives in DC has released people from Gitmo who went right back into the battlefield killing my brothers-in-arms. This very day."

The big lawman paused for a moment. "For what? He traded them for one soldier who deserted his post and got people who thought he had been taken by the enemy killed trying to find and rescue him. He lets these heartless scumbags out of Gitmo to kill more of our soldiers, for this creep?"

Marshal Cahn reacted angrily. "The country, John. I work for the country. It doesn't matter whose ass is planted in the Oval Office. They come and go . . . the country remains."

John quieted his mind and thought about the response but was still searching for an answer to this dilemma. His trust in Cahn had not waned, but he could not truly understand how anyone of integrity could rationalize a way to continue to be part of the government during that time frame.

He felt as if he had hit a stone wall. "We're sitting out here with this info and have nowhere to go with it. Makes no sense." He began pacing like an angry tiger. Looking left, the big lawman tried to walk his way to a place of understanding. The more he thought, the more frustrated he became. How could this be happening here in the United States? Had everything he held in his personal beliefs been knocked to the ground while he just stood by watching? He did not remember ever seeing anything quite like that, and yet here it was, actually happening. There he stood, in the darkness of the Arizona desert, feeling helpless to prevent what he knew was going to befall the country within the coming hours. Nowhere to turn. No one who held the national trust, who could absolutely be counted on without doubt. It was absolutely mind-blowing.

"We can't wait on this. We're gonna have to roll the dice and trust someone in DC." Cahn's words voiced his decision.

"Marshal, the only thing I can say is, I think you should trust your gut on this," John said somberly. "Let someone know, who you feel can initiate something to stop what's coming. Don't see any other way on this." John trusted the system less than anyone he knew, but he understood the grim reality born in waiting too long before trying to do something.

"Okay, I'm going to pull the pin that could easily get out of control and come back to have dire consequences and seriously bite all of us in the ass," Marshal Cahn said resignedly.

"Serious consequences? For who?" John asked.

"For the ultimate and only 'tyranny fail-safe net' we have in this country."

"Not sure I'm following you."

Cahn took John by the arm and guided him away from the others before he spoke. "This is for you and you alone to hear. I wish there was another way to do this, but there isn't . . . so here goes." He took a deep breath. "There is a group of command officers within the military and in other places, people who guard us as a nation and who, for the last five years or so, have been doing things under the radar to try to protect us from the enemy within."

John smiled slightly. "Go ahead." He was thinking about the relativity of this to the Shadow Wolves.

Marshal Cahn went on. "The only reason I know about any of this is because of what I did in military intelligence before my appointment to US marshal. When the current administration started asking strange questions of career people in national security positions and when most of them who didn't follow their protocol started falling off the organizational charts, this group formed and coalesced naturally. It wasn't hard to read the writing on the wall. These sons of bitches that wove their way into office are in the process of unraveling the fabric of this country, and these people, me included, have no problem with doing what must be done to stop them."

"That's kind of what I have going here with my Shadow Wolf brothers and sisters. Actually, at this moment, it's exactly what we are wrestling with," John emphasized.

Cahn was feeling a bit better about his decision to let John in on this secret group. "This is not a simple troop of boy scouts. These are people who, if they were found out and properly prosecuted, would be hung for treason. Make no mistake, the only reason you are hearing this is because there is no other way to prevent what seems to be coming at us. And I use the word treason because it is in the same spirit of the 'treasonous acts' performed by our patriots during the Revolutionary War." Cahn looked at John, filled with an emotion that was pulling him in several different directions. He was telling John his most closely guarded secret, and the only reason he was doing so was because of the desperate position they were in. Eric Cahn was a sterling guardian of secrets, and relating this one did not rest easy with him. At that moment in time, he was betting everything he had on the belief that John was the man he thought he was and hoping he was right for doing so. For he knew beyond a doubt that what he did next and whom he did it with could have dire consequences, but there were no other options.

John said quietly, "I think you oughta know that my mother's a full-blooded Mohawk, and her ancestors had a little bit of skin in that war in those days too."

Cahn acknowledged John's proud comment and then said resolutely, "I won't tell you any names of the members of this group. Actually, I can't tell you." He dropped his eyes, then looked back up at John, who was four inches taller than him. Cahn was muscular all the way up to his neck, and that gave him the appearance of a weight lifter. His shaved head topped off a look of fierceness you don't see in many others. He was a former soldier and a current lawman down to his toes. He smiled and turned into the night as he dialed his phone. "Come with me, John. I'm going to need you to talk with someone."

"We'll be back in a few minutes," John said to the group. "You better get yourselves ready for the next 'adventure.' It could make this one look like a walk in the park." As he stepped away with Marshal Cahn, he watched them checking their gear and taking stock of what they had left or needed.

Cahn was talking with someone quickly, relaying the information he had and identifying John to the person on the other end as someone who could be trusted. He handed the phone to the big lawman and nodded as indication that he should speak. What followed was an accounting of everything he could recall from the reporter's recorded notes, the story he had been told by Jimmy Begaye, and what Gato said on what information he could talk about. The man on the other end quietly asked to speak with Jimmy and Gato, so the phone went back to Marshal Cahn as John went to find Jimmy and Gato.

Within a few minutes, John, Gato, and Jimmy came trotting back to Cahn. John explained to both that they needed to tell everything they knew about the coming attacks, in detail, to the man on the other end.

Gato asked cautiously, pointing at the phone, "Who's on the other end?"

Cahn replied, "I can't tell you that yet, but considering the situation, I recommend you give him what you have. He's one of us, Gato. I vouch for that."

Gato looked at him, considering his words. Then he nodded and took the phone. He relayed most of what he had already told John and then handed the phone back to the marshal, who handed it to Jimmy, saying, "Here, talk to this man."

"Who is he?" Begaye was fearful that he could be saying the wrong thing to the wrong person and maybe get his mother and brother killed as a result. He eyed the phone before he slowly put it to his ear, looking like he was afraid it was going to bite him. He studied John's face and understood that he could be trusted on this, then relayed everything he knew. When he was done doing that, he handed the phone to the marshal. The call ended, and they rejoined the group at their vehicles.

Noche asked in his usual stoic manner, "I wonder who it is that's gonna clean up that mess?" He nodded his head toward the bodies strewn about him.

"We don't have time to deal with it right now. There are way more important things lying ahead of us. Besides, they won't know the difference. Don't think time matters to them anymore," John said

200

quietly, respecting the fact that they had just killed a small group of men.

"But whoever has to come to the crime scene and do the clean up is gonna have a pretty nauseating job on their hands," Noche commented. "Looks like two of them messed their pants."

"Great observation, Noche." John paused for a moment. "I think we had better bring Armando into this." He looked at Cahn and asked, "Marshal, I need you call him and say that you needed us and asked us for assistance because you didn't have time to do anything else."

"I can do that. Where do I go with it if he starts wanting a lot of detail?"

"Make up something good. He's no dummy, so I would keep the conversation as short as possible."

"How much do you want me to tell him about where we're going and what we're gonna do?" Marshal Cahn was not a good liar, and this scenario was far from comfortable for him.

"Just say that we have to finish up something, and you don't have time to explain it now, that you have deputized us and that removes liability from him," John advised.

Cahn made the call to the task force commander and said exactly what they had discussed he would say. Word for word.

John called the rest of the pack and asked that they come to meet up with him ten miles south of the cave. He gave them the exact coordinates.

Perky got on the phone and told John, "I got a call from Bellamy, asking for a ten-seven on Alicia. He said his sister, who's a nurse at the Chandler Hospital, thought she saw her pushing some older woman in a wheelchair into the emergency room. She couldn't talk with her because of her needing to get to a patient's emergency. She said she couldn't find them when she got back to her station, but wanted to offer her help if she needed it."

"What did you tell him?" John asked.

"Told him he should call you."

"What did he say then?"

"He said that he didn't want to get you upset . . . it being your mother and all. He wanted to check with Alicia about what was going on."

201

"Thanks, Perky. He'll probably call soon. I got it."

———————

Bellamy went to the hospital where Amma Gode had been taken by Alicia. While driving there, he was on the phone with Special Agent Douglas Wilson, who told him, "I want you to get to the old woman and put her lights out, and find a way to do the same to Gode's girlfriend. You got that, Bellamy?"

"Yeah," he responded.

Then I want you to call Gode and tell him that his mother and lady were killed and you think it was done by the cartel."

"Yeah?" Bellamy wondered where he was going with this.

"I want that son of a bitch so messed up that he comes out of his skin and does something stupid. Insanely stupid. You good with that?"

"Of course."

———————

Fifty miles south of Phoenix, the Islamic jihad-Mexican cartel caravan arrived at the place where they were to have their ceremonial celebration. It was the last night before what they planned to be the beginning of the end of western civilization and the rise of the Islamic world caliphate.

The cartel crew began assembling the encampment while Ali Maloof used his satellite phone to pass on the confirmation that they were readying for the attack on the Grand Canyon. He spoke in code to the jihadist control center and listened to their encoded response. The air was filled with promise for him in one sense and with dread in another. For if they failed at any part of this mission before breaking the American spirit, there was no way of knowing for sure what would happen as backlash. He knew that only wounding a king was not the way to defeat him. The only option is to kill the king, and the king in the eyes of the entire world was the United States. He would do his part in crippling the soul of its people and would therefore ride the tide of Islamic extremist power, as the American way of life slowly crumbled in the many quarters around the world. They were using the corruption engrained in the American system to defeat it. That corruption was fed by the greed and arrogance of the perceived self-entitlement of those who held power. Power that was given to them by an uneducated, distracted segment of the country's population.

They set about erecting their tents and starting up the generators as they put out security on all four points, protecting the site from any surprise threat. The mood was intense and at the same time they were confident that the coming hours would bring the beginning of the end of the Great Satan, and they were to be part of the cause of it happening.

Ali eyed the crew as they moved quickly in the darkness, setting up a scene that would be a bizarre mixture of reveling and barbarous execution. As the generators began their purr, the lights broke through the desert night, creating shadows on the cacti and bushes that surrounded them. Suddenly he realized he had not heard from the man he had sent north to the cave with weapons and ammunition. It troubled him that he had not heard from the young man, about whom he had questions. Not serious enough to take him out of the strategic thread of what he was about to do, but troubling enough to want to keep him closer than he had done by sending him north to the cave. He pulled his phone from his pocket and dialed Jimmy's number.

———

The phone buzzed in Jimmy Begaye's pocket. "Uh-oh," he commented automatically after seeing who was calling.

"What's wrong?" John's focus was immediately on him after hearing Jimmy's reaction to the phone call he was receiving.

Jimmy waved at John, signaling a need for silence as he automatically answered, "Yes, boss."

Maloof asked, "Where are you at this moment?"

"Uh . . . on my way back." He was scrambling.

"Where are you now?" the jihadist demanded.

"Not sure, but I'm heading your way. That is, after I fix the flat I just got. I hope my spare is good."

"How are things at the cave?"

"It was all good when I left," Jimmy responded.

"How long ago was that?" Ali pushed.

"About twenty minutes or so."

"Twenty minutes?"

"Yeah, about that. I should be back up and running within fifteen minutes and on my way again."

"That's good." To Jimmy's relief, Ali Maloof ended the call.

"What's that?" John asked, pointing at the phone, referring to the conversation.

"That was Maloof, and I get the feeling that he senses something is heading his way. He's a freaky guy. He seems to be ahead of people." Jimmy looked at John. He took a shallow breath and went on. "He makes me think that he can read me like a book sometimes. You know what I mean?"

"He's right about something heading his way. Just hope he's not ready for it," John said quietly.

"Something . . . like?" Jimmy was trying to coax out of him something he was hearing in his head.

John said it. "Hell . . . is headed his way . . . because we're coming, and hell is coming with us."

Jimmy chuckled and commented, "Ain't that a line from that movie about Wyatt Earp?"

"None other," Marshal Cahn interjected. "None other." He tapped Jimmy on the shoulder and went on. "Seems like you know your movies."

"Yeah, I do."

Cahn cautioned, "But don't you go thinking that this is some sort of movie plot. Okay?"

"No . . . I understand that, but you know how Hollywood can always take something bad and make it worse."

John said, "This is badder than worse. So let's not get caught up in that shit." He looked at the carnage in and outside the cave and made it obvious through the look in his eyes that it was going to get a lot worse before it could get any better. "Let's get going."

As he walked toward his vehicle, he noticed Marshal Cahn on the phone, with his left hand waving in an expression of what he was saying over the phone. He was saying certain words, but John couldn't weave them into coherency. What he did get made no sense, but then, what about this moment did?

They loaded up into their vehicle convoy and headed south, in the middle of the Arizona desert, on the blackest of nights. With not one of them knowing if they would live to see the sun rise.

---

Bellamy entered the hospital from a side door and walked quickly toward the emergency room, arriving just as Amma, slumped in the wheelchair, was being taken into the treatment area. He dropped into a chair and picked up a newspaper that was sitting on a seat next to him. Hiding behind the opened paper, he observed Alicia going in with her and a few moments later coming back out with her phone to her ear, walking toward the hospital security office.

He got up and followed an orderly into a storage closet. Locking the door, he raised his weapon that was already sporting a silencer and fired, instantly killing the unsuspecting man. He dumped the body into a rolling clothes basket, threw some clothes on top of it, and quickly threw on a set of blue scrubs he found on the shelves over his clothes. Exiting the closet, he scanned the area for surveillance cameras. He found none as he moved swiftly into the treatment area, searching for Amma Gode. It didn't take long before he had his target in sight. He moved to her bedside swiftly and pulled the curtain around the injured woman's bed.

"Can you get me some water?" she asked weakly.

"You won't be needing that or anything—" His words were interrupted as the curtain was pulled open by a nurse.

"What are you doing here?" she asked as he signaled her with a finger to his lips to be quiet and closed the curtain once again. Pointing the gun at her, he said, "Shut your mouth, and nobody gets hurt. Okay?"

She nodded yes. He got behind her and Amma realized she was in great danger. He put the weapon to the back of the nurse's head and prepared to take his shot. But before he could finish, she fainted, falling to the floor and dropping the tray she was holding. A voice cried out "What happened?" as staff started rushing toward their area.

With the curtain being drawn back, Bellamy stated loudly, "She just fainted," pointing at the fallen nurse as he began to walk out of the room with the gun tucked into his shirt, a fatal mistake. Alicia arrived with her weapon in hand and a security officer beside her.

"What are you doing here, Bell?" she demanded when she saw the look of terror on Amma's face as she pointed at the rogue task force member with trembling fingers. His scrub shirt fell open as he drew his weapon. The silencer raised up in her direction, and immediately everything fell into place.

Two quick rounds from Alicia's Sig Sauer put an end to the Judas in their ranks as he fell dead at her feet.

# 29: GHOST WARRIORS

ON THE STRIP in Las Vegas were three separate groups of well-trained jihadists poised in hotel rooms, ready to strike three casinos at the same time with explosives and automatic rifles.

A team of crack Qud-trained jihadists was in position near the glass bridge of the Grand Canyon, with rocket launchers that were primed and ready to demolish that structure beyond repair.

At the same time, a large truck was parked on Cadman Plaza in Brooklyn, New York, less than one mile from the Brooklyn Bridge. Two men were sitting in it, ready for the signal to drive onto the bridge and stop in the middle of the span. They were to take a motor scooter from the cargo bay and speed off toward Manhattan, where they would remotely detonate the deadly cache of explosives in the truck, effectively taking down the middle of that bridge.

At the Mall of America, a truck was parked in the lot outside the main entrance, loaded with explosives and ready to be driven through the doors into the middle of the structure, to be blasted into the mind and spirit of Middle America.

In Chicago, a janitorial crew had been infiltrated and had planted explosives throughout the lobby, hidden in the bottom of trashcans. High heat chemicals in the bombs were designed to weaken the foundation of the country's tallest building.

On a power boat docked at a pier in Red Hook, Brooklyn, were three jihadists with rocket launchers ready to set sail toward the Statue of Liberty to do it some serious damage from the water, then hightail it for New Jersey and abandon the boat, booby-trapped with high explosives.

At the New York Stock Exchange, there were a dozen suicide vests hidden by some on the janitorial staff who had come into the United States as refugees from Syria and at the mayor's insistence, were hired instead of the veterans who were originally promised the jobs.

It was all in place. The devastation would begin in Las Vegas and like a wave, sweep across the country. Ali Maloof thought, "What fools these Americans are. They brought upon themselves their own destruction by their naive concept of justice and fairness. True justice will be ours! Fairness will go the way of their other weaknesses."

The tents were up and the activities were beginning as a group of women arrived and began moving about the encampment, kissing any man who came into their path. Middle Eastern music was blaring through the speakers placed throughout the encampment, and the smell of hashish filled the air. There was dancing and festivities as the "moment of truth" approached. Ali Maloof felt this was the "night of change" so many of his brothers had died to bring about, and he had the supreme honor of being part of bringing this "change" to the West. What filled his heart was the knowledge that there were believers in elected offices in America who were part of this change. "Brothers who were elected through the greed and stupidity of the American electorate. What a moment in time! What a great irony," he thought. There were brothers entrenched around America as lawyers, dentists, bankers, doctors, and in the media in control positions.

Wilson showed as the merriment was in full swing. He found Ali and embraced him warmly. "I'm going to miss working with you, Ali. This has been quite an experience." He looked around at the celebration. "This world will never be the same."

"That's true, Douglas. Oh so true," came Ali's response, which startled Wilson. His first name was never used by people with whom he interacted, with the exception of Mandrell. This set the rogue agent to quickly revisiting his prior conversations with the principal jihadist.

"I want to be out of here and out of the country as soon as possible. You understand, I'm sure," Wilson said while running the use of his first name through his mind.

"You will be, as you have been assured."

"Where is the key code for my money?" Wilson asked.

"I have it right here in my pocket, Special Agent Wilson. Or should I say, 'such a special agent' Wilson?" Aloof chuckled maliciously.

"What does that mean?" Wilson asked, slightly annoyed.

"Nothing more than the fact that you will always be special to me." Ali patted Wilson on the arm as he spoke. "I'm only jesting, my friend."

"Oh yeah, I get it." But Wilson did not like the exchange. He felt that Maloof was untrustworthy, and were it not for the payday he was receiving, he would have taken the son of a bitch out long ago. But money always reigned supreme with him, and that demanded his tolerance.

"Do you?" Maloof smiled.

"Do I what?" Wilson was becoming visibly agitated with the conversation.

"Do you realize how very special you are, Agent Wilson?" Maloof laughed.

"Okay, you can have a laugh or two on me, but that gets stale after a while. I don't have a sense of humor. You should know that," Wilson said tersely.

Ali did not respond to that comment, rather, he reached into his pocket. As he did, Wilson put his hand on his holstered weapon. The jihadist said, "I think you'd best relax, Special Agent Wilson. I mean you no harm . . . Here." He handed the agent a small replica of a crescent moon. "This is the key you will present to the bank in Dubai."

Wilson took it and examined it closely. "What's the code?"

"Two words . . . Blended Reason," he uttered.

"Hmmm . . . Blended Reason. Okay, that's easy enough to remember."

"That is the idea, my friend." He took Wilson by the arm. "Come and join our celebration." He walked him toward a group who was toasting the night, some waving their arms like hippies at a rock concert.

As he approached them, Wilson thought, "I wonder when they're going to pull out their cigarette lighters and hold them over their heads as they begin to dig the scene." He chuckled to himself because what he was watching firmed his conviction that the hippie culture was the easiest led. And usually led by charismatic fools. He wondered if some of these people were just looking to party anytime, anywhere, like Deadheads.

––––––––––

They had no idea they were being silently surrounded by John Gode, US Marshal Eric Cahn, and a sizable contingent of Shadow Wolves. With a plan beginning to form, the lawmen knew that they could put down the plan to blow up the casino and hotel, but they needed hard intelligence on the entire plan of destruction, in the most detail possible, in order to stop the attacks that were about to happen. They did not know about the dirty bomb. John felt instinctively that the person, or persons, who could give up where all of the attacks were to take place and in what order was somewhere in this encampment. It wasn't hard to figure that out. What was hard was getting to that person, or persons, who had that information, and it had to be done quickly. The most important challenge was to get to him or her without getting killed. And then making certain he or she was still alive when they were reached.

Cahn and John observed the activities from a vantage point hidden from the eyes of the security team who were covering the encampment, which in this case was the east side.

"Gode, we need to get moving on this. What's your feeling?" Cahn asked quietly as he observed the activity before him.

"There has to be guards of some sort out here, and my gut is telling me that we're not too far from them where we are sitting." John peered into the darkness with more than his eyes, then looked at the marshal. "Wait here. I'll be right back." He blended into the night silently and without hesitation, moving toward a position he was being drawn to by his instincts . . . and something else.

The marshal tried to caution him about going it alone, but before he could utter a sound indicating that, the big man faded into the night. The marshal sat poised and ready for just about anything, with an alertness learned through his experience in Iraq and Afghanistan black ops. He listened to the sounds of people celebrating the approaching death of his beloved country. He was getting the feeling that he was going to enjoy capping them before going for the higher-ups.

John moved like a spirit toward and behind the prone figure who was observing a span in front of him that somehow did not include John Gode. It wasn't until he felt the blinding pain of his throat being sliced did his observation end. John pushed the dying man's face into the ground, stifling his last gasps. The big lawman returned to where Cahn was positioned and led him and the Wolf pack past the dead sentry, directing them to fan out in a line, ready to assault the unsuspecting reveler terrorists. Those jihadists, who were lying on-point guarding the encampment on the remaining three points of approach, were each taken out quickly and silently by other Shadow Wolves.

Cahn pointed toward two men who were in deep conversation near a raging fire. They were slapping one another on the back and at times, laughing loudly.

John's eyes narrowed with fury as he said quietly, "Son of a bitch. That son of a bitch."

Cahn asked, "Which one?"

"That blond-haired prick right there. Special Agent Wilson."

"Well I'll be a donkey's ass, that motherless prick came to me last year wanting his men deputized to expand their jurisdiction in the 'Fast and Furious' investigation. The first time he came by, I couldn't give him an answer. Then he came back a week or so later and identified himself as being part of a unit with DHS, so secret that even most of that agency didn't know they existed."

"Tell me you didn't deputize him," John implored.

"No way was I doing that."

"What stopped you?"

Cahn let out a breath. "I didn't like him or the way he acted. Arrogant, and he seemed to go out of his way to antagonize. I thought about throwing him out on his ass."

"Whoever he really is, here he is committing treason, and I'm not surprised . . . not even a little." John's bad feelings for him continued to build.

"Keep your cool, man. He may be the guy we're looking for who knows the big plan. I suggest we try taking both of those two alive," Cahn said with a growing intensity.

John immediately passed the word down the line that the "two by the fire" were to be kept alive if at all possible. Then he gave the order to move out.

They moved closer and closer, looking for the most opportune moment to strike. And strike they did, taking out the two hooded guards who were standing near the truck holding "those who were about to die." Two silent shots dropped both men like drapes, which caused one of the women nearby to start screaming. Shots rang out almost instantly from several other hooded guards who came running toward the truck. They went down quickly as the Shadow Wolves began spreading out through the complex, firing their weapons.

John and the marshal moved rapidly toward Ali Maloof and Douglas Wilson, who turned and ran toward the edge of the encampment. In an instant, John was on Wilson, knocking him to the ground and kicking the gun that the downed agent had grabbed out of his hand as he rolled away. His agility as he sprang back to his feet surprised Cahn, who lunged at him without realizing that he was leaping on a man who was holding a razor-sharp knife in his hand, awaiting the marshal's body. It caught him in the heart, instantly killing him.

John grabbed Wilson's wrist and flipped him backward, ripping his shoulder apart as he flew through the air and landed hard on the ground.

"Listen to me, Geronimo," Wilson warned with a face full of pain. "You think you've got a chance to win this one, but you are so far from reality, it's amazing to me that you are standing here at this moment, you piece of ignorant garbage. But you won't be standing long now." He started to pull another gun from his pocket as he spoke, but John's weapon pull was much faster as he drew a bead on the rogue agent.

"You drop that, Wilson, or two things are gonna happen." John centered himself as he spoke. "First, you're going to hear a loud crack. Then you're not going hear anything ever again." He waited for Wilson's reaction.

Wilson paused, silent. He looked up at John and shrugged his shoulders as he said, "Okay, you got me . . . Here." He brought the weapon down, pointing it at the ground like he was surrendering, then stopped. "You know something, Go-day? You have the same look on your face that your friend Sunday had when I put one through his head. He had no idea it was coming and neither do—" He twirled the gun in his hand, gripping it and starting to squeeze the trigger. John put a round right between his eyes.

The big lawman watched him fall, then moved quickly to Marshal Cahn's body and saw he was gone. He said a short prayer for this man, whom he had known only a short time but had ignited a strong feeling of trust in him. After a few seconds, he surveyed the area where he had seen the other man run into the intense darkness. He took Eric Cahn's phone from the dead man's pocket and moved like the dark animal he had become, depending on his acute senses and the "something else" that seemed to be guiding him.

He struggled to find the other man as the sounds of screams, gunfire, and confusion rained behind him. The Shadow Wolf leader moved past a tent, stopping just beyond it, straining for an indication of where his prey might be hiding. His wait wasn't long, as he had to dodge a slicing swipe from a crescent blade. John rolled in a manner he had learned in Aikido. Another swipe came dangerously close to his head as he rolled away once more.

"Infidel, please give my regards to Allah. Tell him Ali Maloof continues to serve him by sending evil ones, like you, to him for his judgment."

"I'll do just that. But first, I have something planned for you."

"What is that?" Maloof asked from an unseen position in the darkness. Somehow, he was not worried about John shooting him. John felt that this man thought he couldn't kill him for some reason.

"You know something I need to know, and I will get that out of you before I'm dispatched to face your bullshit god."

"Hmm, interesting response. But it changes nothing. The reality of your demise is still at hand. You'd best prepare. Allah's will always prevails."

John got a make on where the Islamic terrorist was standing, and he moved on him like a ghost before he could wield his blade once more. John took Ali's arm as he swept his foot, throwing him to the ground. He snarled, "And now, my hateful friend, I will introduce you to some of the desert's friendly denizens."

Ali Maloof was now beginning to get a sense of the doom that awaited him in the coming moments.

John guided him into the darkness, saying, "There are snakes all around us. Snakes that dwell in pits during the mating season. I know where one of those pits might be. I heard sounds coming from it as we approached your camp. I'm surprised that you didn't know about this pit." John pushed the Islamist leader along toward a depression in the ground that he had almost stumbled into when he went to take out the first sentry. The snakes were rattling in a chorus of frightening proportions, especially to Ali Maloof. "I dropped a pig into that pit just an hour ago. A pig for the reptiles to feast on, commemorating your great festivity," John lied.

Maloof was becoming more frightened by the second, realizing from the tone of John's voice what might lie just ahead of him.

The big lawman said, "I'm going to make you the offer of a lifetime. Are you interested?"

"Go ahead." Ali's persona was now that of a terrified man. His former gusto was nowhere to be seen or heard as John walked him on his march of certain death.

"You want to be with Allah. No?" John asked.

"Yes, of course, but not yet. What do I do? What can I do?" He was starting to plead. Facing death was turning his spine to liquid.

"Here's my offer. I'll only make it one time. One time only," John said convincingly.

"Go ahead, please. Go ahead." They had reached the snake pit, and the sound of the reptiles was loud and overwhelming.

"I will let you live and watch you walk away into the night and go wherever you want to go."

"What do I have to do for that?" Ali dropped to his knees, looking pleadingly up at John as he waited for the deal.

"Or I can drop your ass into this here pit, where I believe you will die an extraordinarily harsh and painful death."

Ali Maloof was turning into liquid at the thought.

John continued, "I think the pig lasted a while even with all the bites it took. You know, those snakes don't like to be interrupted when they're getting some. Funny how that goes." John watched Ali squirm. "I'd hate to see what they're gonna do with another interruption."

"Okay, okay. What is it you want from me? Money? I got lots of money. Women, I got lots of women because I got lots of money. Hashish? I got lots of that too. You can have it. You can have it all."

"No, what I want from you is this . . . where are the attacks going to be? When are they going to be? What are they going to be?"

"They can't be stopped. I can't stop them. Take my money . . . I got lots of money. Let me go. You can't stop this. If it could be stopped, I would do it. I would do it. I would do it," he kept repeating.

John doubled down on him. "Where are the attacks going to happen? Now! Tell me now! Where? When? How? Or you will be snake-bit in a just a few minutes, and I'll stand and watch you die."

Ali knew if he told John all he knew about the attacks, his life would be worthless anyway, but to die this way was beyond comprehension. He weighed the offer and the possibility of his survival as he knelt there, cowering.

"Stand up," John ordered.

"I can't tell you that. I don't know what you're talking about." The cowering terrorist moaned.

"Okay. Say hello to Allah for me." John held him by the collar and started to push him into the pit as Ali jerked backward, screaming. The snakes were intertwined in massive rope-like groups, rattles blazing like a wave of cicadas coming at them with the overpowering sound of their collective song. Ali dug his feet into the ground and started to push himself away from the slithering mass in font of him. As he did so, one foot slipped, causing him to fall, throwing his leg forward. Instantly, he was struck by two angry snakes on the same leg. He screamed as John yanked him back from the frenzied den.

"Look! Look at what you've done. I'm going to die. The pain is unbelievable . . . It's very bad. Do something!" Ali shouted.

"And it's gonna get worse. I can stop your leg from rotting off, but you gotta give me what I want," John said, almost in a whisper.

Ali twisted side to side in absolute agony as he struggled to his feet and into the clutch of John Gode. "I can't . . . I can't," he muttered.

"Okay then, I'll just have to leave you here." He released his grip on the writhing man, allowing him to drop to the ground again, rolling to and fro, screaming in pain.

Noche came up behind John and saw what was happening. "Snake?" he asked.

"Two snakes."

"He won't last long without anti-venom," Noche said stoically.

Ali looked up at him pleadingly, screaming for help, trying to push himself away from the frenzied snakes.

"I'll go and find Jerry. He's got some in his pack." Noche turned and started running back to the encampment.

"No need to. He's a goner. I'm just gonna leave him here." John looked down at the anguished Ali, who was in full-blown agony. John turned away toward the clamor of what was left of the battle.

"No!" Ali shouted. "No!"

John had just started on his way when Ali grabbed him by the ankle. "Treat your virgins well when you see them, asshole." The big lawman stepped out of his grip.

"I'll tell you . . . please do something."

"I'm listening." John stopped dead in his tracks.

"It will begin on the Strip in Las Vegas," Ali said quickly.

"When? Where on the Strip?"

"Please give me something for these bites," the jihadist begged. "I can't think clearly. I need to stop the pain."

"Get Jerry over here, quick." John dragged Ali back toward the encampment as Noche broke into a dead run toward it. He returned, still running, with one of his Shadow Wolf brothers, Jerry. The anti-venom was administered quickly as Ali's eyes went back and forth between Jerry, who was injecting the life-saving medicine, and John and Noche. Fright filled his face.

"Talk to me," John said as he knelt down next to him.

Ali gave him the entire plan, step-by-step, hoping it would suffice to make the Shadow Wolf leader get him the medical aid he needed.

John took the marshal's phone and hit the number last dialed by Cahn. He heard a man's voice say, "Go ahead, Eric."

"This is John Nan Tan Gode calling to give you the information that my friend Marshal Eric Cahn can't."

"What do you mean, 'can't'?"

"He's dead." The Native American lawman told everything he had learned from Ali Maloof.

The information went up the line to those trusted by US Marshal Eric Cahn. It was now up to them to do what they could without going through the normal process of dealing with thwarting a terror attack on American soil, because that process could no longer be trusted. They would have to find another way.

———————

A few days later, the Arizona desert sky was full of color as the sun set, and the spirit of the night began to stir. The clouds, a brilliant orange, were hanging on the horizon with sunrays lighting them from the bottom up as the daylight crept behind the mountains, off in the distance but not too far from where a man named John Gode was standing. A dust devil was dancing across a place between him and the setting sun. This tall, lean man, who in the approaching darkness could have easily been confused with a saguaro cactus, was breathing in the beautiful scene before him. He was fully aware of a man standing behind him about eighty feet away in the desert foliage. At first, that man seemed to be taking photos of the evening desert that lay some thirty miles south of Phoenix and less than ten seconds from Washington, DC.

He could hear what sounded like clicking behind him as the sound rode the desert air to his animal-like ears. There were others who had joined the man, but there was no conversation accompanying their arrival. The one with the camera device used hand signals to communicate with them.

About twenty feet from where John was standing was a rise in the land. He proceeded with what he was doing despite the action behind him, moving slowly toward it while shaking his fist in the air. This was his grandfather's "old ways" method of bidding the sun a good-night and asking it to return in the morning. As he was ceremonially dancing and chanting toward the rise, he suddenly dropped to his knees. There he began his shaman-natured ritual celebrating the spirit of the wolf, the dominant creature of the night. As he chanted, a shadowy wolf slowly approached him out of the encroaching darkness, kissed his forehead, and stood there for a moment, watching him. After a moment, the animal turned and looked at the men who had stopped dead in their tracks as they approached from behind. The mysterious wolf's fierce eyes glared at them as they froze in place. He then slowly turned his glance back to the kneeling Native American, kissing his forehead again before disappearing back into the shadows. At that point, John heard movement coming from what sounded like three men. He got back to his feet and continued dancing his way into the darkness. He went behind the rise from where he was able to observe them, but they could not see him. He was a Ghost Warrior known as a "Shadow Wolf." One who could easily blend with the night. Disappear into the darkness at will.

They spread out, moving swiftly without making a sound, closing in from different directions on the place where they last saw him. All three had been startled by the appearance of the wolf and prepared themselves should it attack them.

John's first thoughts were that they were sent by one of the drug cartels to take him out because of his success with intercepting their supply lines into Arizona. He remained part of the darkness, blended with the desert landscape, observing them, totally hidden from their eyes, his Sig Sauer in his hand, poised at the ready.

As suddenly as they appeared, they were gone. Motionless, John held his position for another ten minutes to make certain that they weren't doing the same and waiting for him to move. After a short time, the night sounds of the desert and his spirit wolf helped him to know they were gone.

"I thought that we had gotten them all, but maybe I was wrong. Never underestimate the Deep State," was John's lingering thought.

# Epilogue: Our President Under Siege

THE RADIOACTIVE MATERIAL never arrived at the dumpster on the reservation in Arizona, but the explosives were detonated and killed twenty people who were working on the grounds along with several guests in the casino hotel. Jimmy and Sweet Tooth's mother was not one of them. Jimmy, Sweet Tooth, and their mom all disappeared into the Federal Witness Protection Program.

An attack on the Las Vegas Strip was met by an anti-terrorist SWAT team. Two officers were killed. Three civilians died. All twelve terrorists were killed on that boulevard.

The glass bridge at the Grand Canyon was no more. It was blown up by a team of radical Islamists who escaped after successfully firing handheld rockets into it.

The Mall of America witnessed a huge explosion in the parking area just outside one of the main entrances as a truck was surrounded by law enforcement. A lone terrorist detonated the vehicle, killing himself and wounding four police officers.

In Chicago, the Sears Building was shaken by the heavy explosives that severely damaged the ground level from the front to the rear. But no one was killed because the building had been evacuated and closed in time.

On Wall Street, a suicide bomber detonated an explosive vest on the trading floor as the closing bell rang, killing thirty-five people and sending the financial infrastructure of the United States into a tailspin that it would not recover from for several years.

Just off Red Hook in Brooklyn, New York, a powerboat was blown out of the water by a Coast Guard cutter as it failed to stop on their command as it made its way toward the Statue of Liberty. All five aboard the powerboat were killed.

A truck, which had been parked on Cadman Plaza, in Brooklyn, New York, rolled onto the Brooklyn Bridge, where it stopped suddenly. Two men fled the truck on a motor scooter that had been stored in the back of it. They escaped. The bridge was severely damaged by the explosives in the truck, but it was not brought down.

Richard Penelope, Special Counsel was placed under arrest and charged with high treason.

Mandrell went unidentified and disappeared.

Peppy Costa and Antonio Septuan left the United States for parts unknown and were placed on an international fugitive list and hunted by the United States Marshals Service.

The former POTUS was in full disaster mode, leading an effort to discredit and drive his successor from office. Fully funded by a multi-billionaire outside the country, rioters were being recruited and paid for by this cabal and were waging war against the Constitution and the will of the American people.

John Nan Tan Gode was appointed as the first Native American United States marshal for the federal district of Arizona. His appointment was intended as a mechanism by those in the swamp to control his actions. To say "that didn't work" would be an understatement of immense proportions.

Finally, there was a feeling of tremendous change that began sweeping across the land as a new president was sworn into office and was immediately set upon by the Deep State and those left behind from the previous administration. But he was stronger and smarter and far more adept than any of them had ever imagined.


THE END OF THE BEGINNING

# Glossary

For the sake of authenticity, abbreviations are used throughout the book as they would occur in normal conversation. Below are their expansions.

**34th** 34th Degree Bubba (a rank not known to the other 33 degrees)
**35er** 35th Degree Bubba (a rank not known to the other 33 degrees)
**36er** 36th Degree Bubba (a rank not known to the other 33 degrees)
**C/O** Case Officer (Clandestine Service officer of the CIA)
**CIA** Central Intelligence Agency
**FBI** Federal Bureau of Investigation
**FEMA** Federal Emergency Management Agency
**GFE** Government Furnished Equipment
**LEA** Law Enforcement Agency
**NSA** National Security Agency
**OTM** Other Than Mexican
**SAC** Special Agent in Charge
**CCS** Central Security Service
**MO** Modus Operandi

Printed in the USA
CPSIA information can be obtained
at www.ICGtesting.com
LVHW021324171123
764112LV00092B/4067